# Rylee Rising

by

## Mayzie Sterling

ISBN: 978-0-9882036-5-5
Published by
Marsha Hinton
dba New Meadows Media
PO Box 535
Lewiston, Maine 04243-0535
United States of America
writer@marshahinton.com

For Mom.
1933 - 2023

With special thanks to my family who love me despite my madness.

# Chapter 1

"This powder is totally awesome, and there aren't many people here yet. This is great!"

Thom looked up at Chip's extended hand. "Look at the snow!"

"Exactly, Thom. Look at the snow. It's starting to get heavy."

Chip pulled Thom to his feet and then pointed at the overcast sky.

"Keeps the noobs off the slopes."

Thom resettled his goggles and grinned. "Race you to the lift!"

The two men stumbled and ran through the deep snow to the chairlift. Thom tried to use his snowboard to block Chip, but a wind gust caught the board and sent it flying off down slope instead.

While Thom was retrieving his board, Chip arrived at the

lift and found it shut down. He looked up at the sky.

"Hey, buddy, looks like we're done here. Might as well head back in."

"What? No way!"

"Thom, it's a blizzard."

"It's not snowing that hard. I can still see my hand in front of my face." Thom argued. "Oh well, the family might be here by now. I can't wait to see Lexie in her snowsuit."

"The one that's going to make her look like a Panda?"

"Pandas are cute."

"That poor kid isn't going to have a choice. Her first pair of real shoes will be ski boots."

"What's wrong with that?"

Reproachfully, Chip replied, "I guess with your mother nearly making it on the Olympic Ski Team, it must be in your genes."

"Alternates are officially on the team."

Suddenly animated, Thom added, "Hey! I have one of those neat little wooden sleds for Lexie. She'll be riding on the slopes tomorrow! Why wait until she can walk?"

Chip gave Thom a disapproving look, then shook his head. "You are one sick puppy."

"I'm just glad that we arrived early enough to enjoy it before the snow police shut us down. It will be nice to take Lexie out this afternoon. Might as well head back to the cabin. We could have been out on the snow even sooner, but you decided to sleep in."

"Did not. I don't drive a rocket on four wheels like you do. Maybe if I weren't a starving student and was getting paid what I was worth by a certain very junior representative who pretends to be a practicing lawyer, I could have a fast car."

"Chip! I'm wounded. Truly cut to the quick. According to the newspapers, I'm a very junior representative who pretends to practice law and playboy boss. And don't you forget it!"

"Uh-huh."

Chip pushed Thom and tried to run, but fell in the deep snow. Thom started laughing and sat down on Chip's chest.

"Very, very junior representative who pretends to practice law, playboy boss. Say it. Say it!"

"Never! I'll go to my grave before I submit. Besides, you haven't been sworn in yet. I might leak a juicy scandal, and they will kick you out or something. That way, you'll be a pretend lawyer."

Thom stopped laughing as the wind suddenly picked up.

"Man, we'd better get back to the cabin. Mom probably has hot chocolate with marshmallows waiting for us. I love cocoa with marshmallows. It's nice that she still thinks I'm ten."

By the time they reached the family lodge, the blizzard had developed. As the pair struggled through the snow to the massive front doors, the wind stung their exposed skin.

"Wow. They're not here yet," Thom said.

Chip stripped off his snow gear and turned on the radio for the local news and weather. The two men, still cold and now increasingly uneasy, listened intently as the news reported a major accident on a nearby state highway.

Thom said distractedly, "They must be stuck in that accident. The news guy said traffic was backed up for miles. However, the good news is that it looks like we've seen the worst of the storm. We should be able to go out again tomorrow. Did you see the highchair I got for Lexie?

"Can she even sit up yet?"

3

"Yes. Well, sort of."

Given how you pamper your niece, I dread the day when you have kids of your own. They'll be spoiled rotten."

The two men stood motionless for a moment more, anxiously listening to the radio.

With a hint of apprehension in his voice, Thom said, "Well, I'm certain they'll be here soon and will be hungry. I reckon we should rustle up some grub. How does chili sound to you?"

"Made by you?" Chip smirked.

"I can cook. I fry a mean egg. However, Mom has some chili in the freezer here."

"Oh. If it's your mom's chili, then it's okay."

"To your room, young man, until you learn to respect your elders."

The doorbell rang, and they looked out the window to see a police SUV. Thom walked toward the door.

"Steve said he was stopping by to see Mom and Dad."

When Thom opened the door, he was greeted by a sober-looking uniformed officer. Thom jabbed at the guy.

"Steve, good to see you, buddy. Mom and Dad aren't here yet."

"I know. Can I come in?"

## Chapter 2

### Six months later.

"You waiting for your beau, young lady?"

"No. I'm waiting for my tardy friend."

Rylee's smile faded as the elderly couple walked into the restaurant, leaving her in a swirl of emotions.

She stamped her foot, trying to shake off her frustration.

"Well, where is Lisa?" she muttered, her voice tinged with impatience and worry.

A wren, prospecting in the nearby flower bed, chirped and hopped further into the landscaping. Rylee's cheeks turned pink with embarrassment, making her feel guilty for scaring it away.

"I'm sorry. Come back out," she said softly, bending down to search for the wren. But it was nowhere to be seen, and she stood back up, her gaze fixed on the restaurant door with a mix of hope and annoyance.

Rylee jerked her left arm up, glancing at her watch. "I knew I should have picked her up," she sighed.

Feeling a pang of regret. She let her arm drop, the weight of disappointment pulling it back to her side.

The wren reappeared, inspecting a cigarette butt before dismissing it, then moved on to a promising wrapper.

"Didn't find anything you like? If you go out back by the dumpster, you'll probably find better pickings. Let's see if I can find something for you."

She was unsure whether to focus on the wren or her own predicament. Rylee took a step but pulled up suddenly. She slowly eased the foot she had stamped from her shoe, feeling the sting of her earlier impatience.

"Serves me right for losing my temper."

She watched the wren flutter to the top of a nearby shrub.

"I don't think you'll find much worthwhile around here."

Rylee breathed deeply and pushed her long chestnut curls from her face. Her eyes darted toward her car. Biting her lower lip, she shifted her purse. "You and I both need to decide here. We're spending too much time looking for something we're not going to find."

Rylee's face wrinkled as her foot gingerly found its way back into her shoe.

"That's it! I'm hungry. One of us needs to find something to eat." Rylee turned to the wren. "I'll bring you some food, little one."

The bird darted deeper into the bush as the parking lot erupted with the sounds of a car scraping over speed bumps and a tinny horn echoing off the surrounding buildings.

Rylee's eyes rolled as she turned to face the parking lot. The door of the little car opened, and a coppery head emerged.

"Hey, Rylee! I made it!"

Lisa lurched across the parking lot, stopping often to swat at her skirt.

"Look at you with your arms all crossed! Are you mad at me? How could you be mad at me? Can you believe this static cling?"

Lisa struggled with the offending garment.

"That must be the ultimate static cling. Your skirt looks

like it's alive," Rylee teased.

Lisa pulled at one side of the skirt, only to have it rebound against her leg. "What do I do to stop this?"

"Are you wearing a slip?"

"No."

"Uh-huh. That may be part of the problem."

The wren emerged to find a morsel to its liking at the spot where the wrapper had been. It plucked up the tidbit and flew away. Rylee tore her eyes from Lisa's writhing skirt to watch as the wren rose in the air.

"At least the bird got something to eat!"

"Hey! I'm here with plenty of time to spare."

Rylee's mouth drew into a tight line. Lisa stood, allowing her skirt to dance unhindered around her legs.

"I know I'm late. I know that you're thinking you should have picked me up. And I know you need to arrive before your class starts. But I also know that you will forgive me because you adore me."

Lisa beamed at Rylee, turning her irrepressible personality on full. Rylee's mouth remained a tight line, but her eyes softened in the face of Lisa's cheery incandescence.

"You're correct. I do think I should be there before parents start dropping off their children. Therefore, Ms. Ten O'clock Scholar, you must decide what you want to order before the waitress gets to our table," Rylee warned.

"Yes, Sergeant! Ginger pancakes with the lemon glaze, it is."

With a genuine smile, Rylee took Lisa's arm. "Lisa, you're a pill."

"See. You do love me."

## Chapter 3

They marched together into the restaurant, Lisa's skirt still twisting around her legs.

Lisa's right eyebrow crept toward her hairline.

"Oh, my! Look at our waiter," observed Lisa. "Isn't he a dish?"

Rylee, unable to resist, turned to look at the young man approaching the table.

Lisa leaned across the table. "Do you think he saw me walking in?"

Rylee watched the lethargic waiter. Feet dragging, he arrived at their table. He pointed vaguely at the menus while staring out the window.

"Today's specials are on the flyer inside the menu. What do you want to drink?"

He turned from staring out the window to staring in the direction of the kitchen.

Lisa beamed at him.

"Oh, we're ready to order now. I'll take the ginger pancakes and a cup of coffee with cream. Could you bring some extra lemon sauce with those?"

He started writing on his pad without looking at Lisa.

Lisa cocked an eyebrow at Rylee.

"So, how did you get the weekend shift?" Lisa said.

"Huh?"

"How'd you get stuck on the weekend shift?" repeated Lisa.

"Just worked out that way."

"Well, what days do you have off?"

Ignoring Lisa, the waiter looked at Rylee. Lisa's eyes widened and then narrowed quickly. Rylee repressed a smile.

"I'll take the Cowboy Scramble with an English muffin and a cup of hot cocoa," Rylee said.

"Anything else?"

He looked over his shoulder at the door. Lisa frowned.

Suppressing a grin, Rylee said, "No, thank you."

The waiter moved to the next booth and didn't look at the people sitting there.

"I bet he gets the order wrong. I don't think he was even paying attention," Lisa griped.

"Well, I do agree that he seemed distracted."

Lisa snorted.

"Just like you to be nice, saying he is distracted. I think he's stuck-up. I mean, who could ignore me?"

"Is that the definition of stuck-up? Ignoring you?"

Lisa crossed her arms and huffed. "Rylee, you know what I mean."

"You assume that he's stuck-up just because you think he's ignoring you. He might not be feeling well, be shy, or have had a horrible day so far. You might try being kind," Rylee suggested.

"And what if he is just stuck-up?"

"Then you need to be kind to him anyway."

Lisa rolled her eyes.

"Rylee, you need to look harder for things to complain about. What fun are you?" Lisa tilted her head to one side and tightened her mouth. "So, tell me. Have you even looked at anyone since Greg?"

Rylee shifted under Lisa's scrutiny.

"Lisa, stop. No more matchmaking," Rylee hissed.

Lisa's eyes continued to bore into Rylee's. She looked away, but Lisa's unusual silence drew her gaze back.

"Okay. No. Not really. Greg was nice, and I still like him. There was just something missing. Something didn't click for me. Happy now?"

A smug smile played at the corners of Lisa's mouth. She leaned back in her seat and put her hands flat on the table.

"I told you not to date someone boring."

Rylee suddenly felt warmth in her cheeks. "Greg is a good man, a committed Christian, and will make Kristi a wonderful husband. He just wasn't the guy for me," Rylee responded.

Rylee's words were firm, but her heart was less confident. Lisa was right; despite all Greg's outstanding qualities, he was so dull.

"Because you are looking for Mr. Excitingly Perfect. You know you are. Something like that smarmy waiter thinks he is," Lisa said.

"Okay. You're right. Greg is not exactly what I'm looking for. I hoped he would be. He is a fine Christian man."

Lisa waved a dismissive hand in the air. "Yes, yes. He's a good Christian. He will make an excellent husband and father. But Rylee, in your heart of hearts, you are a wild woman. You need someone who will get you going."

Rylee's face burned. "Lisa, you should be ashamed of yourself. Life isn't all about excitement."

"It isn't? Prove it. You're looking for excitement. You just haven't looked in the right place. You need to start looking somewhere different. Somewhere you haven't looked before."

Rylee's throat tightened, and she dropped her head to stare at the floor.

"Did he talk about anything other than fishing? I think all his neckties have a fishing theme," Lisa said.

Defensively, Rylee's head jerked up. "Greg likes to fish! There is nothing wrong with that."

Lisa yawned. "Come on, Rylee. No matter what, Greg always drags the conversation back to fish."

Rylee's eyes hardened as Lisa's words chaffed against her.

"I just can't see you spending the next sixty- or seventy-years gutting fish. Gutting fish fun for you?" Lisa waved her spoon at Rylee.

Rylee shivered.

"If I remember correctly, you broke it off. You need to let me help you," Lisa offered.

"No. No more matchmaking. None. Can we change the subject now?"

"You're just playing it too safe. Broaden your horizons!"

"Enough, Lisa. Just stop."

Lisa swallowed her retort when she caught sight of the tears welling up in Rylee's eyes. Reaching across the table, Lisa took Rylee's hand. Hot tears streaked down Rylee's face.

With emotion in her quiet voice, Rylee spoke. "It's so hard to watch Kristi planning her wedding. And Ruth, too, is coming to services with her new baby. I've been thinking about joining another congregation to find a guy."

"That's my girl! I'll go with you!"

Rylee smiled, blinked back the tears, and squeezed Lisa's hand.

Lisa, that's not a good reason to change your membership. And I've already tried dating non-Christians," Rylee said.

"Ouch. I remember. Those guys didn't work out so well, did they?"

"No. It was much too uncomfortable for both of us. I should stick with Christians. Unfortunately, Greg was one of the last single Christian men I knew."

Lisa giggled.

"Doc Hooper is a widower," Lisa teased. "Sure, he's a little old, but he likes you. And his stories are a lot more interesting than Greg's."

Rylee sat up straight, squared her shoulders, and stuck out her chin. "I don't need a husband to be fulfilled or to be acceptable to God."

Despite the show of confidence, Rylee's heart sank. If she really believed what she was saying, why was she so concerned about finding the right guy?

"The waiter returned, and without looking at either Rylee or Lisa, asked, "Who had the pancakes?"

Lisa blazed at the waiter with her smile. The waiter showed the only animation Rylee had seen from him so far, and it looked like fear.

The waiter shoved the plate at Rylee without taking his startled eyes off Lisa.

"Oh, uh, here's your eggs."

"Could I have some hot sauce with this?" Rylee asked.

The waiter's head swiveled around. He snatched a bottle from another table and plopped it in front of Rylee. He turned and fled from the force of Lisa's attention.

Lisa turned a smug face to Rylee. "See? I was nice."

Rylee's laughter rang out.

## Chapter 4

As the girls burst from the cozy, bustling restaurant into the bright daylight, Lisa gestured toward Rylee's car with a playful nudge.

"Look, Rylee," she teased, her voice light and singsong, "some guy is ogling your car again. Maybe you should sign up for one of those dating services and mention that you own an old car."

The dark blue GTO shimmered in the golden sunlight, its sleek, muscular contours capturing the attention of an older man. He paced around it with keen admiration, his eyes tracing every curve of the well-preserved machine, savoring its classic beauty.

"Not funny, Lisa. And it's a classic car," Rylee retorted.

A smile played at Lisa's lips as she rolled her eyes. "Old, classic, whatever. Guys seem to go wild over it. You should use it to your advantage. I certainly would."

"Get going, or we'll both be late."

As Rylee strode toward her car, she noticed the man still circling it, his gaze full of appreciation. Seeing her approach, he tipped his hat politely and called out to her.

"Is this your car, Miss?"

"Yes, sir. My father gave it to me."

Her pride was evident in her tone as she watched Lisa's little car bounce out of the parking lot, leaving a trail of dust in its wake.

The old gentleman's white eyebrows shot upward with surprise.

13

"Just gave it to you?"

"Yes. He said it wouldn't crumple like an aluminum soda can in an accident."

The older man nodded sagely.

"That's true; it's no soda can. Is it all original?"

"No. My dad replaced the carpeting and gave it a fresh coat of paint, installed an alarm system, and did other little things to keep it in top shape."

"Miss, I would say it's pristine. It's a '74, isn't it?"

"Yes, sir. It is."

"Well, Miss, you're fortunate. You really do need more than just an alarm system. I'm surprised it hasn't disappeared already."

The man ambled away, shaking his head with a chuckle, and frequently glancing back at the car with longing eyes.

Rylee knew she had to hurry to avoid being late. Her mind whirled with conversation and emotion, like the dust kicked up by Lisa's car. She knew she shouldn't care, but Lisa's words about her future and finding the right guy echoed in her thoughts.

She was looking for someone special, but how hard should she be looking—and where? If she couldn't find him at church, where would he be? Using an online dating site seemed as likely as meeting him at a five-car pileup, and just as safe.

Rylee shook her head, trying to clear away her thoughts. She slipped behind the wheel and turned the key, listening to the engine roar to life. The GTO's powerful engine growled beneath her as she merged into traffic, its capabilities tempting her to defy the speed limit. As she drove, Rylee recalled the little wren with a wry smile. "If I can't fly, at least I have a car that does," she mused, feeling a thrill of freedom as the road stretched out before her.

## Chapter 5

"Looks just like every other stupid church!"

Hard, blue eyes glanced into the rearview mirror to check on the baby in the car seat.

"What am I doing?"

With a quick motion, Thom flipped off the turn signal and continued driving down the road past the parking lot. He pulled up and stopped at the intersection.

His head snapped up at the sound of a blaring horn. "Hey, buddy, you having a heart attack or something? Get moving!" The car behind him pulled around him, and the man driving it glared at Thom as he passed. "Wake up, you idiot!" the driver shouted.

Thom's blue eyes found the mirror again and softened, seeing the baby still asleep.

"Well, we're here. How bad can it be?"

Thom's hands tightened on the steering wheel. He sighed as he looked down the road that would take him home. He rubbed the wrinkles from his forehead and turned the car around at the first gas station he came to.

His eyes flicked from the reflection of the sleeping baby in the mirror to the road back home as he pulled into the church parking lot. The stone walls of the edifice loomed to his right.

"Yup. Just like I remember, every head swiveling around to check out the new person, or the new car, or the new outfit, or the new couple. You would think that it was gossip central instead of a house of worship."

Smiling faces turned his way.

"What am I doing here?"

He started to turn the car around to leave when he heard the echo of his own words again. A desperate promise made to a dying face. He rubbed his forehead and slowly straightened the steering wheel.

Thom looked over his shoulder at the building and slid down in his seat. Shaking his head, he bit his lower lip as he pulled into an open spot.

"Everything I've learned tells me not to act based on emotions. It always leads to trouble."

His jaw tightened. His hands clenched the steering wheel until his knuckles whitened. He looked at the people milling around the entrance.

People ready to judge him.

People ready to force them both into neat little molds.

People who had no understanding of his pain.

The promise reasserted itself and rang through his thoughts like a bell. He shut off the car. His hands ran through his unruly hair, and his eyes squeezed shut.

"I don't have to do this. No one would expect me to."

He rubbed his forehead again.

"I'm going back home. I don't belong here."

Defiant eyes locked on his reflection in the mirror as he jerked the car into reverse. The motion caused the baby to blink. As Thom watched, she stretched in her car seat.

Carefully shifting into park and turning off the engine, he waited as the baby slowly awoke. With a forced smile in his voice, he turned in his seat to look at her.

"Hello, sunshine. Did you have a nice nap?"

Lexie's sober eyes found Thom. After a moment, she smiled. Thom's eyes crinkled.

"How's my girl?"

The cold grey stone of the church building dominated the view from the car's rear window. Thom bit his bottom lip. His eyes moved down the gray building to the people gathering around the entrance. He turned back to Lexie, only to have her erupt into giggles.

"Well, since we're here, we might as well go inside."

Thom took a deep breath, threw the door open, and reluctantly planted his left leg on the pavement. He watched a car enter the parking lot from the street. The vehicle pulled into a nearby spot, and a family spilled out.

"What am I doing here?"

Thom exited the car and moved around to the passenger side.

Lexie, all smiles and giggles just moments before, became a reflection of Thom's discomfort. Arching her back as if her spine were a reed, she managed to resist Thom's efforts.

"We should just go."

"Excuse me, young man, may I help?"

"What?"

Thom jerked around to face the voice. His eyes were immediately drawn not to the old gentleman who stood in front of him but to the man's massive handlebar mustache. Thom stared at the sharp points of the mustache curling up the man's cheeks. The man stepped forward.

"Now, let's see what you're about, little bit."

With a few soft words and quick movements, he removed an unresisting Lexie from the car seat.

"There. That wasn't so hard, was it?"

Smiling, he tapped her nose gently and turned to hand her to Thom.

"Uh, thanks," Thom said.

"Oh, no trouble at all, young man. Pretty little girl. I'll see you inside."

Thom rubbed Lexie's back and reached for the diaper bag. Still fascinated with the enormous mustache, he watched the old gentleman move across the parking lot, returning greetings from others.

"Hey, baby, I want to go back home. How about you?"

Sober brown eyes regarded him, and then Lexie curled up on his shoulder. Thom hoisted the diaper bag over the other shoulder, patted Lexie's back, took another deep breath, and headed across the parking lot toward the stone building.

"You would think that the money they spent on this monstrosity could have been put to better use, like, I don't know, perhaps feeding the poor. These people talk about doing good, but it seems like all they do is build ugly buildings."

Using the diaper bag as a buttress and grunting out chilly good mornings, he made his way through the gauntlet. He eyed the open maw of the entrance and stepped back to avoid the people passing him on the front steps. Lexie squirmed against his firmer hold. The guilt driving him warred against every fiber of his being. Eyes flitting for an escape path, his gaze passed over the people surrounding him. Only fools would worship something that didn't exist. He looked up at the opening, and his eyes found their way to an inscription over the entrance.

"I rejoiced with those who said to me, 'Let us go to the house of the Lord.'"

As the congregants continued to move around him toward the front door, he smoothed Lexie's top over her leotard as he looked back toward the freedom of the parking lot.

"Okay. This isn't working here. Time to go home." Thom squeezed his eyes shut as Lexie cuddled closer. Her mother's swollen face and pleading eyes lost the battle to Thom's will. His face darkened with defiance, and he spun on his heels toward the parking lot.

Abruptly, lilting laughter filled the air and hummed its way toward him. Lexie straightened and turned to find the source as two young women rushed around the corner. Their faces were bright, and their conversation animated.

Thom's attention centered on the young woman with smoky hazel eyes and dark, root-beer-colored hair that tumbled to her shoulders in loose curls. Her movements, though hurried, retained fluidity. The form hidden underneath the soft blouse and long pleated skirt whispered of a beautiful shape disguised. Thom froze in place and held his breath, fearing the vision would dissipate.

## Chapter 6

Rylee had managed to catch up with Lisa's underpowered car at the church's parking lot entrance. She impatiently guided the GTO around it and came to a screeching halt before bolting out of the vehicle.

"Rylee, slow down."

Lisa hissed, jumping out of the car and smoothing her skirt.

"I'm getting all tangled again."

No matter which way Lisa pulled the fabric, it puckered and clung to her legs, seeming to retaliate by forming even more clumps.

"I don't have time to slow down." Rylee headed toward the building. "I can't believe your mother never taught you to wear a slip."

Lisa gave up the battle and started to laugh. She hurried to keep up with Rylee, who moved with the speed of a heat-seeking missile. Catching up, she came even with her friend just as the static started to erupt from Rylee instead of her skirt. Eyes flickered back and forth between Rylee and the man with the baby. A sly grin spread over Lisa's face.

Rylee's heart lurched as she skidded to a halt, suddenly entrapped under the piercing scrutiny of a surfer-looking guy striding toward the parking lot. His ice-blue eyes drilled into her with a piercing intensity that made her skin burn with an almost unbearable heat.

Her gaze swept over his unruly, golden, cowlicked hair—wild and untamed—before settling on the soft, delicate brown curls of a baby cradled on his shoulder. The infant's appearance jolted her, a breathtaking contrast to the man holding her.

With deliberate caution, Rylee inched toward the newcomers, anxious not to startle the little girl whose presence overshadowed any urgency to prepare her classroom. She exchanged a glance with the man before bending to brush the hair back from the baby's forehead. The baby's eyes, unblinking and fiercely present, locked onto Rylee's with unnerving intent.

"Good morning."

Rylee's voice held a hesitant warmth as she smiled up at the man.

For a fleeting second, Thom was robbed of words as she raised her eyes to his, eyes that burned with a dark, almost black hazel intensity—a detail that sent his mind into a frantic spin even as their gazes met.

"Hi."

Thom's voice was thick with disbelief as he struggled to formulate the simplest greeting. His eyes followed the cascade of her dark, flowing hair.

Rylee's smile deepened as she bent down to Lexie, whispering, "Hello, sleepy. I hope to see you later."

Then, she pivoted back to Lisa, whose teasing grin radiated unspoken challenges. Rylee's cheeks flushed fiercely as the silent, explosive question burning on Lisa's face demanded an answer.

Thom adjusted Lexie's position as the baby twisted her small body to catch a final glimpse of Rylee disappearing into the distance. Inhaling sharply, Thom caught one last, potent waft of her clean, honeysuckle scent that had nearly overwhelmed him earlier. His feet, which had been poised to escape moments before, now marched on instinctively up the steps, as if commandeered by an unseen force even as his tormented mind fought against it.

"I'm not going to be lured in by just a pretty smile," he murmured bitterly.

Nearly inside the building now, Thom drew one final, resolute breath and patted Lexie's back in a fierce, protective gesture.

"The things I do for your mother." His tone was a mix of defiance and fierce responsibility.

Squinting as his eyes adjusted to the darkened interior, he peered inside, straining to spot the radiant young woman and her dangerously inviting smile. Another deep, deliberate breath filled him as he lowered his head to examine the baby once more.

"Well, Lexie, let's do this."

The small child sat up straight, her somber eyes reflecting the weight of his words, before bursting into a cascading fit of giggles. Rubbing her back tenderly yet firmly, he stepped into the shadowed doorway.

## Chapter 7

A middle-aged, balding man thrust out his hand. "Welcome."

Thom offered a soft smile, his eyes darting past the man in search of the captivating woman with dark hazel eyes. Reluctantly, he turned back, trying to maintain his focus. With a practiced smile and a slight shrug, Thom indicated that his hands were full with Lexie and the diaper bag.

Laughing, the man withdrew his hand. "Been there, done that."

"This little lady would like to attend your Sunday school. Do you have one for her age group?"

Thom already knew the answer; he had researched this congregation. His mind was caught between wanting to be there for Lexie and the disquiet he felt in a church building.

"We sure do! Sorry, but I didn't catch your name."

The man left the question lingering, adding to Thom's unease.

"Thom. And this is Lexie Simms."

"My goodness, doesn't she have brown eyes. Dimples and brown curls as well."

The man casually scrutinized Thom's blue eyes and unruly blonde hair.

"She must look like her mother."

Thom's practiced smile faltered, a hint of tension creeping in. He shifted the conversation. "Where can I find her classroom?"

"Just down the stairs. I think the cradle roll class is the
23

second door on the right."

Thom negotiated his way down the stairs, careful not to bump into anyone else. The scene in the hallway was chaotic and noisy. The harsh glare of the fluorescent-colored walls seared his eyes, and he found himself weaving briskly around a stampede of rambunctious children. Every surface in the area radiated the raw, electric energy of a wild, good-natured rebellion.

Amid the frenzy, Lexie's eyes darted as she tracked the children flitting in and out of classrooms. Her head spun with the vibrant disarray. Wrapped in Thom's arms, she wriggled, desperate to take in every detail before Thom managed to pinpoint the right room.

Then, there she was—THE young woman— meticulously shuffling a stack of papers at a small table. Her scent snaked its way into Thom's senses, compelling him to step inside.

"Excuse me."

Thom all but shouted to be heard over the mayhem behind him, his voice cutting through the clamor as he fumbled with the squirming Lexie in his arms. Rylee turned, her sharp gaze locking onto them.

For a moment, Thom was utterly transfixed as he watched Rylee smooth her root beer-colored hair behind her ear almost as an afterthought. The woman's smile ignited something untamed in him as she leaned down close to Lexie.

"Hello, little one."

She straightened smoothly to face Thom.

"Hi, I'm Rylee Vance. I teach the cradle roll class. I'm glad to see this sweetheart is joining us."

Thom's startling blue eyes swept over her face.

Despite herself, Rylee's composure wavered, her cheeks aflame with an undeniable blush. In that charged moment, Thom's entire world narrowed to the enchanting pink that crept across her face.

"Doesn't she have a name?"

"Oh. Sorry. Yeah. Her name is Lexie, uh, Alexia."

Rylee grinned and looked at the baby. "Lexie."

Lexie stilled, her large brown eyes locking onto Rylee with a piercing intensity. Thom glanced down at her, a wry smile flickering at the corners of his lips.

Rylee couldn't help but respond to Thom's smile with a gentle warmth.

"Well, Lexie, I'm happy that you're here."

Her voice was a soothing promise chasing away his discomfort.

As Rylee reached out to claim Lexie, Thom instinctively tensed and clutched Lexie closer. An invisible barrier had slammed into place between them. Rylee's confusion was palpable as her arms dropped. With a quiet nod, she smiled knowingly.

"You can stay with her if you'd like. Or, if you'd prefer, you can take her upstairs to one of the adult classes."

Thom's eyes darted away, embarrassed and conflicted. "No. That's fine. It's just I haven't left Lexie with—"

Rylee nodded in understanding. "Someone you don't know. I get that."

With a playful wink aimed straight at Lexie, she lightened the tension.

Thom's voice was low and guilty. "I'm sorry. I'm just a little too overprotective, I guess."

"No. Not at all. Children need our protection—they

can't shield themselves from the chaos out there."

She bent once more to lock eyes with Lexie. "Come here, Lexie, and let me show you some pictures."

Lexie's face brightened, her smile bursting to life as she bounced up and down. Her plump arms reached out frantically toward Rylee.

In that moment, a small voice in Thom's mind whispered that he could take Lexie and go back home, yet the magnetic pull of the scene in front of him kept him rooted as he entrusted Lexie to Rylee.

"Have you been here before?"

A soft smile curved on Thom's lips as he shook his head in denial.

"You're more than welcome to stay with her if you'd like. We often have parents join our class."

She glanced at Lexie, who had already nonchalantly popped her thumb into her mouth, cozily draping herself over Rylee's shoulder.

Thom smoothed Lexie's hair. "Well, you look happy, baby girl. How long does the class last?"

Thom glanced out at the hallway as Rylee settled Lexie into a tiny, vibrant chair.

"About 45 minutes. We have several adult classes. You might be interested in attending the one in the auditorium. I will bring this pretty girl up to you after class. Or you could stay here if you want."

Inside, Thom was mildly surprised at his unexpected comfort with the situation. "I'd be as happy as Lexie to stay here with you, Ms. Rylee," he silently vowed.

Thom's eyes wandered over the tiny, brightly colored chairs

and the scattered array of hand puppets as he studied Rylee, who had now begun softly singing to Lexie. Her voice, sweet yet resonant, carried the simple tune of 'This Little Light of Mine' through the charged air. In that moment, Thom's legs were weak and reluctant to obey him. He lingered, letting the plain melody anchor him in place. His gaze drifted back to the larger chairs before returning to watch Rylee singing.

Then, as if on cue, a woman carrying a small, squirming boy brushed past him into the classroom, shattering the spell. Thom blinked, stepping aside as the interruption tore him from his reverie.

"Oh, excuse me."

The woman barely paused before handing the lively boy off to Rylee with a few hurried words, then swept past Thom like a gust of wind.

"Is the auditorium just up the stairs?" Thom asked, his voice edged with lingering urgency.

Now holding the wriggling little boy close, Rylee looked up quickly.

"Yes. I'll bring Lexie to you as soon as we're done here."

Thom waved weakly at Lexie, but, like Rylee, she was utterly absorbed by the unruly energy of the little boy. Disheartened, Thom made his way up the stairs to the auditorium, the echoes of chaos and tenderness mingling in the air as he ascended.

## Chapter 8

"Frankie, don't take Bobby's crayons."

Rylee moved to intervene amid the hostilities.

"Sit still, and I'll help you with your crayons."

Her efforts to avert the budding crisis between Frankie and Bobby kept her busy, but her mind was a whirlwind of unwanted thoughts, taking her attention away from the children. Shaking herself, she forced her mind back to the task at hand. The hard truth was undeniable—if she were going to have Lexie in her class every week, she would need reinforcements. She kept singing resiliently as she deftly lifted Frankie, moving him to a seat on the opposite side of Lexie and safely distanced from Bobby's possessive reach.

Her attention shifted between the feuding toddlers and the unwelcome, and Rylee was sure, sinful thoughts that refused to be hushed, even by the commanding sound of her voice.

Across the table, Lexie sat as still as a captivated statue, her wide brown eyes glued to the colorful drama unfolding around her. Rylee cast a glance at Lexie, offering a reassuring smile through the din of the turmoil and the disarray of her thoughts. Lexie mirrored the smile with gleeful assurance, but even that smile couldn't still Rylee's wandering thoughts.

"Lexie's father is unbelievably amazing looking," the thought ambushed her, accompanied by a burning blush that radiated across her cheeks. Desperate to divert her thoughts, she considered Lexie.

"Lexie, you must look like your Mommy."

Without missing a beat, Rylee's eyes darted around the

table, scanning for new disturbances. She spotted Bobby again, this time with an apostle figure halfway to becoming a snack.

"Bobby," she said, firm but loving, "don't eat the apostle. Here, put him with the other apostles. See how good they are as they listen to Jesus?"

Her fingers gracefully plucked the tiny object from Bobby's hands, and she resumed singing cheerfully, clapping rhythmically to bring the children's wandering attention back to order as she circled the table, helping them with their crayons.

But even as she moved, singing and clapping her way through the mayhem, she couldn't silence the persistent musing about Lexie's father. He seemed so unlike Lexie, yet both were disturbingly fascinating. His wild blonde hair and easy movements made her think he must be a surfer.

"A married surfer," she reminded herself pointedly.

Still, the way he looked at Lexie, with such consuming and evident love, made something twist quietly inside her. It was the look she secretly wished someone would cast on her someday. The more she tried to set her mind to other matters, the more Lexie's father became the focus of her inner thoughts.

"He can't be happy," a sly voice inserted itself. "He's here by himself with an infant. Where is the mother?"

Rylee frowned and tried to push the thoughts aside. "He's not unhappy. He's just trying to navigate a new place, new people. That's not unhappy," she retorted to her internal thoughts.

"That's not true," she countered, her resolve wobbly.

She shook her head. "He's just the overprotective type. The married, overprotective type."

Unable to influence Rylee, her thoughts shifted in another much safer direction as Freddie started throwing crayons.

"We need volunteers. Lexie's father could volunteer down here. We always need volunteers. It wouldn't hurt to suggest it," a conspiratorial whisper urged. "Maybe then he'd linger, maybe talk to you a bit more."

Her inner thoughts suddenly escaped into an audible outburst.

"Rylee, stop it! He's married,"

The children froze, startled by her sudden declaration, their eyes wide as saucers.

## Chapter 9

"Hey there."

Thom's heart wasn't in it as he numbly nodded to the balding guy stationed at the door. His thoughts were fractured as he wandered forward, each step more uncertain than the last. He hesitated outside the auditorium door, his mind churning over the sameness of these spaces. They were all familiar yet profoundly empty, echoing with memories that he would rather stay buried.

Thom slipped inside, grabbing a seat at the back pew, his eyes moving warily to the mustache-clad instructor up front, who was already deep into some fervent spiel. His ears perked at the name Hosea. Try as he might to tune out, his thoughts clashed and tangled.

"How could a loving god send a poor soul to marry a prostitute?"

The question gnawed at him like a bitter worm burrowing in his brain, a stark reminder of the irreconcilable gap he felt between doctrine and reality. "Was there a point to being here amidst all these hollow declarations?"

Thom looked around, his skepticism unyielding.

Mustache guy droned on, glorifying Hosea's supposed faithfulness and rambling about mercy and providential care. The more he preached, the more Thom's soul rebelled; the lofty claims felt increasingly like veiled platitudes, insincere covers for life's harsh truths. Eyes shifting to the exit, Thom noted the bald guy still loitering there—a silent specter of Thom's own feeling of entrapment in a role he never chose. Frustration welled within him, and he let out an audible sigh, the sound echoing his conflicted sorrow.

An old lady nearby frowned deeply, her disapproval slicing through his stormy reverie and reminding him he didn't quite belong. In a flash of rebellious humor, Thom waved back at her, acknowledging the absurdity within himself.

As he refocused, he turned to face the window, watching tree limbs sway with the breeze. Ms. Vance popped into his mind, with her calm presence that promised a different sort of peace, battling his brimming cynicism like a lighthouse in the storm. Her warm smile and the gentle way she sang to Lexie flooded his thoughts.

In Ms. Vance, there was a spark of hope in a blush. Those eyes, so filled with light, were both what he craved and what he despised for their hopeful innocence. Yet, here he was again, caught between worlds he couldn't reconcile, unable to silence the clashing voices in his head.

"Why am I doing this to myself?"

The question loomed large. It echoed as loudly as the bald man's obnoxious, 'Hi, welcome!' when he passed through the door. It shouted whenever he saw a complete family, unlike his own. It screamed when he imagined Lexie's future and the empty places in her life. Thom hated that he was here and hated more that he couldn't leave it behind. He hated not knowing which side he was on, which voice in his mind would win out.

Yet there he sat—his mind as divided as ever, until he thought of Lexie downstairs and the way she cuddled into Ms. Vance as though she'd known her forever.

Even in his worst moments, thinking of Lexie brought

him a kind of peace. His thoughts went to his promise.

"Andie, am I going to be able to stay true to my promise to you?"

Determined not to run, Thom forced his eyes to the front and tried to ignore the old lady's stare of disdain.

He retreated again inside himself, distracted by the chaos unfolding in his heart. His mind drifted back to Ms. Vance and her brightly lit room. He visualized her stunning smile and that blush that had spread across her cheeks when she would hand Lexie off to him. He thought of her knowing eyes, how quickly she'd caught on that he didn't have a clue what he was doing. He thought of her offer to join them in the cradle roll class, all of it colliding with the bible lesson he was half-hearing, and leaving him more uncertain than ever.

And yet, even knowing nothing had changed, even knowing he could never commit to this, he felt a strange pull to see if Ms. Vance still smiled when she came upstairs.

## Chapter 10

Lexie was the last child left in the room, and even if the mothers hadn't arrived yet to pick up the other toddlers, Rylee would've known the end was near; the absence of children always coincided with her supply of patience running out. Today, she ran out early, and she was a little surprised it wasn't Lexie's dad who brought her to the end of her wits.

"He's certainly been a distraction."

She was exhausted. She sang and clapped and danced her way around the room, blurring together a frantic medley of 'This Little Light of Mine,' 'Jesus Loves Me,' and 'How did Jesus love them?'

By the final verse of the last song, she was unsure of the answer herself. It was all she could do to keep the children from eating the apostles, fighting over crayons, and throwing the papers on the floor, let alone making them listen to her.

In the end, Frankie and Bobby seemed as determined as ever to put her on the fast track to martyrdom.

Ashamed of herself for trying to figure out a way to get Thom into the classroom with her, she mulled the idea of getting parents to help. As the mothers arrived to pick up their children, she broached the idea of volunteering in the classroom with them. She decided to meet with the church leaders and broach the idea with them.

She turned to look at Lexie quietly sitting at the table, watching her with large brown eyes.

Next week, when the children come back, will Lexie's dad be with them? Would he stay with the children and volunteer? Would he sneak up to the auditorium again? Would he have a smile for her when he returned to the room? Would he care if she didn't have the nerve to smile back?

"Rylee! Stop it!"

She was desperate to keep her mind from wandering even further. She busied herself with picking broken crayons and bits of torn paper off the floor and was finally distracted enough to stay on task when Angie, Frankie's mom, showed up to collect her son and did her best to look apologetic.

"Did he behave?"

"Well," Rylee said, her own voice a dusty mix of wear and exasperation, "as good as any toddler who has an appetite for the apostles."

Angie looked relieved, as though Rylee's answer was exactly what she'd expected.

"I wish she wouldn't teach him those songs," Rylee whispered to no one as Angie left, too quickly to say goodbye. "Belting out 'If you've got the money, honey, I've got the time,' is not appropriate for anyone."

She scooped up Bobby and carried him to the door, handing him off to a breathless young woman who'd hurried her way down from the auditorium.

"Did you have fun, Bobby? Of course you did! Let's go see Daddy."

The last of her energy ebbed away with the last of the toddlers. Despite the mass exodus and the exhaustion, Rylee reminded herself it wasn't a bad day. In fact, it may have been the best day she'd had since she started teaching cradle roll. At least as far as Lexie was concerned. She hadn't known what to expect, hadn't known how Lexie would do in class, especially if the way she clung to her dad was anything to judge by. She was worried that this first time would be the last.

Any kind of separation can be difficult at that age. Rylee knew that from experience. She knew it from watching the children and their parents, and from watching herself. Any kind of separation can be difficult at her age, too.

She prepared herself for weeks of coaxing Lexie from her father's arms, and she prepared herself for the kind of disappointment she was most familiar with when the dad decided it wasn't worth it and stopped bringing Lexie with him.

She thought of all this when she turned from Thom and settled Lexie into her tiny chair and wondered if she'd have the courage—or the strength—to suggest he keep bringing her with him.

"Have you been here before?" Rylee had asked him, her voice lilting with surprise as much as hope.

Her surprise intensified—and her hope as well— when Lexie stretched out her chubby little arms with an urgency known only to toddlers and reached for Rylee. Her dad's leaving didn't bother her in the least. Once he was gone, it didn't seem like he'd ever been there.

The thought that three months could pass and the same would be true of Lexie's attendance streak lingered in Rylee's mind as the last toddler made his exit.

But right now, Rylee reminded herself, Lexie was still here. And at least for today, she and Thom had separated without incident. That was more than Rylee could say for most of the other parents, and more than she'd expected for this first week.

If he brought Lexie next week, if they separated as easily as they did this time, maybe she'd have the nerve to suggest that Thom do more than drop Lexie off. Perhaps she wouldn't be too flustered to get the words out.

If he brought Lexie next week, if he looked at Rylee with the same piercing blue eyes, she hoped she'd have the spine to look back from beneath the root-beer colored hair she knew he noticed.

If he brought Lexie next week, she desperately hoped she could avoid another outburst brought on by sinful thoughts.

If he brought Lexie next week, maybe she'd have a volunteer and some help taming the apostle-hungry toddlers.

If he brought Lexie next week, maybe she'd have more than a glimmer of hope.

The passing thought gave her enough courage to face her fear of disappointment, and she managed to summon a last burst of energy as she gathered Lexie up and exhaled a weary, satisfied breath.

"You are a perfect angel."

Rylee said, planting a kiss on Lexie's forehead and thrilled that, for once, the words weren't hollow.

## Chapter 11

Thom had been waiting at the top of the stairs, only to be pushed back by the rush of children. He backed off to a corner and out of the tangle of small bodies. Rylee waded through the tide of children with the same grace as Venus rising from the sea. Thom stood transfixed, watching Rylee float toward him through the chaos.

Lexie again twisted around, trying to get a look at everything that was happening as the children swarmed past. By the time Rylee reached Thom, Lexie was altogether distracted by the perpetual commotion.

"She was a dear; you should be very proud of how well-behaved she was. Was this her first time in a class?"

Despite himself, Thom found himself wanting to talk with a church woman. He was entrapped by her voice as if her words were chains.

"Yes. So, she did all right, huh?" He mentally kicked himself for saying something so stupid. He felt the need to say something more intelligent, like, "Did you know I'm a lawyer, a state representative, and moderately wealthy?"

"She was a very good girl," Rylee responded.

Thom racked his brain for something to keep the conversation going when the balding guy walked up again.

"You really do have a cute little girl there," the man said. Thom jerked back to reality as he interpreted the friendly comment through his church-people-avoidance-radar as a subversive way to get more information out of him.

"Yeah, I think so."

Thom looked at Rylee and added, "It was nice to meet you, Ms. Vance. I'll see you next week." He turned abruptly and hurried to the front door.

"Hope I didn't scare him off," the man said as he watched Thom walk away.

"Of course you didn't, Scott," Rylee said.

Rylee patted him on the arm and smiled encouragingly before walking into the auditorium.

"That was kind of weird," she thought.

"And who were you talking to, Rylee?" Lisa put her arm through Rylee's.

"Oh, Lexie's father. I wanted him to know how well-behaved she was. Bobbie and Frankie were," Rylee wrinkled her nose. "Well, you know how rowdy those two can be. I feel sorry for their mothers. It was a blessing that Lexie was so good. I don't think I could have handled it by myself if she hadn't been such an angel."

"My honest opinion is that he's a total honey, just in case you're wondering."

Rylee ignored the comment.

"Lexie's father wasn't very talkative, and I wasn't able to get a phone number or any other information out of him. We were talking, and I thought that he might share some contact stuff with me, when he just ran away."

Lisa laughed. "Ran away? Seems all the guys we meet lately are running away."

Lisa gave Rylee an appraising look. "Must be you."

Rylee scowled at Lisa. "Behave."

"No. Why did he run away?"

"I don't know. He ended the conversation with the speed of a guillotine and scooted out the door."

"You asked him if he was married, didn't you?" Lisa gave her friend a disapproving look.

"No. Of course not! Do I look desperate?"

Lisa became uncharacteristically serious.

"No. But I do know electricity when I see it. I've been watching the static all morning. It's worse than this stupid skirt."

Rylee's eyes snapped angrily at Lisa. "Will you stop?" Taking a deep breath, she asked, "Was he in your class this morning?"

Lisa suppressed a grin.

"No, sorry to say that he wasn't. If he had been, I'd have all the pertinent information about him. You really need to try to be more aggressive there, Rylee girl, or I might draw his attention away from you."

Rylee bit her bottom lip. Sometimes Lisa was exasperating.

"Lisa, focus, please. He's married, and I think he might be a surfer."

"Well, Ms. Rylee, he looks like he knows what he's doing with the baby. I can't see a surfer being able to care for an infant. I, on the other hand, have no prejudices against surfers. I'll bet he looks yummy in a pair of baggies."

Lisa raised her hands to ward off Rylee's glare. "Okay. Okay. Try Jim's class. New people tend to stay in the auditorium's adult class. He may have parked his handsome little self in there."

"Right. He may have. Thanks."

Rylee abruptly excused herself to wander the auditorium in search of Jim Hooper. She was relieved to escape from the uncomfortable conversation with her friend. "Doesn't Lisa realize that he is a married man?" she mumbled.

When Rylee finally found Jim, he was discussing high school football with several young men. Rylee joined the group and waited until they had finished discussing a rival school's football program.

Jim Hooper, a retired physician, was most famous for his huge handlebar mustache. He was also the driving force behind the state's free clinics. After several years of successfully administering the state's free clinics, he had turned the task over to younger men and, at seventy-two, entered retirement.

Rylee had been surprised when Jim had asked her to help at the local free clinic. At the time, she was working as a secretary. She wasn't a medical professional by any stretch of imagination and didn't know what she could do to help. It turned out that every office, even a free one, needed administrative support personnel.

"Well, Ms. Vance, what can I assist you with today?" Jim asked as he turned to face her.

"Jim, did you have a blonde guy in class this morning?"

"Yeah, sure did. Came in and sat right in the back. He left as soon as all the kiddies came up from class."

"So, you didn't get to meet him either?"

"No. He was quick. Didn't say anything in class; while I can't be certain, I don't think he opened a Bible the entire time he was here. He just stared at the ceiling and out the window all during class."

He regarded Rylee with the practiced eye of an observer.

"Nice looking fellow. Why are you looking for him?" Rylee's blush did not go unnoticed by Jim.

"His daughter Lexie was in my cradle roll class, and I just wanted to meet her parents. She's a real charmer."

Jim's grey eyes twinkled as he nodded his head. "Well, I'll have to agree that she is a little cutie. How about I trip them up and hold them down next time until you get up here?"

That famous handlebar mustache appeared to be pulling his lips up into a smile.

## Chapter 12

By the time Thom made his way through the bleak parking lot, carrying Lexie like a fragile secret, he couldn't help but feel torn apart. Lexie had grown fussy, and every step he took only deepened the nagging doubt about his sanity. A promise had compelled him to enter this place where he no longer belonged.

Lexie's tiny fingers clutched at his collar as if pleading for comfort, while his eyes darted around—there wasn't a single soul in sight. He imagined that inside the building, everyone was still wrapped up in their rituals, maybe singing hymns or indulging in long, drawn-out amens, gossiping about the mundane absurdities of the week. None of them were slipping away early like him.

"Good," he murmured.

His statement was laced with guilt as if he had just robbed a candy store. Having the deserted lot all to himself felt like a temporary relief—a clear path to escape the relentless barrage of inquisitive stares and intrusive smiles. He longed to avoid another awkward prying interaction with earnest church members. He hungered for another moment when Rylee's hopeful eyes would meet his. Suddenly, he felt embarrassed by running away like a thief.

The weight of it all was overwhelming; he felt irredeemably misplaced; caught between the hated burden of a promise he couldn't escape and the allure of the young woman with root beer-colored hair.

Lexie squirmed as he tried, with unsteady hands, to

secure her into the car seat, her little struggles echoing the rebellion brewing within him. Desperation took over as he rifled through the diaper bag for a bottle of juice, clinging to the hope that it would pacify her and help him vanish from this place unnoticed.

"Here you go, pretty baby. Who's my good girl?" Crooned softly, the words meant more for his own reassurance than to soothe the restless child.

Crouched beside the car, he held the bottle in place, watching slowly as Lexie's eyes locked onto the promise of juice, her wriggling finally subsiding. He lowered himself so he could meet her gaze while also keeping watch at the entrance of the building. He told himself it was to avoid anyone coming after him for more intel. But in truth, he knew it was hope that Rylee would reappear with her disarming yet daunting charm.

Every split second, his heart pounded with the anticipation of another unwanted interaction. Minutes ticked by until it was undeniable that no one was coming. He allowed an exasperated sigh mingled with relief to escape.

Thom whispered, "Let's go home, Lexie."

Sliding into the driver's seat, he sat frozen for a moment, his mind awash with the surreal mixture of freedom and inescapable entanglement. He felt like a fish gasping in unfamiliar water, desperate to find its way back to the safe, familiar pond.

Before turning on the engine, he stole one last glance at the building through the rearview mirror. Was it sheer madness that caused him to linger as he both dreaded and hoped for a glimpse of Rylee?

A part of him craved something more, something he

knew would be dangerous, beyond the bounds of shattered faith. As tension twisted the lines around his eyes and his reflection stared back in a silent challenge, he could only mutter to himself: "I must be crazy."

## Chapter 13

"Ick! They have liver and onions on the menu!"

Lisa's top lip curled as she punctuated her comment by pointing out the offending offering on the menu to the entire table.

"Some people enjoy liver and onions," replied Rylee. Pious distaste illuminated Lisa's face.

"I'm certain that somewhere in the Bible it says eating liver and onions is a sin, and probably licorice as well. You don't really like liver and onions, do you?"

"I must confess that one of my sins is a preference for licorice. I have tried liver and onions, but I would prefer the chicken. At least I tried them before passing judgment."

"Thank goodness you're not entirely overtaken by sin; there's hope for you yet!" Lisa said.

Rylee had always enjoyed being with this group.

They were usually fun and always noisy. The topics changed quickly when they were together, and it was sometimes hard to keep up with the flow of conversation. They had leaped from the sin of liver and onions to the contemplation of what to do that afternoon.

"Rylee, wake up." "Huh?"

"Our down-to-earth Rylee appears to have gone to another planet."

Lisa leaned closer to Rylee before she erupted into a broad smile.

"Don't tell me that you are daydreaming? It wouldn't have

anything to do with that honey we saw on the way into services this morning?" Lisa asked.

"She was adorable, wasn't she?"

Lisa crossed her arms and raised her eyebrows as she looked knowingly around the table.

"Yeah. That little, Brown-Eyed Susan was endearing, but sweetie, I was talking about the tall blonde one."

Rylee blushed, which drew hoots from the now attentive group.

"I hardly spoke to her father," Rylee defended.

Lisa leaned toward Rylee, with green eyes glimmering.

"True. But you really tried hard to talk to him."

Rylee's mouth tightened as she struggled to remain calm.

"I just wanted to encourage her parents to bring Lexie back. Besides, Lisa, he's a married man with a baby. It's just wicked to—"

Rylee trailed off at Lisa's amused look. Lisa was bursting; everyone else at the table was alert.

"Are you telling me that you didn't look for the ring? You didn't, did you? If he is married, where is his wedding ring? I looked. There was no ring or sign of a ring having been there. And he's slightly tanned."

Rylee's mouth dropped open; her face flamed.

Delighting in the scandalous nature of the conversation, Lisa added, "Of course, I checked. He's cute, and that shirt fits him well. And he didn't look that bad walking away either."

There were several more hoots from the table.

"He could still be married and just not wear his ring," Dave interjected.

Lisa turned her full attention to Dave.

"Oh, right. He probably takes his wedding ring off and goes trolling around churches to pick up girls with his baby. Is that something that guys do all the time, Dave? Are you planning on doing that?"

Dave's response to Lisa started a different, equally animated conversation at the table, to Rylee's relief.

"Why would an unmarried guy bring a baby to church? Maybe he was divorced. Great, a surfer with baggage," Rylee thought.

"Rylee, do you want to come or not?" Lisa asked.

"Where?"

"Still distracted by Blondie, are you? I think you've got it bad."

Rylee frowned and asked in a firmer tone, "Where?"

Lisa waved a dismissive hand at Rylee.

"Miniature golf. Can't stop thinking about the cute guy, can you? You aren't going to be able to focus on anything else today."

Irritation painted Rylee's face.

"I've got to wash some clothes this afternoon," she snapped.

"Uh-huh. And daydream some more about Mr. Good-Looking without having me there to tease you," Lisa said.

## Chapter 14

The next morning, Rylee buried her head under the pillow, trying to muffle the harsh, grating sound of her alarm clock. Like somebody rudely banging on a metal trash can, it thrust her from the comfort of sleep into the chilling reality of Monday morning. She held a small hope that if she ignored it long enough, it might stop on its own or, even better, magically reset itself to a more civilized hour. It did stop—eventually—and Rylee peeked one eye open to glare at the device responsible for her rude awakening. Can it really be morning already?

With a resigned sigh, she swung her legs over the side of the bed and rubbed her eyes, trying to shake off the remnants of sleep and any lingering thoughts of the previous day's conversation. Her yellow-striped cat, Squeaker lounged on the bed, completely unimpressed by any displays of human irritation, his eyes merely slits of disapproval.

"Oh, so sorry, Squeaker. I didn't mean to disturb you," she quipped, her voice dripping with sarcasm.

Squeaker, oblivious to the irony, stretched luxuriously. He arched his back like a victory celebration, then curled back into a contented ball on the blanket, secure in his status as the least industrious member of the household.

Rylee glanced out the window, noting the golden rays of sunlight streaming in, casting a warm glow across her room.

"At least the sun is shining even though it's Monday."

She poked Squeaker gently, half-heartedly hoping he'd wake up and offer some sympathy. But he remained unfazed, dozing in peaceful serenity, immune to the struggles of her adult responsibilities.

It wasn't until the clatter of her preparing tea in the kitchen rattled through the apartment that he suddenly, miraculously, revived. Now animated, the cat leaped from the bed and dashed to the kitchen, meowing loudly in demand for his breakfast as if he had been starved for weeks.

An hour later, after ensuring Squeaker was once again curled up and satisfied, Rylee headed out the door for work. She drove to the small, unassuming building on the edge of town, home to the manufacturing company owned by Mr. Halpern. Inside, the office hummed with activity, a stark contrast to this morning's leisurely pace. Rylee worked under the watchful eye of Mr. Halpern's executive secretary, Ms. Blackman. Her tasks entailed anything that Mrs. Blackburn didn't want to do.

"Good morning, Ms. Vance. Did you have a nice weekend?"

Ms. Blackman's greeting tone was as predictable as her starched white blouse. Rylee often imagined she could recount fantastical tales of alien abductions or brain transplants, and Ms. Blackman would merely nod, unfazed.

"Yes, thank you. It was very quiet," Rylee replied, her voice steady.

"Good. I left some credit card receipts on your desk that Mr. Halpern hadn't given to me. Fortunately, I occasionally check his desk. He's hopeless with these important details," Ms. Blackman remarked, her lips curving into a self-satisfied smile.

"Not a problem, Ms. Blackman," Rylee said, hiding her

amusement.

Ms. Blackman snorted, a dismissive sound Rylee had come to expect. Despite Ms. Blackman's self-importance, Rylee knew the real driving force behind the company was Mr. Halpern. While Ms. Blackman liked to project an air of authority, she was just another secretary, much like Rylee. And Mr. Halpern, for all his disorganization, never sought Ms. Blackman's counsel on business matters, a fact Rylee found quietly satisfying.

As the day dragged on, each hour felt more extended than the last. Phones rang with unwavering persistence, demanding immediate answers to questions that seemed increasingly irrelevant as the minutes ticked by. Orders were placed, corrected, and sometimes misplaced, adding to the chaos that was the company's daily routine. Rylee found herself flagging each small triumph with a silent cheer, marking the path to quitting time with growing anticipation.

"Where are those receipts I left you?"

Ms. Blackman's voice broke Rylee's focus on the mountain of paperwork in front of her.

"Right here," Rylee replied, holding up the neatly organized stack.

She knew exactly where they were, unlike Mr. Halpern, who probably didn't even know that they existed.

"Good," Ms. Blackman said, as if she expected anything less would be a monumental failure.

"Make sure they're done before you leave today."

"Will do, Ms. Blackman," Rylee confirmed, not even glancing up.

She calculated the time left until she could escape to do what she enjoyed—a mere two hours and twelve minutes.

After work that evening, Rylee headed directly to the Orchard Street Free Clinic. Working at Halpern's paid the bills, but volunteering at the Free Clinic made her feel like she was doing something worthwhile. She couldn't wait to get there.

Chapter 15

Rylee slipped on her worn sneakers and stepped out into the cool, gray light of early dusk. The clinic was just a short walk from Halpern's, and Rylee could leave her car in the private lot instead of having to find parking on the street.

The city was beginning to hum with the evening rush. The neon sign flickering above the clinic entrance was a welcome sight. Volunteering there wasn't just a way to spend her spare time; it filled her with a profound sense of purpose, a small but steady belief that her efforts could brighten the lives of those who struggled every day.

Inside the clinic, the atmosphere was a mix of urgency and tender care. Rylee had discovered early on that, behind the compassionate smiles and hopeful conversations, running a free clinic required more than just good intentions.

This was where her knack for numbers and organization became indispensable. She meticulously balanced the clinic's books at her desk, poring over donation records and state reimbursement forms with a concentration that rivaled the antiseptic calm of the examination rooms.

Despite her efficient work, every spreadsheet and carefully logged donation told her a heartbreaking story of people in desperate need. When she first started working, she was amazed at the weight of the responsibility.

"How did Jim and his colleagues manage to shoulder this full-time," she wondered, "when so many patients arrived with needs that went far beyond a simple check-up?"

Determined to make a broader impact, Rylee transformed herself into a valuable resource hub for the clinic's patients. She scoured community bulletin boards, combed government directories, and even contacted local charities until she compiled an extensive file of addresses and contact information for food banks, daycare services, clothing drives, and housing opportunities.

She kept the information on this list meticulously updated, ensuring that those stepping through the clinic's doors could be guided to additional help—a network of support that she had built with both relentless effort and a hope for better futures.

Though Rylee couldn't share her deep faith by preaching directly, she found comfort in directing patients toward compassionate, Christian-run programs.

Sometimes, after handing out pamphlets about local soup kitchens or affordable daycares, she received quiet thanks that reassured her she was making a meaningful impact. It was enough for her to know that her indirect guidance planted seeds of hope while colleagues who were more versed in direct outreach took the next steps.

Standing in the clinic's modest foyer, Rylee greeted her co-workers in a warm, steady tone.

"Hello everyone," she began, her voice soft but carrying an undercurrent of resolve.

Murmurs of concern quickly reached her ears, and worried faces turned toward her.

"What's wrong?"

June Stuart, standing near a desk cluttered with papers

and a computer humming steadily, pursed her lips.

"Rylee, there's a new bill in the state legislature—a bill to cut taxes that might, in turn, slash funding for a lot of services, including our free clinics," she explained, her voice laced with apprehension.

Rylee's eyes widened as she tried to absorb June's news, a frown replacing the calm resolve on her face. June moved to her cluttered desk and tapped on her computer screen, inviting Rylee to take a look.

"Read it for yourself," she said quietly.

Leaning over June's shoulder, Rylee scanned the dense paragraphs on the monitor and then shook her head in confusion.

"June, this document doesn't mention free clinics at all," she murmured, tracing a finger along the printed words.

June scrolled back up to a highlighted section that discussed the duplication of health and human services already reimbursed by Medicaid or Medicare. June remained still to let Rylee read the critical lines.

"What it means is if a local hospital provides these services, the state won't need to reimburse the free clinics. It's all wrapped up in bureaucratic jargon meant to mask a larger cutback."

Her words came out in a low, indignant whisper as her eyes flashed with barely concealed outrage.

"No way! How could they possibly get away with that?" She leaned back, her mind racing with questions.

"How did you find out about this?"

June leaned forward over her cluttered desk, her tone even but urgent.

"I'm always monitoring the health and human services documents, and legislature links to catch potential funding sources or cuts. I came across this one during my daily scroll. It's all here," she said, her finger now circling the fine print on the screen.

"How could they do this to people who need help?"

"It hasn't been voted on yet—it's not law until a majority decides it. But from the looks of it, they're pushing it through faster than anyone's noticed. We could try talking to our representatives, but it's a long shot. At first glance, most legislators see nothing but tax cuts, missing the deeper consequences until it's too late." Her expression hardened as she said, "It would take more than just the two of us to get their full attention on this hidden crisis."

Rylee's head spun with the enormity of what was unfolding. She had never been all that interested in the intricacies of state legislation, and now, with every word, she felt the ground shift beneath her feet.

An ominous feeling crept over her. This bill wasn't just a change in numbers on a page, and she had no idea how to fight it.

## Chapter 16

As the evening dragged on at the clinic, Rylee felt as if she were drowning.

"How could this happen?" she thought.

Emotionally exhausted, she went through monotonous paperwork, trying to focus on what was in front of her instead of the what-ifs and whys she couldn't answer.

She yanked at her desk drawer to retrieve an envelope and, predictably, it jammed halfway out. Instinctively, she reached for the nail puller she kept handy to wrench it free from its decades-old track.

"This drawer is so battered," she thought, her eyes narrowing in on its mangled edge.

Her glazed-over stare suddenly snapped into a wild, sharp focus as realization struck her.

"This entire desk is battered and bruised!" she thought.

Rylee scrutinized the desk's scarred surface beneath mountains of paperwork. Her gaze expanded, taking in the entire room and its threadbare furnishings. Even her chair was patched with army green duct tape, and she was astounded by how she had never registered its dilapidated state before.

"How could it be that anyone could claim free clinics didn't need every last penny they could muster?"

Her numb frustration evaporated, replaced by a burning, righteous rage.

Slamming her hand down on her desk, she said, "I bet the duct tape is secondhand, too!"

She stood abruptly.

"It's outrageous! We're not living it up in luxury here. There's nothing lavish or indulgent in this place."

June's head snapped up from her computer screen.

Rylee pressed on, fueled by disbelief.

"We've got three ancient computers, for heaven's sake. Even the magazines are last year's editions, scavenged from the hospital. And don't get me started on our medical equipment! How can anyone say we don't need the funding?"

She glanced at June and Rob Patterson, both highly skilled professionals who offered their expertise without payment. Even the rest of the medical staff provided their services free of charge.

Rylee's foot slammed against the floor. Her words were heavy with determination.

"This is unacceptable. We must stop this bill." Her face took on a resolved grimace. "No, I must stop this bill."

"Yeah, you and what army?" Rob challenged, his voice dripping with skepticism as a slight, knowing smile curled at the corners of his lips.

With her chin raised defiantly and eyes blazing, Rylee glared at Rob.

"I'll raise one!" she declared.

Wide-eyed, June and Rob watched in stunned silence as Rylee spun around and dropped into her chair. Rob shook his head and sighed, then resumed making phone calls. June's face was a question mark, but her lips remained sealed as her fingers tapped urgently on her keyboard.

Rylee sat motionless for a moment, frozen by the enormity of the task she had just vowed to take on. Then, with renewed resolve, she dove back into the piles of paperwork.

# Mayzie Sterling

"Holy Father," she prayed silently, "please guide me to a way to prevent this disaster. Illuminate the path so that the work here can endure."

## Chapter 17

After leaving the clinic late in the evening, Rylee slept fitfully. Her dreams were tangled and restless, haunted by images of the empty clinic and state legislators strolling triumphantly through its rooms.

She awoke in the middle of the night, struggling to remember every detail of the proposed bill. As the first light of morning seeped through her windows, she sat up abruptly in bed and jotted down a list of ideas to fight the bill. She filled the page with contact numbers, meeting dates, and names of local groups she could contact for support.

Over breakfast, her mind spun with frantic energy.

Everything she read in the paper leapt out as a potential threat—or a potential opportunity. She planned to corner Jim later that day to discuss organizing a formal protest, but knew she'd first have to bring him and the others at the clinic fully up to speed. Rylee was determined to push forward, even if it meant facing doubts from people who didn't understand what was at stake.

That evening, she met Lisa for aerobics class. Rylee hoped the exercise would help her sort some of her racing thoughts, but she found herself distracted, her resolve splintering and bending in all directions with every beat of the music. As the class wore on, she realized her friend was watching her intently, curiously.

Rylee slipped to the back of the group, but Lisa followed her as the music pulsed around them.

"What's going on?" Lisa whispered, her tone amused but perceptive.

Rylee blinked at her, unsure of how much Lisa had already guessed.

"What do you mean?" she replied, sounding casual.

Lisa punched the air, keeping time with the instructor.

"You're a million miles away," she said. "I've never seen you miss a step, and today's routine is practically aerobics for toddlers."

Rylee laughed, a bit helplessly. "A lot on my mind, I guess."

"Yeah?" Lisa prodded, unfazed by Rylee's brevity. "Does that 'lot' have to do with Mr. Good-Looking?"

Rylee sighed and shook her head, giving up the pretense of focus.

"No."

Lisa stopped working out. "No?" She frowned at her friend. "Well, something's got you all worked up."

"You could say that."

"It would be more fun if it were Surfer Dude."

Now, Rylee paused her workout. She noted the instructor looking at the two of them.

"Can this wait until after class?"

"Okay, spill. What's got you so worked up?" Lisa asked, straight to the point. "I can't wait. This has got to be good," Lisa said, a grin spreading across her face.

"Well, you're going to have to."

Lisa lowered her arms and head-bobbed to the music, shifting to a softer dance as she kept chatting.

"You'll feel better when you spill it."

They moved in sync, slowing to a swirl of arms, then to a rhythmic sidestep.

Rylee didn't take her eyes off the instructor until class was finished, ignoring Lisa, who continued to pelt her with questions.

"All right, all right! I'll tell you. Just let me shower and change first."

Smirking, Lisa patiently waited as they gathered their things and slipped into the crowded locker room, where women from other classes filled it. As they changed clothes, Rylee jotted a few more notes on a scrap of paper.

"Paperwork even here?" Lisa teased, catching sight of the scribble.

Rylee rolled her eyes. "Something like that."

The locker room emptied in a whirlwind of chatter and hairspray, leaving the two friends to walk out at their own pace. Lisa was determined to hear Rylee's complete account of the situation, but she resisted the urge to pry until they were well out of the door of the gym.

Rylee could see the thought balloon forming above her friend's head.

"Lisa's not going to let me leave without knowing every last detail," she thought. "She's like a dog with a bone."

"You've got that look on your face again—and I'm not talking about the dreamy one from yesterday when you were swooning over Mr. Cute New Guy. This is different, something gnawing at you that's far from charming."

Rylee glared at her friend.

"His name is Thom Simms." Lisa's eyebrow shot up.
"Oh, my goodness."

"Lisa, no teasing. I'm distraught."

"That's more than obvious. While a discussion about Mr. Thom Simms would be fascinating, I need to know what's eating at you. You've got that deep furrow between your eyes that only shows up when you're truly distressed."

Rylee let out a sharp laugh and draped her arm around Lisa. "Thanks for the wrinkle reminder. I'm not even sure where to start."

"Woo-hoo! This screams Coffee Café! Let's go; I'm absolutely craving one of their pecan sticky buns."

Rylee exhaled, tension loosening its grip. She enveloped Lisa in a fierce hug.

"Thanks, Lisa. If anyone can pull me out of this, it's you. I'll meet you there and spill everything over coffee and doughnuts."

"Uh, that was pecan sticky buns, thank you very much."

## Chapter 18

"Oh, these are phenomenal. Look, Rylee, it's impossible to wallow in misery when you're indulging in these. I swear, I feel lighter already!"

"You're not the one dwelling under that furrowed scowl between your brows that you so helpfully pointed out,"

Rylee took a measured sip of her coffee while glancing at her friend ravenously devouring a pecan bun.

Lisa, her hands sticky and determined, wiped them on a napkin and leaned forward. "Spill the tea. What's with the long face?"

Rylee leaned back, gripping Lisa's hand as if to steady herself. "You know I spend time at the free clinic."

Lisa nodded, her expression encouraging.

"Well, one of the other volunteers discovered a bill hurtling through the state legislature. If it passes, reimbursements to the free clinics will be slashed to nearly nothing."

"But I thought it was a free clinic—it doesn't cost anyone."

Rylee sighed and shook her head.

"It is free for the patients. Every single person working there is a volunteer. Yet, the expenses keep piling up—rent, utilities, and more. We're living on donations from private organizations and generous individuals, but those funds have limits.

Sometimes, equipment is donated, but often, we must

purchase used, worn-out gear. And medicine? Medicine always comes with a price tag. I've become a relentless battler against Medicaid and Medicare, trying desperately to recoup any costs for patient care."

Lisa's eyes darkened with a pensive gravity. "Oh."

"When Jim Hooper first asked me to volunteer, I was clueless about what I'd get into—I thought they only needed clerical help, filing and typing and stuff."

Rylee squeezed Lisa's hand.

"Lisa, they need so much more. And now, the state plans to strip free clinics of reimbursements for services they provide, pointing out that hospitals already provide those services. Many patients avoid hospitals because they're hit with forms declaring they're liable for payment. The free clinic is their sole refuge."

Rylee's voice trembled with urgency as she sipped her coffee. "Lisa, I can't say how critical this is to me. I want to halt this bill, but I'm overwhelmed by how to fight it."

Lisa's demeanor shifted from concerned to razor-sharp. "Oh, is that all?"

Rylee nearly slammed her cup down in despair.

"Lisa, it's not that simple. It requires an army. Where do I scrounge up that kind of force? I know nothing about the inner workings of government, and I doubt you do either. Who do I address? How do I make them listen? One single voice is a whisper in a hurricane. The vote is looming, this is unfolding too rapidly, and I'm not even sure if we can stop it anymore. Where do I begin?"

Leaning fiercely across the table, Lisa's emerald eyes blazed.

"I can't believe I'm the one with all the answers while you, Ms. Smarty Pants, are floundering." Lisa sat up straight and wriggled. "I feel exceptional right now. This is nice."

With her mouth agape and a look of shock, Rylee slouched back. Lisa drained her cup and stood.

"We're going to need more sticky buns. Being brilliant is exhausting."

Rylee scowled as she watched Lisa stride toward the counter. Moments later, Lisa returned with more sticky buns, piping hot chocolates, and that same infuriating, smug smile.

"Lisa, you don't understand," Rylee argued, tension coiling in her voice.

Lisa re-settled at the table, meticulously arranging her napkin. She handed Rylee a cup of hot chocolate.

"I figured we needed something more substantial than coffee. Rylee, there are people you know who know the system inside out. We must start asking the right questions. You're brilliant; you can decipher this mess."

"We? What do you mean, we'?"

Giggling lightly yet resolutely, Lisa grabbed Rylee's arm. "Rylee, you have an entire army waiting for you—an army that you obviously never even realized existed. All you have to do is wake them up. I know you know this, girl," Lisa continued, her grip firm and eyes unwavering. "In moments of panic, your clarity gets clouded. You're connected to a legion of people bursting with resources and information— college students, our vibrant young adult group, and even Dave, who's deep into government studies. What better force could you rally than that?"

## Chapter 19

"Lexie? Where's Lexie?" Thom called out, filling the cozy room with his playful voice.

He feigned confusion, peeking under cushions and behind curtains as Lexie's giggles erupted from under a soft, pastel blanket.

Her laughter echoed like a sweet, tinkling bell, and Thom couldn't help but join in with a chuckle. He pulled the blanket back, revealing her bright eyes and cheeky grin. Lexie squealed in delight, her tiny, chubby hands reaching for the blanket to hide her face again, eager for more peek- a-boo.

"Oh, funny girl," Thom said with a warm laugh, bending down to scoop her up. He lifted her easily into his arms, her tiny body nestled against his side.

"We've got to get ready to go play with your friends," he told her, bouncing her gently as he walked.

"Time for breakfast," he announced, carrying her down the hallway.

Family photos lined the walls, capturing smiles and memories that grew with each passing day. Thom's cheerful, off-key singing accompanied them as they entered the kitchen.

Sunlight streamed through the expansive windows, casting a golden glow across the room and making the polished wooden table gleam. Thom settled Lexie into her highchair, buckling the straps securely around her tiny waist. He presented her with a spoonful of mashed banana, but she batted at his hand in playful rebellion.

Her eyes sparkled with a spunky determination, almost daring him to try again. Thom grinned, knowing this routine all too well now. It was hard to believe that just six months ago, everything about caring for a baby had felt so alien to him.

The bottles, diapers, doctor visits, and lack of sleep had once overwhelmed him, leaving him frazzled and second-guessing at every turn. He'd felt like a fish out of water, gasping for air as he navigated the newness. His worries had piled up like an insurmountable mountain, the constant need for attention and affection weighing heavily on his mind.

But as days turned into weeks and Lexie settled into his heart, the challenges seamlessly melted into joy. Now, he moved through the daily routine with the natural ease of someone who had been doing it for years.

"Come on, little rebel."

Thom expertly dodged Lexie's attempts to evade the washcloth. Her mischievous hands pushed against him, smearing banana on his cheeks and nose, but he was not so easily deterred. He gently stroked the cloth across her face, leaving her clean and giggling. It was a skill he never imagined he'd master, yet he felt like a pro.

Later, as he readied himself for work, Thom tucked papers into his briefcase and felt something bulky and familiar. He pulled out a well-chewed book of nursery rhymes. The frayed edges and tooth-marked pages were a testament to how loved it was.

Six months ago, a discovery like this would have left him flustered and scrambling to understand this new life. Now, it only brings warmth.

It was a joyful reminder of how Lexie had transformed

his world entirely, filling it with a love and purpose he hadn't known he was missing. He smiled, his heart swelling with gratitude and disbelief at how right it all felt.

Thom swung the diaper bag over his shoulder and grabbed the car seat, feeling like the world's most fulfilled man as he headed out the door with a pleased Lexie in tow.

## Chapter 20

Chip closed the file drawer that he had been looking through.

"Hey, boss."

"Morning, Chip. Did you get out on the water this weekend?"

With his leather briefcase in tow, Thom made his way through the narrow reception area and into the only office in the small space.

"Yeah, tried out my friend's new skidoo. It was a hoot. I need to get one of those for myself. You should come sometime."

Thom laughed.

"Ah, to be young and carefree."

"Bring Lexie along. We'll strap her car seat to a boogie board."

"Yeah, that's what I'm afraid of."

"So, what did you do this weekend?"

"You would never believe me." Thom turned to face his paralegal. "What do you have for me today?"

Chip raised an eyebrow but didn't ask what Thom had meant. He picked up the calendar and strode into Thom's office.

"George Dawson wants to meet with you today or tomorrow about the tax cut."

"Really. Coming here? I bet they're counting votes. When am I seeing him?"

"Tomorrow, early afternoon. No way I was letting him in here on such short notice. I figured that if it were during lunch time, he wouldn't want to stay too long."

"Thanks, Chip. What else do we have?"

Chip ran down the list of appointments, senate business, court deadlines, and things on Thom's desk that needed signatures or attention.

"Good, sounds like a light week. How's school going?"

Chip shrugged. "Oh, you know what it's like."

Thom began perusing a file on his desk. Chip turned to go.

"Got any offers?" Thom queried.

"Offers?" Chip paused at the door of the office.

"Yeah. Clerking for a judge or interning at a law firm. You know, offers."

Chip approached Thom's desk.

"Why? Has someone been talking to you?"

"Yeah."

Thom started reading another file. Chip stood at the desk quietly. Thom, suppressing a smile, looked up at him.

"Something you want, Mr. Fallon?"

"Yeah. Who's been talking to you, Thom?"

Eye's wide with surprise, Thom said, "My goodness, Chip. It seems that you're acting like my partner."

Thom locked hard blue eyes with Chip. Chip did not break eye contact, and Thom lost his fight to keep from smiling.

"Interested, buddy?"

Chip stammered out, "What? What?"

"Chip, you are much more than a paralegal here. You might as well be my partner. Pretty soon, you'll take the bar and be a real attorney. We don't make much money here, and I spend time fiddling with politics, but I think the caseload could support more than one attorney. Just look at this week: I will be chasing my tail around as it is, and I think it's an easy week. If it wasn't for you, I couldn't have done it. I think the practice has grown enough that I can share the caseload with a partner."

Chip stood still with a genuinely shocked expression.

"That is, unless you have a better offer. And to tell you the truth, I wouldn't be surprised." Chip fell into one of the chairs. "Partner?"

"Yeah. Partner. Shoot, you could even draw up the partnership agreement yourself."

"But I haven't finished law school yet – let alone passed the bar."

Thom was getting a little concerned. His thoughts swirled. "What if Chip wasn't interested? What if he had acted prematurely?"

He looked at Chip and smirked.

"You'll pass the bar. But if you want to take a little time to think about it—"

Still shocked, Chip repeated, "Partner?"

Thom laughed. "Take your time, Chip."

"I don't need time." Chip stuck out his hand.

Grinning, Thom stood up and took it.

"I had been hoping that you would hire me as an attorney. Wow – partner. This is so cool."

Chip pumped Thom's hand.

"Yeah. It is cool, partner. Let's get to work."

"What do I do now?" Chip said, still stunned.

Thom handed him a file. "We're going to need a partnership agreement.

But first, we need to get an ad for a legal secretary in

the afternoon edition of the paper. And then stand back for the tidal wave of responses."

Thom knew that legal secretary resumes would come in as soon as the ad hit the paper. The last time he ran an ad, he received over two hundred applications. On top of what his week already looked like, it was going to get moonbat-crazy.

## Chapter 21

Chip spent the morning fully absorbed in his work, his fingers tapping rhythmically on the keyboard as he crafted the advertisement for the legal secretary position. He aimed to capture Thom's unique voice—a mix of assertiveness and playful wit, much like the man himself. The clock ticked away, and Chip barely finished the ad in time to get it in the evening edition.

Then, with a little more nervousness, he dived into the intricacies of the partnership agreement. Occasionally, he paused to admire the header, where the names Richardson and Fallon stood united in bold, black letters, symbolizing a monumental shift and the vast potential of this opportunity.

Meanwhile, Thom sat at his desk, surrounded by towering piles of paperwork. Having the state senate president want to talk with him about the tax cut bill, Thom wanted to ensure he understood it completely. Time flew by while he was engrossed in the bill's complexities, his mind a whirlwind of strategies and logistics.

Finally, Thom leaned back in his leather chair, stretching his arms above his head.

"What do you say, partner? Feel like grabbing a bite to celebrate?" he proposed.

He flashed a grin that hinted at more than just a meal.

"I found this awesome-looking restaurant and want to try it out."

Chip welcomed the pause, as he had been stressing about perfecting the partnership agreement language. He raised an eyebrow with curiosity.

"Sounds great, but I sense there's a plot twist here.
Since when have you scoped out restaurants? You're a food truck kind of guy."

"Well, we should meet with our realtor while we're out. He has an office space he wants to show us. The restaurant is just across the street. If it's any good, that will be a bonus for the location."

Thom's eyes were gleaming with excitement at the prospect of expanding their horizons.

Chip was momentarily wordless as he glanced around their small, utilitarian office that had served them well. He noted the crammed file cabinets, the precariously stacked legal pads, and the coffee stains ingrained into the worn carpet.

"That's why you were so eager to move. You've been planning to ask me to be your partner for a while," he realized, piecing together the clues.

"Yep," Thom confirmed, tucking the gathered paperwork into his briefcase.

"You'll need your own office unless you want to sit out here with the secretary."

"Guess it depends on the secretary," Chip replied with a wink, imagining who might fill the role in their soon-to-be lively new space.

Thom snorted, his way of returning the banter.

"Okay, boss."

"Okay, partner."

They both laughed as they exited the office, Thom holding the door for Chip as they stepped into this new chapter of their professional journey.

## Chapter 22

"I'm driving. Can't pick up girls in your minivan."

Chip declared with a smirk, jangling his keys confidently. The café Thom had mentioned was right across the street from the prospective office and provided a good view of the building and traffic.

The café served simple dishes, but the food and coffee tasted good. This was a location plus in Thom's book.

"This isn't a great part of town, is it?"

Thom's eyes scanned the scene outside the café window. The street was lined with a patchwork of small businesses, each with a story etched into its facade. Chip followed Thom's gaze, taking in the worn but bustling area.

"Well, you know that the folks down here need attorneys too, even if they don't make six figures," Chip replied.

Thom could hear a hint of determination in his voice.

"Ah, still the starry-eyed dreamer out to save the world," Thom remarked.

Chip leaned forward, resting his elbows on the table, and fixed Thom with a knowing look.

"Oh, don't try that with me. You didn't charge anything for probating that estate a few months ago."

"The family will come back to me next time they need something—just good marketing. There wasn't much to probate anyway," Thom countered with a shrug.

"Uh-huh. If I remember," Chip began, but Thom cut him off.

"Shh. Attorneys aren't supposed to be nice. Remember,

we're heartless sharks and blood-sucking scum. It's on the bar exam," Thom interrupted, his tone dripping with mock seriousness.

"Yeah. And you're in local politics for the money, right? Just so we're clear, I'm not the only starry-eyed dreamer here. Besides, I don't see any other law offices around. That smells like opportunity to me."

Chip gestured at the street. "Look no law offices."

"You noticed that too. So smart of me to make you my partner."

They crossed the street to the prospective location. The business, though not high end, were alive with the hum people and the murmur of traffic. They found the realtor waiting for them inside, a welcoming smile on his face.

"Not a bad location. Visible from the street, but with plenty of parking out back." The realtor intoned.

Thom, surveying the area with a critical eye knew that Chip was correct. There weren't any law offices even close. He had driven around the area with Lexie on Saturday to check that out. It was also conveniently located in the middle of the district he represented.

"I get dibs on the office with the good view," Chip quipped.

Thom saw no remarkable views from either office. The realtor led them on a guided tour of the building. The interior was in good shape, with street-level access offering a bright reception area, a cozy conference room, and a handicapped-accessible bathroom. Upstairs, between the two offices, there was an open space for support staff, a compact kitchenette, and a good-sized storage room. These amenities were upgrades from their current office, which lacked kitchen facilities and a conference room.

After the tour, Thom extended a hand to the realtor, shaking it firmly.

"We're going to take a walk around the neighborhood. This looks good. My partner and I will get back to you. Thanks."

Thom's mind was already envisioning this new location's possibilities.

Thom and Chip took a mental inventory of the neighborhood surrounding their prospective office space as they strolled along the street. The sun cast long, golden rays driving back the shadows as Thom quietly absorbed the sights and sounds of the area.

The hum of middle- to lower-income businesses buzzed around them, a symphony of urban existence. Unpretentious coffee shops exuded the rich aroma of freshly brewed beans, thrift stores displayed eclectic collections in their windows, and mom-and-pop boutiques and grocery stores stood proudly, each jostling for attention like colorful characters in a lively play. The upper stories of the buildings contained offices or apartments. There was a bail bondsman and, catching Thom's eye, a private eye, but no lawyers within walking distance.

The business district eventually turned into lower-income single-family homes. Again, a potential marketing venue.

Foot and automobile traffic was moderate. A few bums lived in the alleyways, but mostly, it appeared to be a vibrant working-class community. Thom mulled over these observations, struck by a sudden appreciation for the diversity and spirited energy that thrummed in the hustle around him. His current office is located near the state capital building and surrounded by many law firms. The idea of escaping their old, stuffy office began to feel electrifyingly real.

He nudged Chip and mused aloud, "You know, having an office in a neighborhood like this is gonna reach a clientele that we couldn't back in the old place." Thom's thoughts were fresh with possibilities.

The neighborhood pulsed with potential for Richardson and Fallon, a promising spot for their new partnership to flourish and grow. Thom's mind raced through the prospects, one vision after another. Maybe Chip was right after all. This location could be a marketing dream, especially with the lack of competition from other law offices. A range of businesses, with everything from pawn shops to quirky diners, this vibrant neighborhood offered a chance to connect with an untapped clientele who avoided the big law firms downtown. The surroundings were perfect for a practice that wasn't interested in charging big-city rates. Something about the lively, variegated atmosphere felt like the start of an exciting chapter. Unlike their old office, this space had potential. It was teeming with possibilities while not straying from Thom's vision.

The idea of moving felt real, adventurous, and strangely exhilarating.

## Chapter 23

"Rylee, I'm so glad I caught you before you slipped out the door! You don't pay a lick of attention to your phone at work."

Lisa's voice exploded through the phone, vibrant and insistent.

"Listen up: tonight, at Mackie's Barbeque, we're assembling."

The declaration hit like a thunderclap. Rylee, fighting a burgeoning yawn and a surge of disbelief, struggled to decipher her friend's fervor this early in the morning.

"Lisa, I'm no psychic. What are you on about now? Who's assembling, and for what cause?"

"Seriously, Rylee? We don't need an excuse to come together—and please, your memory isn't as sharp as it used to be! The newly minted army is meeting to devise a plan to crush the insidious free clinic closing bill."

Lisa's excitement spilled over like an uncontrollable fire.

"It's a genuine 'Let my people go' moment. Aren't you fired up?"

A newly minted army? Rylee's heart pounded. Hadn't she and Lisa mulled over this idea only last night?

How on earth had her friend swung into action before breakfast?

"Army? Lisa, what have you been up to?"

"Dealing with the government isn't a problem," Lisa said dismissively. "Dave is in the mix, and he's finally going to prove he isn't just coasting through on a slacker major. He's set to blow our minds with his supposed brilliance."

Rylee blinked hard, trying to catch the rapid-fire momentum of Lisa's relentless enthusiasm.

"Lisa, I'm not sold on this. We barely sketched a plan, and the guys might not like being forced into helping!"

"When will you learn that I've got this locked down? We fine-tune everything tonight."

Rylee could almost hear the exasperation in Lisa's tone.

"A solid plan is coming, trust me. I told everyone there's a bill that could stamp out the free clinic if it passes and that we need all the help we can get. If they're game, they'll show. You've been the fixer for everyone else long enough—now it's your turn to be helped."

Lisa's words hit Rylee like a speeding freight train.

"I'm running the show here, and I love it. I even rallied Dave—he said he relishes the chance to fight governmental injustice. Chill!"

Rylee's sigh was heavy with resignation. This was classic Lisa—before she had uttered a complete idea, Lisa had already whipped up a chaotic motley crew. Losing control of the finer details terrified her, yet deep down, she was grateful for Lisa's all-consuming zeal.

"Alright, Lisa, slow down just a second. When exactly are we converging?"

"Six o'clock at Mackie's Barbeque. And don't you dare chicken out," Lisa snapped before the line went dead.

Rylee stood rooted, phone still pressed to her ear, reeling from the explosive conversation. She ought to feel thankful that her friends were ready to rally, but it all felt like a raging whirlwind had descended to hijack the very fabric of her day.

## Chapter 24

Rylee was again waiting outside a restaurant, scanning the street until June finally arrived.

"Thanks for inviting me. I appreciate being included in your brainstorming session," June said, her voice tinged with gratitude and curiosity.

"I wanted to personally walk you in and make introductions. The group can be spirited, and I didn't want to scare you off," Rylee replied, ushering her inside with a hint of urgency.

As they entered, June's concern skyrocketed upon seeing the youthful group gathered around the table, their energy buzzing like a live wire.

"June, this is the brainstorming group. I'll let you make your own introductions because it will save time. I hope you like barbeque."

Rylee pulled a chair for June and then sat next to her. "They may resemble a band of barbarians, but don't worry, they don't bite. They just must be steered in the right direction. They may not seem like it, but they can be quite effective. Dave here," she gestured toward the young man at the far end of the table, "is studying government."

June's optimism crumbled like a house of cards. The cacophony of youthful chatter felt aimless and unfocused. How could she tell Rylee that this was a disaster waiting to happen?

At that moment, Lisa leaned across June, jabbing Rylee with a playful poke, her gaze locked on a retreating waiter.

"Isn't he delicious?" Lisa mused with a mischievous grin.

Rylee and June turned their heads to appraise the waiter. Uninterested, Rylee returned her attention to her menu.

"So young. So very, very young," June lamented internally.

"Oh, that's right, you've got your eye on the cute guy with the kid," Lisa added with a sly glance.

June's eyebrows shot up, silently demanding answers from Rylee. Lisa filled the silence with the air of someone privy to all secrets.

"There was this guy at church on Sunday with an adorable baby. He didn't stick around after class. Probably just there for the Sunday school for the baby, which Rylee teaches," Lisa confided, her tone conspiratorial.

Rylee shot Lisa a look that could cut steel.

"She suspects he has a wife somewhere but wasn't wearing a ring. I think he's available," Lisa said with an edge to her voice.

Rylee's glare was fierce enough to strip paint, while Lisa winked at June, unfazed.

Finally, the orders arrived, and June felt a wave of relief. Just as she picked up her fork, the raucous noise around the table abruptly ceased.

Looking up, she was taken aback to see the once-wild group now bowed in serene, silent prayer.

## Chapter 25

"So, ladies, are you really going to leave us groping in the dark? What's the plan?"

Lisa barked, her voice slicing through the clamor like a laser beam.

"June, why don't you take this one? You've got the grip on this mess far better than I do."

Rylee was relieved to hand the reins to June.

June's eyes flicked over the assembly of determined, almost ravenous faces. She doubted any of them possessed the sheer nerve required for such a colossal undertaking, yet their stare burned with raw hunger and anticipation. Perhaps, with relentless focus and fiery passion, they could pull this off.

"So," June challenged, "how many of you actually grasp how a legislative body operates?" Her query set the stage like a gauntlet thrown down.

In an explosive moment, Dave's hand rocketed upward.

"Choose me! Choose me!" he thundered, waving his arm with ferocious energy.

"Except you, Dave," Lisa shot back sharply, an eye- roll punctuating her words.

Undeterred, Dave kept up his wild theatrics, spouting exaggerated "ooh" sounds like an overzealous alarm.

Seeing no one else daring to step up, June exhaled sharply and pointed her finger at him. "Alright, Dave—you own the floor."

Dave grinned, chest out like a battle-hardened warrior, and launched into his explanation.

"Okay, here's the deal: It all starts when some guy—or maybe a crew of guys—cooks up an idea for a new law. They hammer out the exact wording, and then it lands in a committee's crosshairs. If it survives that gauntlet, it's thrust onto the floor." He paused dramatically. "Along the way, parts get axed or bolstered until it's finally put to a vote." He sank back into his chair, a glint of triumph in his eyes.

"Exactly. A bill has been rushed through committee and is about to hit the floor for a vote. Its mechanism will slash Medicaid or Medicare reimbursements for duplicated services."

She made eye contact with each person at the table. Her voice intensified with every syllable.

"If hospitals can provide those services—which, mind you, includes but isn't confined to medical care at free clinics—they'll see that duplicate funding vanish."

"Why?" came the question from several. "They claim it's to cut taxes," Dave stated.

"But slashing taxes isn't a bad idea," Lisa countered. June's nod was resolute.

"Yes. Tax cuts sound splendid on paper. But in truth, this one is a ruse to free up cash, so they won't have to hike taxes. It's hardly a legitimate tax cut—its money earmarked to funnel into other projects. They already have spent it.

Right now, the state's reimbursements for free clinics are modest, but they are the lifeline keeping those doors open."

She leaned forward; her intensity undimmed.

"I know you're all thinking, 'Free clinics are free,' but that's a myth. They rack up costs—electricity, rent, supplies. None of that comes gratis."

"But wait, can't you just go to an emergency room? They're

compelled to treat you!" someone asked.

"Yes, but then they make you sign a form, pledging to shoulder the steep care costs. Not everyone can handle that burden. Not everyone feels they can make that kind of financial commitment."

The debate exploded like a volcano, ideas erupting in a furious, overlapping torrent.

Dave rose again with a determined clatter, tapping his glass with a fork to seize control.

"We need to seize the legislature's attention—and we need it now."

"All right, Mr. Smarty-Pants, so how exactly do we do that?" Lisa fired back.

Before chaos could claim the room again, June waved her hand to quiet the group.

"We grab their focus by convincing them that a vote for this bill will cost them reelection!"

"But how exactly do we pull that off?" Lisa persisted.

June's eyes locked onto Dave's as he puffed himself up, straightening his imaginary suspenders in preparation for another impassioned tirade.

"We mobilize—lobby relentlessly, flood the airwaves with letters to the editor; we hold protests; we spread the word among every friend and acquaintance. We hand out fliers, make those phone calls to legislature members. We let the public know with unyielding force that this is a disastrous idea."

"But, like I said, slashing taxes isn't evil. People want lower taxes." Lisa's rational slicing through the heated chaos.

"True," June countered sharply, "in theory it is. But when it inflicts harm on the people who rely on these essential services, it becomes intolerable. We must underscore that those relying on these clinics are the ones who can barely manage a doctor's bill, let alone a hospital invoice."

Someone shouted from the table's far end, "Why don't we just run an ad?"

Dave's head shook in emphatic disapproval.

"Ads cost money. Letters to the editor are free. That's the currency we must flood the system with. One letter can trigger a wave of support; if the noise is loud enough, the newspapers are forced to take notice. Boom—free publicity!"

The group dove back into the fray, their energy surging with a new, relentless intensity. Dave scribbled note after note and quickly made assignments.

Rylee stepped forward, declaring herself the primary liaison for their state representative so she could leverage every bit of knowledge of how free clinics operate. With a determined nod, June vowed to draft the first letter and dispatch it that very night.

Rylee's eyes swept over her impassioned friends, her heart swelling with newfound resolve. For the first time, she truly believed they could shatter the status quo. Together, they were an unstoppable force.

As the meeting blasted to its end amid raucous laughter and triumphant high fives, they bowed their heads—not in silent prayer but in a fervent, fiery plea for strength, marshalling every ounce of their conviction to fight back against the relentless assault of the bill.

## Chapter 26

When Rylee got home later that evening, the soft hum of the city still echoed in her ears as she stepped into her apartment. The intense discussions and shared resolve from the meeting left her heart pounding with high-voltage energy. She kicked off her shoes by the door, reached her cluttered desk, and powered on her aging laptop. The screen's blue light revealed a browser filled with open tabs as she searched for any scrap of information about her state senator. With a few determined clicks, she landed on a sparse profile page featuring the name Thomas Richardson, alongside scant details about his background and a phone number for his office.

Casting a quick look over her shoulder at the sleeping cat curled up on the bed, she addressed him softly, "Well, Squeaker, it's just 8:00. Not too late to call, it'll probably go to an answering service or something anyway. I'm just asking for an appointment."

Rylee tapped in the number for the from Richardson's webpage. As the recorded message started, she became nervous. She ended up rambling off something about stopping bill and hanging up.

"Oh, no. I didn't leave my name or that I wanted an appointment."

She blew out a breath and hit redial. This time she waited for the message to play out and calmly left a message asking for an appointment, leaving her name and phone number.

"At least I've got tonight to figure out what to say to him. I don't want to tank our chances by sounding like an idiot." She grimaced. "I already sound like an idiot."

The cat, nestled under a rumpled quilt, let out a series of tiny, rhythmic snores, blending gently with the soft brush of the night outside.

Rylee shifted her focus back to the screen, her fingers pausing above the keyboard as doubts crept in. Could she muster the courage to call him? What if her words stumbled, or if the urgency of the cause came off as clumsy? With a deep, steady breath, she began drafting her message. Her fingers danced over the keys as she typed frantically, then paused to delete and rearrange her sentences. She organized her thoughts into clear bullet points, each a building block of a message meant to convey the fiery urgency of the meeting. In her mind's eye, she pictured Senator Richardson—perhaps distracted by his busy schedule, maybe too jaded to notice the conviction behind her words—which further galvanized her determination.

Meticulously, she revised her script until every sentence shone with precision. Rereading the draft repeatedly, her eyes traced each word as she polished phrases and tightened the language until it could almost leap off the page with conviction. Memories of the impassioned rally, the fervent voices, and determined faces surged through her, filling her with renewed resolve.

She made herself a sandwich and went to her computer to reread the bill. Finally, she printed it out, picked up a highlighter, and got straight to work. She flipped on a light as it grew darker, adding to her growing list of questions, consulting the dictionary beside her and doing Internet searches occasionally.

"Squeaker, they may say this is a tax reduction bill, but it doesn't reduce taxes by one dime."

Her head hurt. She hadn't studied this hard in a long time.

"They're cutting spending, but only to put the money into these other bills."

She waived several pages at Squeaker, who batted at them.

"And they're telling us these other bills will cost the taxpayers nothing."

With eyes flashing, she threw the papers down on her desk.

"And as far as I'm able to see, these 'no cost' bills would not benefit the citizens of this state at all. Someone has decided that they would get money for their unnecessary pet project by cutting funding for important things, like free clinics. These politicians are trying to gain votes by greasing palms," she said to her disinterested feline.

Rylee sent an e-mail with her discoveries to Dave and copied it to June. If she was correct, this was bigger than just free clinics.

Energized by her discovery, she was more determined than ever to stop this bill.

At last, satisfied, she clicked the print button and watched as the crisp pages emerged, their edges still warm from the printer. She neatly tucked the final draft into her bag for the morning, her pulse quickening at the thought of stepping into this challenging new arena.

As the night deepened, the soft glow of her computer competed with the lamplight, casting long shadows on the walls.

With one last glance at the peaceful, slumbering Squeaker and the reassuring dim light of her screen, Rylee methodically switched everything off and carefully flicked out the lights. Climbing into bed under her soft, familiar quilt, her mind buzzed with possibilities and plans. She closed her eyes as Squeaker's steady, comforting purr filled the quiet room, carrying her into a night cradled by determined dreams and whispered promises of tomorrow.

## Chapter 27

That night, Rylee tossed and turned as she drifted into a vivid dream about Thom Simms, the image so clear it felt like reality.

Thom stood before her—tall, confident, and arrestingly handsome—on a sun-drenched beach. With the ocean glistening in the distance, he seemed every bit the rugged hero of a Hollywood romance. His baggy shorts flapped did nothing to diminish his appearance. He grinned at her, the sunlight making his eyes even bluer. A surfboard was casually tucked under his arm, as if he had just conquered the waves. She felt the warmth of the sun and the sharpness in his gaze, which softened into something more tender.

He stepped closer, pulling her into his arms, and Rylee felt the strength and safety of his embrace. She sighed as he leaned in, his lips teasingly close. But just as she was about to melt into the moment, a cold reality intruded.

Thom's dark-haired wife appeared out of nowhere, inserting herself between them with abrupt finality. The dream shattered like glass, and Rylee jolted awake. Her heart thudded, and her lips tingled with the ghost of a kiss that never happened. She lay there, willing herself to breathe.

"What is wrong with me, Squeaker?"

The faint light from the window barely illuminated the room, casting long shadows like the doubts gnawing at her sanity. She knew the truth.

"He's married. It was just a dream." She touched her lips.

"But it felt so real."

The memory of the sun's heat was still on her skin, and the closeness of Thom's imagined embrace lingered like a sweet echo.

Squeaker twitched in his sleep beside her, blissfully unaware of her turmoil. She swung her legs over the edge of the bed, trying her best to shake off the vivid residues of the dream. Those piercing eyes wouldn't leave her alone.

"This is madness," she scolded herself. "It is pure insanity to even entertain the thought. He's not yours. You barely know him, girl. Time to snap out of it. Get a grip."

She stormed out of the bedroom, hoping movement would chase away the clinging dream remnants. The kitchen light was jarringly bright, and she squinted as she flicked it on. Squeaker was at her feet the second she opened the fridge, his little nose twitching with anticipation.

"You don't miss a beat, do you, cat?"

A flood of meows erupted around her. He was like a tiny, furry alarm clock set to hungry.

"I'm not feeding you yet. If I do, you'll expect food at this hour every night, and guess who'll be awake?"

She gently nudged him with her foot, but Squeaker dodged her attempts and kept up his noisy serenade. With exasperation that bordered on amusement, Rylee finally caved and tossed him a treat. Of course, he pounced on it with reckless glee.

She poured herself a steaming cup of herbal tea, trying to find comfort in the ritual, and opened a box of cookies. Sitting at the small kitchen table, she munched her snack, watching Squeaker sniffing around for more treats with a zeal that made her smile despite herself.

"If you were the dog I had growing up, you'd be loyally sitting by me as we rode this crazy wave of emotions together."

Squeaker, however, finished his search and began grooming himself as if he hadn't a care in the world.

"Who needs a guy when you've got a cat that takes you for granted?"

She laughed at the ridiculous truth of it.

Grabbing a novel from the bookshelf, the cover dog-eared and familiar, she sank into the old wingback chair she had salvaged from her parents' attic. Its worn fabric was like an old friend, perfectly molding to her as she nestled in.

She hoped this comfortable refuge would allow her to settle back to sleep as she desperately tried to escape her thoughts.

But the quiet of the apartment and the vibrant memories of the dream made it impossible to escape for long. His arms, his eyes, that sunlit beach—they all lingered. As the words on the pages went unseen, time seemed to crawl by.

Rylee poured herself more tea, the warmth a soothing balm to her frayed nerves as she watched the city outside slowly come to life.

## Chapter 28

Rylee lurched awake, the sharp sound of a siren slicing through the dawn. She jolted upright in the chair, dazed and disoriented by the noise that lingered like an alarm clock she couldn't reach. Her heart raced as she struggled to get her bearings.

"Oh, my! What time is it?"

The words were barely out of her mouth before Squeaker, sleeping contentedly on her lap, yowled in protest as Rylee leaped up too suddenly. The movement sent the book tumbling, landing squarely on the disgruntled cat. With a look of wounded dignity, Squeaker trudged off, his tail puffed up like a bottle brush, hissing his displeasure with every step. Her mind was spinning in a million different directions. She rubbed her eyes, trying to clear the fog enough to focus.

A glance at the clock made her heart sink. "Six fifteen!"

She was already running late. Ignoring the chaos she'd left behind, Rylee dashed to the bathroom, splashed her face with cold water, and pulled a brush through her hair. Looking at the results, she tugged the rebellious hair into a lopsided ponytail and ran from the bathroom. She frantically pawed through the laundry basket for anything that was passably clean. The only thing that wasn't wrinkled was a bright pink top she hardly ever wore.

"I look like a flamingo has swallowed me."

Time was slipping away. She had to make do. She grabbed her old tote bag, practically flung her laptop inside, and raced to the kitchen.

Squeaker was still sulking near the fridge, shooting her a look of betrayal.

"I'm feeding you now."

Grabbing a can and popping the lid before dumping it in the cat's bowl. The cat ignored her peace offering, dramatically showing how deeply she had offended him.

She snatched an orange from the counter, then put it back, knowing she'd never have time to peel it. A cold toaster pastry would have to do. As she shoved it into her bag, crumbs scattering everywhere, she was already half out the door, jangling keys in the fumbling haste of her exit.

The street was conga line of morning commuters. She wove through the crowded traffic. Her pulse thrumming to the rhythm of the flow.

Her thoughts darted back to her dream. She couldn't help picturing Thom on the beach, those piercing blue eyes watching her from the shore. Buried under her panic and the late hour, she felt the vividness of it returning like a blush she couldn't hide.

Her unruly thoughts almost made her miss the turn for the parking lot at Halpern's.

"This is madness." she mumbled aloud. Rylee didn't even register the day's beauty as she sprinted across the parking lot.

She stumbled into the office, breathless and disheveled. She could clock in just as the second hand ticked past 6:59 on the time clock. Her pink shirt was too bright for her taste, but at least it distracted from her mismatched socks.

Ms. Blackman looked at Rylee in alarm. "Ms. Vance, you look awful. Are you ill?"

"Sorry," Rylee mumbled.

"Are you running a fever? Are you coming down with a cold?"

"No. I haven't slept well the past two nights. Too much going on."

"Rylee, you haven't started engaging in risky behavior, have you? You've always been such a steady employee."

"No, ma'am."

"Well, okay. Figure out how to get rested. I can't have my girls entering the wrong numbers or misfiling invoices because they are out partying the night before," Ms. Blackman warned.

Rylee went to the bathroom to look at herself in the mirror. The circles under her eyes were pronounced, and her hair needed some real help. She brushed her hair, pulled it back into a ponytail, and washed her face. She studied the results in the mirror and decided that it really didn't do much more than make her face wet. She got herself a cup of coffee before going back to her desk.

She slid into her chair, the soft chime of her computer starting up cutting through the chatter of the busy room. She powered through task after task on sheer adrenaline, hardly noticing as the day blurred past.

Emails were answered with lightning speed. Phone calls were placed with an urgency that caught even Rylee by surprise. She barely paused for lunch, wolfing down the pastry she had stuffed in her bag that morning, and calling Richardson's office again, asking for an appointment stating that the matter was urgent.

When the clock finally signaled the end of the workday, her head buzzed, and her eyes felt grainy from staring at the screen. She was the last to leave the office, exhaustion gnawing at her relentlessly.

Rylee felt like she was navigating a dream, floating through the day in a fog that refused to lift. Her mind was thick with a cloud of fatigue while her body performed its duties on automatic pilot. The office had cleared out long before she left, and the long shadows cast by the afternoon sun made her feel even more like a ghost.

She didn't even remember the drive home, but when she finally crossed the threshold of her small apartment, the remnants of her sleepless night bore down on her with a weight she could hardly support. Keys slipped from her numb fingers, clattering onto the kitchen counter her empty mug from last night.

She barely managed to peel off her shoes before she collapsed into a creaky chair, the sound of it groaning under her dead weight. Her eyes, though barely open, locked blankly onto a pale wall that was as bare as her energy was spent.

Even Squeaker seemed to know she was beyond the reach of his feline wiles, snoozing away in his freshly claimed throne—the chair she had meant to sit in—and leaving her to her exhausted stupor.

Her thoughts were a tangled mess, echoing with shards of her bizarre dream and the insanity of her self- imposed crush. She had left a message at Richardson's office on her abbreviated lunch break, but she was too tired to check to see if they had returned her call. She thought about calling it again just to hear that voice.

She exhaled deeply, a long sigh that seemed to drain the last of her energy as she let it all out. Thoughts of the beach with

Thom flashed vividly behind her closed eyes.

"He's married, and you're nuts. He's also impossibly good-looking."

She silently admitted as her resolve wavered. Rylee felt the tension coiled in her shoulders like a spring ready to snap.

"Time to put on the comfy clothes and crash," she declared, though her voice lacked the resolve to make a proper decree.

Slowly, she pushed herself out of the chair and trudged toward the bedroom. Her feet barely lifted off the floor, dragging sluggishly over the linoleum tile.

She thought longingly of a quick shower, but even that felt like too much effort when all she really wanted was unconsciousness.

Just as she reached the doorway, her phone buzzed rabidly to life in her hand. The screen lit up with a number she recognized instantly, sending a jolt of adrenaline shooting like a bolt of lightning through the fog of her exhaustion.

A faint smile danced on Chip's lips, quickly turning into a full smirk as the messages played back on the senate office line. The voice on the recording was breathless and tangled; he imagined it belonged to some hapless undergraduate girl with an overactive imagination and a quirky cause. Amused, he hit replay and listened to it again, catching the way her words ran over each other in a rush of awkward enthusiasm.

Was it the same girl who had called Thom with that hysterical message about banning plastic forks?

He considered handing this off to Thom, thinking of how entertaining it might be to watch his reaction. But he knew Thom's week was packed tight, and he already had enough on his plate. Besides, Chip enjoyed this kind of thing. It was like a little break from the serious business of law, a chance to sit back and watch the chaos unfold from a safe distance.

Grinning, Chip paid close attention to the timestamps of the messages. The first was left just five minutes past eight the night before; the second just seconds later; the third at seven minutes after noon today. He hadn't had the chance to check this line before heading off to classes, so he'd missed her first attempt to reach him. The poor thing seemed incapable of stringing two coherent words together. He had been out all day, and Thom had been court and busy at the statehouse all day. A pity, he thought; it might have been more fun to take it in person and hear her flustered desperation firsthand, to see if he could even keep a straight face.

He dialed the number she had left behind, expecting a comedy of stammering to unfold. The voice that answered was just as anxious and uncertain as he'd anticipated.

"Um, hello?"

"Good afternoon. Is this Ms. Vance?"

"Um, yes, I'm Rylee Vance."

"Ms. Vance, I'm Charles Fallon, Mr. Richardson's aide."

He paused for effect, imagining her catching her breath in hope.

"Mr. Richardson is currently unavailable, but I would happily meet with you and discuss your concerns."

It was a new strategy for Chip, taking on these more colorful cases himself.

"I have some time available this afternoon."

He glanced at the calendar, where he noticed Lexie had a well-baby check-up at three-thirty. "Between four and five."

Thom may come back to the office if Lexie wasn't hungry and cranky.

"We're located at 679 Elm. I look forward to meeting you."

"Oh, thank you. I'll be there."

His suspicions confirmed that she could not manage a full sentence without gasping for air. He briefly considered telling her he would be in the office until six tonight but ultimately decided it was best to handle this as quickly as possible. He knew these eager young activists. They usually arrived early and overstayed their welcome. If he gave her an inch, she'd run a marathon with it. The sooner he could conclude this meeting, the better.

At precisely four o'clock, Chip settled into his chair, which he had strategically angled to avoid the last rays of sunlight streaming through the window. He began to work on a cover letter to a client with instructions for their upcoming deposition. He imagined Ms. Vance already on the way, cycling through the entire catalog of what-ifs in a frazzled attempt to prepare. Would she bring protest signs? Perhaps a stack of brochures and fliers to convince him of her cause? He wouldn't have been surprised.

A soft chime on his phone alerted him to a message from Thom.

"Chip. Baby's gained three pounds. No shots today! Taking her to do an overnight with Granny. Meet you for burritos at 5:30 usual truck?"

With a quick and satisfied swipe, Chip sent back his agreement. This changed everything. No rush now.

Relaxed, he leaned back, ready to let this meeting run long enough to have some fun with it if it was an especially odd request.

## Chapter 29

Rylee's heart pounded as she circled the block for the third time, anxiously searching for a parking spot—each minute feeling heavier than the last. When she finally found parking, a sudden flash of self-consciousness hit her; she was still wearing blue jeans and the horrible pink shirt, not the meticulously chosen outfit meant to command respect. With hesitance and a trace of panic, she gazed at the lettering on the building: Law Offices of Thomas O. Richardson.

A torrent of conflicting thoughts began to churn in her mind.

"A lawyer! Great, just what I needed."

Convincing a lawyer felt like scaling an insurmountable wall, yet she steeled herself, summoning what little courage she had left.

"All right, best foot forward.

She pushed the door open even as uncertainty clawed at her.

Inside, Chip looked up with a questioning tilt of his head as Rylee stepped into the room.

A cold, weighted brick seemed to settle in her stomach that instant. Her voice trembled with vulnerability as she ventured, "Mr. Fallon?"

Chip replied coolly, "Yes, I'm Charles Fallon. Can I help you?"

His eyes flicked briefly to the wall clock—it was nearly four forty-five.

Rylee didn't miss his glance. As she stepped forward,

extending a tentative hand, she tried to appear composed despite the storm of doubts swirling inside her.

"I'm Rylee Vance. You called and said you could see me between four and five."

Internally, this felt like a betrayal of her expectations. It was a small, cramped office. Not at all what she was expecting.

Chip's gaze shifted again to the clock. Following his glance, Rylee felt a surge of insecurities. When he turned back, she was caught smoothing back her unruly hair, as if trying to iron out the creases in her frazzled composure.

"Oh, yes. Ms. Vance. Please, sit down."

His tone was polite yet laced with unspoken scrutiny that made her skin crawl. Chip observed her with an almost imperceptible censure. In his mind, she matched what he had imagined.

"She looks like a wreck," he thought.

He masked what he thought with a smile. "How can Mr. Richardson assist you?"

Rylee sank into the chair he indicated, feeling a weariness in her limbs and deep in her being as if the weight of the world was pressing down on her shoulders.

"There's a bill going before the legislature in a couple of weeks that would cut funding to the state's free clinics."

Her words felt flat. They weren't the defiant appeal she had hoped to give. That knowledge made her even more flustered.

Chip's eyes darted acutely to the stray lock of hair that defied control, sticking out awkwardly from the side of her head.

"You're opposed to the bill, I take it?"

His tone betraying a mixture of skepticism and concern.

"Yes."

Her voice wavered. "I mean—I'm opposed. I'm not in favor of it."

Each word felt clumsy, as if she was wrestling with her incapacities.

"Are you feeling all right, Ms. Vance? Would you like some coffee?"

Chip's offer didn't sound like he was being kind. It didn't rise above practical professionalism.

His eyes, however, held a peculiar intensity that deepened Rylee's discomfort, feeding the inner conflict of wanting to be taken seriously yet feeling that she had already lost that battle.

"No, thank you. I'm fine."

Chip's eyes were uncertain. The tension in the room built as she hesitated again, her gaze anxious.

"Is Mr. Richardson supporting this bill?"

"Mr. Richardson hasn't made up his mind yet." Chip responded, at once measured and dismissive, as though the answer was meant to soothe and deflect her rising anxiety.

A surge of relief mixed with renewed determination flooded Rylee.

"He hasn't? So there's still time to convince him?"

A glimmer of hope began to fight back against her fear of failure.

"I'll take your concern to Mr. Richardson, and he'll get back to you."

Chip had decided to end this interview. He stood and extended his hand.

At that moment, a tumult of emotions overtook her. The earlier meekness evaporated, replaced by a raw anger intermingled with desperation at this dismissal.

"Mr. Fallon, I might not grasp the inner workings of government fully yet, but I'm learning—and this bill is wrong!"

She yanked the elastic from her ponytail, letting her hair cascade wildly around her face.

Chip's eyes widened in shock as he witnessed the transformation—a timid, disheveled woman now ignited with fierce determination. He resumed his seat cautiously.

"I apologize. Please, continue, Ms. Vance."

"Thank you."

She breathed, steadied by her conviction. "From what I see, this isn't a real tax cut—it's merely a money shifter. Instead of easing burdens, critical community services get chopped, all to fund someone's pet project."

Chip couldn't help but smile inwardly; despite her initial disarray, she now articulated her thoughts with striking insight. Her earlier appearance had masked a brilliance that now shone through.

"That's exactly what's happening, isn't it?" Her smoldering eyes locking onto his, daring him to answer.

"I think I should arrange a meeting with Mr. Richardson for you. He needs to hear your perspective." Chip flipped through his appointment book.

"He's meeting with the senate president tomorrow at one o'clock, so it'd be a perfect opportunity to get rid of the old blowhard," he thought.

"How about at two-thirty tomorrow?" Chip offered. "Oh, I work until two-thirty,"

"Not a good time for you? I could try for next week," he offered hesitantly.

"No. Tomorrow at two-thirty is perfect." She would make it work.

Once more, Chip rose and extended his hand. This time, Rylee didn't hesitate to stand either—her defiant energy overtaking her earlier self-doubt.

"Mr. Fallon, thank you so much for your time. I appreciate that you could see me on such short notice and fit me into Mr. Richardson's busy schedule," she said.

Chip offered his best professional smile, his face betraying a hint of admiration amid his amused thoughts.

"Mr. Richardson is always interested in what his constituents have to say. I'm certain he'll value your perspective."

Walking her to the door, he shook her hand again. Amid his professional routine, he couldn't help but notice the spark in her eyes.

"I'm very glad to have met you, Ms. Vance."

## Chapter 30

"Well, the resumes aren't just coming in—they're storming the door, partner," Chip announced, his voice charged with urgency.

"Yeah? How many are we looking at?" Thom snapped back.

"There were six blazing on the fax machine this morning, a slew of messages seething on the answering machine, and about twenty e-mailed applications bombarding us. I've scattered copies all over your desk."

Thom ripped his hand through his hair, releasing a heavy, weary sigh.

"Thanks. Here I go again. You're not dodging this— the pain is on you too, like a real partner. Any that spark your interest?"

"There are three worth a serious look for the paralegal spot. There are more if we're looking to hire a receptionist in the new place."

"Oh, yeah. We'll need one of those if we take the new place."

"Yep, we will. I purposely left your copies untouched, so you'd give me an honest, unbiased opinion. We'll compare notes later."

With a deep, resigned breath, Thom muttered, "Okay." He swept up the pile of resumes only to toss them down with a clack. Pulling up the tax cut bill, he scoured it once more. He understood its implications, nothing justified stopping people from shuffling money around. And if he dared vote against it, he'd be painted as a spendthrift, a label that could cost him every hard-fought vote.

A knock at the door sliced through his thoughts. "Mr. Richardson?"

Chip called out, pausing at the threshold until Thom's nod permitted him to enter. His behavior was all theater for Dawson.

"Mr. Dawson is here."

Thom's lips curled into a wry, dangerous grin. "Thank you, Charles. Please show Mr. Dawson in."

Swiftly, Thom shoved the resumes and tax files back into his desk drawer as George strode in, radiating an unsettling confidence.

"Thomas, good to see you."

George greeted, his tone laced with charm and challenge. His eyes, sharp and relentless, swept the room.

"My goodness—are these pictures all of you? And trophies too. Snowboarding champ, huh? Didn't peg you for a risk-taker."

Thom moved around the room and sank into his chair, while George prowled about, still taking in the room.

"And the tiny model—is she yours? Didn't know you were married."

A cold glint flashed in Thom's eyes as he thought, "You old fraud. You know everything about me, or you wouldn't be standing here."

"I'm not married." Thom replied flatly. George nodded slowly.

"Ah, public service life has become your mistress, hasn't it, like the rest of us?"

Thom's smile remained measured, though his mind was warily alert.

108

"Cup of coffee?"

George's smirk grew wilder.

"You got something a little stronger?"

"Dr. Pepper, perhaps?"

George chuckled, a sharp edge in his laugh. "Coffee's fine, Thomas."

"I'll be right back."

Thom stepped out and left the door open wide. The office was small enough so that Thom could keep an eye on George to ensure he wasn't snooping around.

Thom handed the steaming cup to him. "To what do I owe the honor of this visit?"

George set the coffee down on Thom's desk with deliberate care.

"Straight to business. I appreciate that no-nonsense approach in a man."

Thom's pleasant smile belied the tension he felt as George settled back into his chair.

"Thomas, we're staring down a series of votes on crucial bills. I've noticed you've barely spoken your mind on half of them. As someone with decades of experience— and you being a junior rep—I thought I'd drop by to help illuminate any legislative darkness you might be fumbling through."

"Thank you, Mr. Dawson; that's very considerate of you."

Thom gave a slight nod, though internally he knew he was being baited.

George continued with the predatory calm of a spider weaving its web.

"Oh, Thomas, drop the formality."

George leaned forward as if to seal a secret covenant.

"We're all colleagues here, united in serving the citizens of our great state. I'd even like to think of us as friends."

His inner voice sneered behind Thom's polite exterior as he thought, "My friends know to call me Thom, you pompous blowhard."

Thom said, "It's reassuring to see your interest in guiding the new blood."

George pressed. "You, from such a distinguished old family, have caught many eyes. With committee assignments looming, we believe you'd be an excellent candidate for a seat on Ways and Means."

And there it was. That was the bait—an irresistible morsel wrapped in flattering expectations. George's eyes gleamed like a benevolent predator, offering Thom advice and an opportunity to advance in politics in exchange for an as-of-yet unnamed favor. All Thom would need was to toe the line for good old George.

"Oh, George, that's one massive bite for someone as inexperienced as I am."

The click of the office door broke the underlying tension. Thom couldn't ignore the creak of George's chair as the older man leaned forward, his grin hardening into something almost fixed.

"Thomas—or do you prefer Tommy? I urge you to consider the real difference you could make on that committee. Or perhaps another? From where I sit, as a battle-hardened public servant, you're one of the rising stars. I pride myself on spotting public-spirited talent and sharing the hard-won wisdom that eases the brutal slog through political chaos."

Thom's eyes flicked to one of his snowboarding photos.

George followed his gaze intently.

"I've always had a passion for slicing through fresh powder. But thank you for the offer."

George's smile stiffened further as Thom rose, his voice firm.

"My assistant has just left, and I've scheduled an interview for a new secretary. Looks like someone will be in a few minutes."

George's momentary confusion betrayed his expectation of a smoother encounter. Thom extended his hand, which George accepted with a calculated grip.

"I hope you'll mull over my proposition. It could propel your political career in this state," he paused, "or far beyond just the state senate. Aim high, Thomas."

George picked up one of the trophies, his voice lowering with a cryptic edge.

"Sometimes, a perfectly groomed trail is exactly what you need."

Thom nodded slowly.

"Sometimes a groomed trail is beneficial. Can I call you back on that?"

He laid a firm hand on George's elbow as he escorted him out with deliberate resolve.

"Certainly, but don't linger too long—you might miss the lift. Fresh power can hide obstacles A groomed trail helps. Remember that." George warned.

Thom paused, his mind swirling with the implications. He hadn't yet mapped out his political future beyond the election. He hadn't even taken the oath of office when his world had shattered. Yet the lure of higher office, the promise of easing his path if he played by George's rules, was almost intoxicating.

As he gazed again at the photograph of Lexie and the vibrant shots from his snowboarding days, Thom felt the fierce tug between the wild thrill of blazing fresh powder and the cautious safety of a marked, predictable trail. In that intense moment, the weight of his choices and ambitions pressed down like a storm waiting to break.

## Chapter 31

After George reached his car, he wasted no time. Revving the engine, he peeled out of the parking lot, his mind already strategizing his next move.

The meeting hadn't gone as smoothly as he'd calculated. Thom was more resistant than expected. He needed Thom's vote so, now it was crucial to up the ante. With swift precision, George hit the speed dial on his phone and barked orders into the line as soon as it connected.

"Get a couple of the girls to apply for a job with Richardson."

His voice betrayed the simmering frustration beneath his polished exterior.

"Yes, that's right. He's looking for a new girl. It would be nice to have one of our people in there."

He paused, recalibrating his chessboard of political maneuvers, and then shifted his tactics.

"And get me some more information on Richardson, Richardson's assistant, Charles something, and any new staff they might add. Get that guy we used before. Bonnie will know who he is. We need to find something we can use. Richardson wasn't as eager to take the assignment as I thought he would be. We will need plan B. If he doesn't take the carrot, we're gonna use a stick."

## Chapter 32

"Ms. Blackman, can I take the afternoon off today?"

Rylee asked, her voice quiet but tremulous as if she were holding back a storm of emotions behind a practiced smile. The fluorescent lamps of the cramped office glinted off her anxious eyes.

"I have an appointment that might take a while."

Every word weighed on her, each syllable a reluctant admission of vulnerability.

Across the desk, Ms. Blackman's eyes narrowed. That sharp, assessing look wasn't merely disapproval—it cut deep, as if Rylee's very right to exist beyond the work was under earth-shattering scrutiny. Her gaze swept over Rylee with the cold probe reserved for those who have dared to dream outside the prescribed limits.

Rylee's stomach churned, her insides twisting in silent protest. She braced herself, feeling the tension in her chest, aware that the next few moments could shatter her fragile composure entirely.

"Well, you know that we prefer more advanced notice than this," Ms. Blackman said.

Her voice was flat and measured, lips pressed into a thin, unyielding line. Every word was deliberate, as if each syllable were a decree.

"When did you make this appointment?"

"Yesterday, after work," Rylee admitted.

Rylee fought to keep her voice steady. She dared glance at Ms. Blackman's face, watching as a deeper frown etched itself across her features.

"The way you're dressed, I would guess that you're off on a date with some handsome young man. Isn't it a little early for such frolics?"

A flush of panic and indignation surged through Rylee. Her heart pounded so loudly she was sure everyone could hear.

"No," she blurted, "I'm going to speak with my state representative about a bill coming before the legislature soon."

"Really?"

Ms. Blackman raised an eyebrow so high it seemed to tear at the seam of her stern expression, as if Rylee's words were too lofty, too contrary to the humdrum demands of office routine to be believed.

"Really," Rylee repeated.

Her tone grew steadier even as uncertainty wavered at the edges of her defiant resolve.

"Can't you do that by email or over the phone?"

"I have already done that. They want me to come in. His name is Thomas Richardson. The appointment is for two-thirty today."

Silence descended between them, heavy and oppressive, laden with the invisible weight of Ms. Blackman's disapproval. Finally, Ms. Blackman's voice slashed through the charged atmosphere like a sharpened knife.

"Well, you know we need you here at your desk, not off playing politics."

Rylee stood rigid, her body frozen, her rage ignited by the injustice of countless similar encounters. She remembered Lisa's warnings that every supervisor, no matter how nice, was never your friend. Ms. Blackman was not a nice supervisor. Lisa's warnings stung all too painfully now.

Swallowing hard, every muscle in her tense frame strained to keep her emotions in check as Ms. Blackman continued.

"Ms. Vance, I'll allow it this time."

Ms. Blackman shoved a file across the cluttered desk with a force that suggested an accusation more than an approval.

"But you must give us at least a week's advance notice in the future. This is unprofessional and unacceptable."

As Ms. Blackman swept a dismissive hand, Rylee's thoughts roiled inside her like a storm.

"What did that mean, 'I'll allow it this time?'" she silently seethed. Every harsh word fed her inner rebellion.

"Who is she to dictate every detail of my life? Doesn't she understand what this opportunity means to me?"

The suffocating confrontation left her body quivering, a cocktail of smoldering anger and burgeoning despair. She trudged back to her desk, her vision blurred by beads of sweat and unshed tears. In the quiet solitude of her cubicle, she murmured to herself beneath the droning hum of the office air conditioning.

"I need to calm down."

She inhaled deeply, trying in vain to anchor herself with controlled, measured breaths while her mind whirled with the injustice of it all.

In a moment of fragile hope amidst the internal chaos, Rylee reached for her phone. With trembling fingers, she called Lisa's number.

"Lisa, this is Rylee."

Lisa's bubbly tone burst through the static, a cheerful antidote to the earlier tension.

"Hey, girlie! What's up?"

"Let's grab some lunch. I need a bit of encouragement."

Rylee's voice steadying just a bit with the promise of respite.

"Oh, yeah—the big appointment with Thomas Richardson. I'm so excited that you scored an appointment so soon."

"Well, it all depends on how things go. Are we on for lunch?"

"Sure. Pick a spot."

She felt the weight of her conservation with Ms. Blackman lifting when she spotted Lisa waiting by the entrance of a small, bustling café

"Quite the outfit you've got on."

Lisa gave Rylee a playful half-smile, her eyes bright with both amusement and genuine approval as she took in the smart yet slightly disheveled look Rylee sported.

"You really don't think it's too much? I just ended up closing my eyes and wearing what I grabbed from the closet."

"That's the best way to do it! I love it!"

"Why don't you start by giving him one of your killer smiles?"

Lisa winked, her tone both mischievous and reassuring.

Rylee let out a soft laugh that mingled with the background clatter of the busy café, feeling at last a tentative easing of the internal tug-of-war.

"Yeah, I might do that."

She drew in a deep, steady breath as the remnants of tension began to dissipate.

"Let's order first, then we can strategize on how to make

this guy really listen."

## Chapter 33

Thom rubbed his temples, feeling the tension build as he surveyed the depressing stack of resumes on his desk. The folders in his inbox had crested the rim and were teetering perilously, threatening to spill their contents across his already cluttered workspace.

"I don't have time for this. I have actual work to do."

The thought of Dawson's enticing offer swirled in his mind like a persistent echo. It was a tempting prize, one that sparkled with opportunity, and he wouldn't mind claiming it for himself. But the clock's hands were marching steadily forward, and his calendar reminded him of the unyielding demands of his job. The folders glaring at him from his inbox were a silent testimony to the constant responsibilities he couldn't ignore.

He longed for a brief escape from the cacophony of obligations of that seemed to slam into him from every side. Glancing at the snowboarding pictures around his office, the idea of calling it a day early flitted through his mind. The allure of a long, indulgent nap before picking up Lexie from her grandparents beckoning him. But just as he began to indulge in thoughts of home, a sharp realization cut through the fog of his musings—the interview with a paralegal prospect!

"Why would Chip schedule one when he wasn't even going to be here? This candidate would be Chip's clerical support, too. This isn't going to happen again."

With a frown on his face, Thom rifled through the pile of resumes, his fingers moving quickly but finding nothing.

It was curious that Chip hadn't prepared the necessary documents for him. Chip, known for his meticulous nature, was almost compulsive about organizing such matters.

"What was the name again? Ryan something?"

Thom squinted at a sticky note, struggling to decipher the scribbled chaos that would reveal the applicant's identity. The writing was a mess, and it seemed as if Chip hadn't even bothered to pen it legibly.

"How am I going to interview someone without their resume? Come on, Chip!"

The sticky note, paired with the time booked out and with no other information on his computer calendar, and the total absence of relevant paperwork, left Thom feeling unsettled. He knew he was missing something.

He contemplated the awkwardness of asking the applicant directly for their name, a scenario he dreaded. Hopefully, the candidate would be organized enough to bring their resume, unlike Chip, who had probably anticipated this mess and had conveniently made himself scarce.

"Next time," Thom vowed, "Chip will be present for the rest of these interviews."

## Chapter 34

Rylee stood outside the office, her heart thumping wildly as she glanced at her watch. There was still time, but her nerves buzzed like she was already late. Her hair fluttered around her face with each gust of wind, adding to her sense of unpreparedness. She looked up at the sign again. It was simple and to the point.

"Law Office of Thomas O. Richardson."

The sign was etched in plain gold letters across a stark black background. There were no frills, just business. As she reached for the doorknob, anxiety and determination wrestled inside her. She needed this to go well.

"Well, Lord," she whispered, swallowing her self-doubt, "here goes. Please let me sound like I'm intelligent."

Inhaling a shaky breath, she stepped inside to prove she could advocate for the clinics.

When he heard the front door creak open, Thom was in the back, trying to slide the hated pile of resumes into a folder. He hoped it was his mystery candidate, so he might get this ill-prepared job interview over as quickly as possible and productively focus on the rest of his day.

"Be with you in a minute!"

Rylee nearly gasped out loud. She knew that voice, but from where? If he looked anything like he sounded, she was in serious trouble. She could listen to that voice all day. Shaking her head to clear the distracting thoughts, she prayed he was an unattractive old guy.

Thom quickly brushed off his pants, slipped on his

jacket, and headed toward the reception area. He was mentally preparing himself for the usual tedium of a job interview when he stopped dead in his tracks.

"Hi, I'm Thom Richardson—" was all he managed to say before his voice caught.

He couldn't believe it. It was her—Ms. Vance from the church. The same Rylee who had practically floated up the stairs and charmed Lexie with her singing.

"How could Chip not mention this?" he thought. "Geez, Chip doesn't know."

His eyes took in her figure, tracing from her long legs to her poised expression. She looked amazing, all the way down to the open-toed pumps. The loose blouse flowed elegantly around her hips, cinched by a striking red sash. He suddenly felt like the air had vanished from the room.

Rylee could hardly breathe. Her carefully planned speech evaporated into thin air the moment she saw him. Standing before her was Thom Simms, whose name was Thomas Richardson. The well-tailored suit emphasized his broad shoulders, his spikey blonde hair only enhancing his professional appearance, and his blue eyes held hers like a magnet.

Her gaze, traitorous and beyond her control, flitted to the mouth she had almost kissed in her dream. She was instantly warm, her cheeks flaming red.

They spoke together, the words tumbling out with mutual shock:

"It's you!"

## Chapter 35

Thom let out a dry chuckle, shrugged off the tension, and strode toward her with deliberate steps.

"You're Lexie's father? Thomas Richardson, right? I always thought you were Simms—doesn't Lexie carry that name?"

Despite Rylee's best intentions to sound intelligent, she was rambling wildly.

Instantly, Thom's friendly facade hardened into a wary scowl.

Rylee, completely oblivious to the sudden ice in the room, chattered nonstop about how Lexie remained calm in the face of the boy's wild classroom antics and her bubbling excitement to meet Mrs. Richardson— each word a warning to Thom to beware of church people.

Thom had to interrupt her ceaseless babble, or he was never going to get back to being productive.

"Lexie enjoyed her time in your class."

His inner thoughts screaming, "This is getting awkward."

"Ms. Vance, shall we begin? Did you bring your resume? I can't locate it among the others."

Rylee's smile froze and her eyes widened in shock. "Did you just ask for a resume? I wasn't aware one was required."

That confused tremor in her tone shifted Thom's irritation, his skepticism about sanctimonious church people now morphed into professional exasperation. His gaze, incredulous and piercing.

"I'm here to talk to you about a tax cut bill."

His eyes flared with surprise.

"Excuse me, Ms. Vance—I thought you had responded to our ad for clerical support?"

"Clerical job? No. Mr. Fallon specifically arranged for me to discuss the tax cut with you. I already have a job."

"Ah, my apologies. I understand now. We just posted an ad for clerical support last night."

He composed himself, donning a tight-lipped professional smile as he stepped aside and beckoned her into the office.

In that charged moment, the realization that Thomas Richardson was the very Thom of her dreams sent an undercurrent of unease through Rylee, as she sensed a tempest of frustration roiling beneath his cordial mask.

"Coffee?"

"No, thank you, Mr. Richardson."

Flustered, the lines she had prepared and rehearsed were gone from her conscious thought.

"Um, well, Mr. Simms—oh, Mr. Richardson—"

His inner thought was a dark whisper. "Here it comes."

Drawing a breath, he leaned forward. "Ms. Vance, you were saying?"

Even as she tried to collect herself, her eyes inadvertently landed on his left hand—a sight that made him instinctively slide both hands under the desk, silently raging. "Not another gold digger."

"Ms. Vance, you wanted to discuss the tax bill?"

"Oh, sorry, Mr. Richardson."

She cleared her throat as she launched into her carefully practiced pitch.

124

"The tax cut bill is a massacre—it will slash funding for free clinics, under the pretense that these services are redundant. For some of your voters, this is the only medical care they can access. I've scrutinized this twisted shell game of a bill. They promise tax cuts, yet no reduction in taxes ever materializes because the funds are merely siphoned off to benefit a small group."

Thom leaned forward, eyes narrowing with a mix of intrigue and challenge.

"Go on, Ms. Vance."

Her eyes darted away from his piercing blue glare. "Um, the promise of tax cuts is nothing but a ruse. The burden stays, only it's funneled to bolster a pet project that could not otherwise get funding."

Thom's nod was slow but affirmative. "She's absolutely nailed it," he thought.

Shifting restlessly in her chair, she pressed on. "That's why I'm here. I need your help to stop this deceitful tax cut bill."

For a heart-stopping moment, Thom's gaze lingered on her exposed shoulder, before he recovered.

"I haven't made my decision yet, but I'll seriously weigh your arguments."

Rising to his feet, he gave Rylee a brisk smile.

"Is there anything else I can do for you Ms. Vance?"

His tone carried a subtle dismissal that did not go unnoticed.

Rylee sat, stunned into silence by the abrupt termination.

"Uh, thank you for your time, Mr. Richardson," she stammered.

"Anytime. My door is always open to the citizens. If you need assistance, don't hesitate to call."

His words were smooth but the smile he gave her didn't reach his eyes.

The cool detachment in his tone told Rylee everything she needed to know. Rylee seethed with a burning impatience, her inner voice a furious hiss, "He doesn't understand the stakes," her eyes went wide. "He's one of them! Now I've spelled out everything for the enemy!"

Her ire rose with righteous indignation.

"Mr. Richardson, its crystal clear you're not going to help. You're merely playing the role of my representative. But this bill? It's a sham—a twisted shell game that will decimate essential community services!"

For a beat, Thom was momentarily speechless.

"Do you get a reward for supporting this sham? And what's with the name change? Make up your mind and stick to it!"

She hurled her hair back defiantly and stormed out without one last glance.

Thom watched her retreat, his arms slack and his mouth agape in silent disbelief.

"She's still on point."

Despite her undeniable allure, he steeled himself against letting attraction muddle his duty—he was sworn to serve the citizens. Thom observed her swaying down the sidewalk with her root beer-colored hair dancing on the breeze.

"And Ms. Rylee, you are way too dangerous for me to ignore."

## Chapter 36

Thom didn't tear his eyes away from Rylee until she disappeared around a corner. Her exit played out like a dramatic scene on a stage performance that left Thom both frustrated and begrudgingly impressed.

The courage she had shown in confronting the issue was something he hadn't expected; despite the storm of anger and distrust swirling around her, she had unhesitatingly declared her stance and left him reeling in her wake.

As Thom stepped back into the building, a delicate waft of honeysuckle enveloped him, the scent wrapping around his senses and reminding him vividly that she had been there. At first, her striking physical allure drew him within the church's stone walls, but now her fierce, unyielding spirit ignited something in him.

Her insistence on lumping him with the enemies she despised simmered in his thoughts. Rylee hadn't just pinned him with her heartfelt declaration; her presence had upturned his day.

"You're not what I expected from a church woman."

Seated heavily back in his chair, Thom wrestled with the inexplicable magnetism that Rylee exerted. Every impassioned word, every charge, and accusation she had hurled in their exchange, stirred him to prove something to her.

He fought the urge to rise and follow her down the street, desperate to prolong the debate or whatever they had been locked in.

The final searing look she had thrown over her shoulder felt like a definitive statement: she'd written him off completely. That fact, instead of disheartening him, steeled his resolve further. The invisible battle lines she had drawn only fanned the flames of his determination.

"Just how did she pull that off?" His head shaking in amazement and confusion.

George's cautious remarks—the subtle insinuations juxtaposed against Rylee's unbridled, fiery honesty.

"Maybe her passion is exactly what's needed to unseat George."

Rylee's words were fanning a growing theory in his mind. A wry, determined smile slowly spread across Thom's face as he considered the bribe of a coveted committee seat against the challenge Rylee presented. Her call to action was not a desperate plea but a challenge ripe with potential.

"Chip must have her phone number somewhere."

Digging through papers and scattered notes only strengthened his resolve. He smiled again. "She's trouble—big trouble."

## Chapter 37

Rylee was fighting a losing battle against the flood of tears. Her grip on the steering wheel was as hard as iron, fueled by raw determination.

"I never should have left the apartment; never talked with Mr. Heartless. He only pretended to care; he's on the enemy's side."

Pulling into the parking lot, her inner fire dimmed to cold defeat. Her throat constricted in silent sobs as scorching tears streamed uncontrollably down her face. In her mind's eye, she could still see his piercing, frigid stare devoid of any hint of compassion.

Fingers shaking with anger, she wiped her eyes furiously.

"How can a heartless jerk end up with such a sweet baby? A baby who doesn't bear even a whisper of his likeness. It's as if someone couldn't cover his legal bills, so Mr. Heartless took the child, just like Rumpelstiltskin from the fairy tale. No wonder he isn't married; who could bear living with someone so utterly devoid of warmth?"

Forcing herself to regain control, Rylee strode to her apartment. Ignoring the persistent mewing of Squeaker, she collapsed onto her bed.

"If we're on our own, then we're on our own." She squeezed her eyes shut.

"I should have worn the stupid gray suit."

The looming meeting with the gang that night was a crushing weight—a stark reminder of her failure.

Glancing into the dresser mirror, she saw puffy eyes swollen from relentless crying and hair whipped into disarray by the wind. Just as she turned on the shower to melt away the day's torment, the phone's insistent ring shattered the silence. Squeaker's meow was a desperate echo of her own inner turmoil.

"Oh, let it go to voice mail." Squeaker began to yowl in protest. "Okay, okay. Hello. This is Rylee."

"Hi, Ms. Vance. This is Thom Richardson. Do you have a few minutes to talk?"

Thom's voice was calm yet edged with urgency as he waited for her response.

Stunned, Rylee's eyes widened in disbelief as she shot a questioning glance at Squeaker.

"Thomas Richardson?"

A warm, almost seductive chuckle slithered over the line.

"Yeah, my parents insisted on christening me Thomas Orlando Richardson. Sounds dreadful, right? So, my friends simply call me Thom."

Rylee looked at Squeaker in surprise. "You can call me Thom, Ms. Vance."

Thom's breath hitched slightly, the tension palpable in every word.

"Ms. Vance, are you still there?"

"I'm here. I'm just—I'm shocked."

"I understand. After you left, I had time to mull over your words. You're exactly right about what's happening. It is going to cut funding to the free clinics. I want to offer you every ounce of help I can. I know you're furious with me, and I can't blame you. So, tell me, how can I make it right?"

Her voice trembled, and fresh tears cascaded down her

cheeks.

"Ms. Vance, I'm sorry for letting you down at the office. Please, let me help you."

Thom's hand slammed against the resume file on his desk with frustration. He could almost feel the weight of her sorrow reverberating through him—it was all his fault.

Then a gentle, vulnerable sound sent shivers down Thom's spine.

"Thank you, Mr. Richardson. I need your help desperately. I'm drowning here—I really don't know what I'm doing. We need you."

Hearing the raw desperation in her plea, Thom struggled to steady his own voice. Why did her pain command such power over him?

"What can I do, Ms. Vance?"

"A few of us are gathering tonight at a friend's place to hash it all out. Can you come?"

"Well, um, I—"

He was caught off-guard by her invitation.

"I'm sorry, Mr. Richardson; I know you have your commitments."

"No, I want to be there. I'm never too busy to stand up for citizens in need. Can I bring Lexie? And please, just call me Thom—everyone does."

Rylee's laugh, a bittersweet sound bursting through her tears, resonated like a spark of hope. Thom felt a warm surge of resolve rise within him as he listened.

"Of course, Lexie is welcome. Who could possibly say no to an angel like her?"

They wrapped up the conversation with directions to

Lisa's apartment. Thom hung up and sank back into his chair, the tension of the day momentarily easing.

"You, Ms. Vance, you almost make me believe in angels."

## Chapter 38

Thom unloaded Lexie from the car, slung the diaper bag over his other shoulder, and began climbing the stairs to Lisa's apartment. Entering a room full of strangers hadn't bothered him while he was campaigning, why was it

bothering him now? He looked down at Lexie in her carrier and paused at the front door.

"You made it with the cutie."

Rylee's gentle voice called to him from the bottom of the stairs.

Gracefully gliding up the final steps, she met him at the landing, reached around him, and opened the door.

"I'm here with show-and-tell," she called into the room.

Lisa's merry voice responded. "Come on in."

Rylee clapped her hands and reached out to free Lexie from the carrier.

"Well, little lady," Rylee whispered, "let me teach you how to make an entrance."

Once again, in the presence of Rylee, Thom was bemused. Lexie all but jumped into Rylee's arms.

By the time Thom entered the living room, Rylee was standing in the middle of a group of people, with Lexie on her hip.

"Let me introduce you to our state senator, Mr. Thomas Richardson and his lovely assistant, Ms. Lexie Simms."

"Oh, my," Lisa said.

She raised an eyebrow at Rylee and elbowed June.

Lisa eyed Thom up and down and patted the couch. "Hi. I'm Lisa. Come and sit by me."

Thom moved toward the couch, as he looked around the room at all the curious faces. One young man stood up and walked toward him.

"Mr. Richardson, my name is Dave. I want to welcome you. We can certainly use your help. Thanks so much for coming."

Thom shook the young man's hand. "Thanks. Call me Thom."

Lisa grinned up at Rylee and rubbed her ring finger. Rylee blushed and started fussing with Lexie, who erupted into giggles.

"Excuse me a moment, Dave."

"Oh, yeah, of course, Mr. Richardson."

"Dave, seriously. Call me 'Thom.'"

Thom excused himself to find his way to Rylee and Lexie. With genuine affection in his voice, Thom bent down to speak softly to Lexie.

"How's my silly girl?"

He gazed at Rylee too and smiled. Her scent was driving him crazy.

Rylee turned to him, surprised by the warmth in his tone and the gentleness in his eyes. There was something about this man. June and Lisa made subtle eye contact before June moved to Rylee and Thom.

"Mr. Richardson, get a plate and we'll talk. The chicken salad sandwich is pretty good."

June motioned toward the food, talking as they walked.

"The problem is the people who come to the free clinic often don't go to the hospital because they can't afford it or just

134

don't want to go to the hospital. When someone is living below the poverty line, they aren't going to want to sign one of those forms saying they are responsible for payment."

"I understand. But the government is funding two programs that duplicate each other. People who go to the clinic can be treated at the hospital. We're paying both to offer the same exact service," Thom replied.

June's forehead wrinkled in a frown, and Thom hurried to stave off her opposition.

"What needs to be shown is that the free clinic is necessary to the welfare of those people who use the clinic. Can you do that?"

"The best way to do that is to talk to the people who work with the clinics around the state. They would be the best advocates," June answered.

Dave interrupted, "We need to get public opinion on our side. The people who use the free clinic often don't pay much in taxes, if anything. The people who are paying the taxes don't like funding services for those that they think are freeloaders."

Thom nodded in agreement. "Smart kid," he thought.

Discouraged, June pursed her lips and looked at the two men.

"Are you telling me that there isn't a way to prevent this?"

Thom shook his head.

"No. But you must be honest with yourselves here. It's an uphill battle, and your best efforts may not be enough. There are some real heavy weights supporting it."

Lisa had been uncharacteristically still as she listened to the conversation. She stood and moved next to June.

"But you're not one guy. We're all in this together. It

doesn't matter if there is an army in support of it; it's wrong, and it would be wrong for us not to fight it. Just tell us what to do and we'll do it."

Thom smiled at Lisa. It didn't matter to her if this group of less than a dozen people were going up against the George Dawson machine. She believed that, because the cause was righteous, they would prevail.

Thom looked around the room again. Everyone here believed it. Where had his own enthusiasm gone? He turned to Lexie, and painful memories returned. He had believed that 'right made might' once as well.

Rylee was puzzled as she watched the subtle emotional shift in Thom.

Dave interrupted Thom's thoughts.

"June submitted a letter to the editor. I checked, and they ran it in the late edition. I already have my letter in support of it drafted and will e-mail it tonight. Hopefully, the paper will run it as well."

Thom's trained mind refocused, and he nodded. Rylee knew that Thom was paying attention, even if part of him had withdrawn. The more she knew about him, the more he became a mystery.

Rylee, picking up a protesting Lexie, moved over to the group. She gathered up a few toys as she went and sat down on the floor beside the sofa. Soon, Lexie was happily playing again.

Thom watched Rylee's movements. She was so patient with Lexie and yet had complete control of the baby. Thom looked down at the top of Rylee's head as she played with Lexie. Her hair looked so soft, he wanted to reach out to touch it and feel it running through his fingers.

Rylee looked up at him. His eyes had softened, and a gentle smile played around his mouth. Rylee felt her heartbeat increase and her breath quicken.

Thom noted that Rylee was becomingly pink again. At that moment, the only person there for him was Rylee.

"...and we could riot!"

Thom was jerked back to the conversation. "What? No. Rioting won't work fast enough. And besides, if the riot is a flop, you'll never get support," Dave said.

Thom smiled down at Lexie and Rylee.

"No. Dave's right. You never know with a riot. What you need is something that people can identify with, something that they can hang onto."

Thom's eyes rested on Rylee's face longer than necessary before he looked up.

"Any other ideas?"

The group stayed busy debating various ideas, but Rylee was only partly aware of the discussion. When Thom's blue eyes locked on her, his words seemed to communicate some private message.

"Well, Miss Lexie, could you pull on Rylee's ear and get her to pay attention to something other than you?"

Rylee startled, her head whipping up to face the speaker.

"Oh. Sorry, Dave. What did you say?"

"Do you have any ideas about something that people might care about as it relates to the clinic? You are, after all, the one that was so gung-ho to get this bill defeated. A pretty face comes along, no offense Lexie, and you just turn to mush."

Rylee felt her face go red.

"Sorry guys, I guess you're right."

She stood and handed Lexie over to Thom. "Okay. Something that people are going to care about. I don't see why they wouldn't care about the clinics closing. It's healthcare for those that can't afford it. Who is against helping the poor?"

Rylee looked around the still room.

"They care more about the tax cuts," June said. Rylee's shoulders sagged.

"I honestly don't really know why someone who doesn't need the services of the free clinic would care about it. And I know that the people who can afford healthcare and pay taxes don't seem to care about the people who use the free clinic."

She dropped her head and remained silent, until she stamped her foot.

"I know that this bill is wrong. It only exists so that the people who wrote it can get funding for projects that are just boondoggles. The writers make themselves look good by standing in the street and shouting, 'I'm cutting your taxes!' while they aren't cutting anything except services to the neediest among us." Finally, Rylee declared, "It's just wrong!"

Her eyes blazed as she looked around the room. The only audible sound was from Lexie, who was getting fussy.

Thom's bright eyes contacted Rylee, and he winked.

"Why don't we contact people who do care about the other services that would be cut?" Lisa suggested.

"Great idea. Do you have a list of the other services on the chopping block?" Thom asked.

"I think I can pull that together. We often apply for the same grants," June said.

Thom looked around the room at the suddenly bright faces turned toward him. This just might work.

138

He smiled as he thought, "George, look out; I'm taking an un-groomed trail."

"Okay. You have my support. If we don't know what people are thinking about the bill, maybe we should go out and talk to them. I can block out some time to drive around the state. Is there anyone else available? I recommend that, if you can, try to go out in teams of two. It's a little safer that way. The number of teams we have will impact how we divide up the state," Thom said.

Lisa started clapping her hands. Rylee was the only one in the room who didn't appear to be elated by Thom throwing his support to the cause. Her heart was breaking as the others happily made plans to storm the state.

## Chapter 39

The meeting broke up shortly after that, and Rylee stayed to help clean up. She was surprised to find that Thom did as well, and even more surprised that he walked her to her car.

"Holy Smoke! Is this your car?" Thom was clearly impressed. "Yeah. My dad gave it to me."

Inwardly she thought, "Great! Another guy is gushing over my car — again."

Thom couldn't help but notice the flat tone in her voice. "So, what's up, Rylee?"

Rylee looked down at the ground. "Nothing. I think that this is a plan that will work. Being able to go out and talk to people will be a great way to get the word out."

Thom shifted the weight of the diaper bag on his shoulder.

"Then why so sad?"

Rylee continued to look at the ground. She could feel the tears in her eyes, and she didn't want Thom to see her crying.

"I'm not sad."

She turned her back on him. She wanted Thom to go away, but then she heard him set down the diaper bag. His voice was soft as he put his hand gently on her shoulder.

"Rylee, what's wrong?"

"I can't go. I must work at a stupid job that isn't important at all. Ms. Blackman told me I couldn't take any more time off unless I gave her a week's advance notice.

She was mad at me because I took off to come see you this afternoon. I know she'll have me fired if I do it again. I need a job so I can live, but this is so much more important."

Embarrassed, she felt hot tears rolling down her face.

"I want to make a difference in people's lives. I want to add something good to the community. I don't want to spend my life filing invoices."

For the second time today, she was uncontrollably pouring her heart out to this man she barely knew.

Unaware that he had moved in closer to her, or that he had placed his free arm around her, she leaned on him for support as she cried.

He felt compelled to protect her, and he was thrilled as her silky hair brushed the back of his hand. Rylee stirred and pushed away from him. Thom slowly let go of her; he wanted to get lost in the sensations awakened in him as he held her.

Rylee turned away from Thom, brushing the tears from her face.

"Rylee, look at me."

Rylee turned, reluctantly. The pupils of her eyes were dilated, making them appear very large and dark, her hair was mussed becomingly. He wanted to pull her back into an embrace and cover her with kisses. It was almost impossible not to reach out to touch her.

"I don't have a buddy yet, unless you count sleepy head here," Thom said.

Rylee laughed and visibly relaxed.

"Thom, I'm so sorry, I don't know what came over me. I don't usually fall apart like this. That's the second time today I've talked your ear off."

"You wound me! Dear lady, I do care. You convinced me the first time we talked. I really didn't like the bill but hadn't made up my mind which way to vote. And to tell you the truth, it would be greatly to my advantage to vote in favor of it. I could curry a lot of favors, maybe even get a seat on a good committee. But you made your argument soundly. I'm not going to vote for it."

Rylee's grin lit up her face.

"And I do care that you must decide between your job and this issue that is so important to you. What do you do for work?"

Rylee was surprised by the question. "I, uh, I'm a secretary."

"Any college?"

Rylee was really puzzled.

"Yeah, but just an associate's degree from a community college up north."

"And you've proven to me that you are also a fledgling political activist. Do you want a job? My firm really needs a secretary."

Rylee regarded Thom. She barely knew him. She looked down at the sleeping baby. He was a good father to Lexie, and Lexie obviously loved him.

"I'm not a legal secretary. You don't even know how well I type."

Thom just laughed.

"Well, if you can't type, then I'll pay you less. As far as the legal stuff is concerned, a secretary is pretty much the same everywhere; Chip and I can teach you the legalese. Do you trust me?"

"Yes, I think I do trust you. And yes, I would like a job."

If Thom had been struggling before, it was everything he could do to keep from wrapping her in his embrace and smothering her with kisses. He hadn't felt this way about a woman in a long time, maybe he had never felt this way. He had to pick up the diaper bag to control himself.

"Good. Don't worry, let me handle it. I'll talk to you tomorrow. I think that there's a solution for both of us."

Rylee was puzzled. "Both of us?"

Thom turned to walk away.

"Yeah, I need someone to go with me and Lexie tomorrow to visit hospitals. I don't think she'll be much help."

He stopped and looked over his shoulder.

"So, get in your hotrod and leave so that I know you got off okay."

"Oh. Thanks."

Rylee wondered what he meant by going with him tomorrow morning. She still needed to give her notice at work. It would be nice to see the look on Ms. Blackman's face when she told her.

Thom waited until she drove away before he moving toward his car.

"What am I doing?"

When he got to his car, he pulled out his cell phone and called Chip.

"Thom, do you know what time it is?" Chip's irritable voice scolded.

Thom grinned at his partner's tone. "Yeah, it's nearly midnight."

"What do you want?" Chip asked.

As he listened to Thom recount the events of the evening, Chip's face changed from a scowl to a look of surprise, and then to amusement.

"I guess your talk with Ms. Vance went well. I've got to say that I wasn't that impressed when she first walked in, but before she left, she had blown my socks off. Sounds good to me. Now, will you get off the phone and let me get back to sleep?"

## Chapter 40

Rylee was greeted by one of her co-workers when she arrived at work the next morning.

"Rylee, Mr. Halpern would like to see you right away." Rylee was alarmed.

"Did he say why?"

"Nope. Just said to have you come see him as soon as you came in," the girl replied.

Rylee's skin prickled, and her throat tightened. She walked down the hall, past Ms. Blackman's astonished gaze, to Mr. Halpern's office. The door was slightly ajar as she knocked. After Mr. Halpern waived her in, Rylee paused just inside the door to collect herself and was flabbergasted to see Thom sitting in a chair.

She took a deep breath.

Mr. Halpern smiled pleasantly. "Come in, Ms. Vance. Have a seat."

Rylee sat down next to Thom. She looked at him, and he winked at her.

"Good to see you again, Ms. Vance."

Mr. Halpern was still smiling.

"Ms. Vance, why didn't you tell us that you were looking for another job?"

Rylee was stunned into speechlessness.

"Mr. Richardson and Mr. Fallon were so impressed with you at your interview yesterday, that they wanted to offer you the position to start immediately."

Thom turned to Rylee. "Ms. Vance, I know that this is

145

probably a surprise to you, but Mr. Fallon and I discussed our needs and decided that we could use someone immediately. Of all the people we interviewed yesterday, we both agreed that you rose to the top."

Rylee's eyes were wide with disbelief.

Thom grinned. "It's true. You don't have to take the job if you don't want it, but just in case you did, I thought that I would take the liberty of talking with your current employer about joining our little firm starting today. If you want the job, it's yours."

Thom turned to Mr. Halpern. "Mr. Halpern has been very kind and is willing to let you go with a good recommendation if you choose to take our offer."

Mr. Halpern returned Thom's smile.

"Well, it was quite a surprise when Mr. Richardson called this morning. He starts work as early as I do. I like that in a man. We usually like to have a couple of weeks' notice, but Mr. Richardson is very convincing. He's probably a very good lawyer."

Both Thom and Mr. Halpern looked at Rylee. Mr. Halpern continued, "It's up to you Rylee. We, of course, recognize your value here and don't want you to leave. After my conversation with Mr. Richardson this morning, you may even be a candidate for executive assistant."

"Oh, um, today?"

Rylee felt unsteady as she looked from one man to the other. Thom had turned to face Rylee. He winked and grinned at her again.

"I not only need a political assistant, but a secretary as well. Ms. Vance, you convinced us that you have just the skills our firm needs. You are articulate, astute, and organized."

There was a rustling sound at the door.

Mr. Halpern addressed the stern-looking matron. "Oh, Ms. Blackman. Come in. You didn't tell me that we had such a fine administrative assistant in Ms. Vance. It appears that someone else is trying to snatch her away from us."

While Mr. Halpern looked at Ms. Blackman, Thom winked again and whispered, "Say 'yes,' Rylee. Trust me."

"What? Rylee Vance?" Ms. Blackman asked.

"Yes. Ms. Blackman, I would like you to meet Mr. Thomas Richardson. He has made Rylee a job offer to start immediately. I have been encouraging her to stay. It's obvious from Mr. Richardson's report that she would make an excellent executive assistant. But you must have known this for some time. In addition, Mr. Richardson tells me she is a skilled political assistant."

"Ms. Vance? Executive assistant? Political assistant? Mr. Halpern, are you looking for another executive assistant?"

Ms. Blackman's face was everything Rylee had hoped for.

"Mr. Halpern, thank you for your confidence in me. But working in an arena where I can make a positive difference in the lives of others is where my heart is. I would like to start immediately with Mr. Richardson and Mr. Fallon."

Thom was elated, but he kept his face in a pleasant business mask. He stood and turned to speak directly to Ms. Blackman.

"I have explained to Mr. Halpern that we just couldn't wait to get Ms. Vance on board. There are important things brewing, and we need our new assistant to start immediately. I know that it will probably be a loss to you, but my partner and I appreciate it."

Thom turned back to Mr. Halpern.

"Thank you for your understanding, Mr. Halpern. May I assist Rylee in packing out her desk, since my partner and I are the ones putting the rush on?"

Mr. Halpern nodded and looked at Rylee.

"Ms. Vance, if you should ever consider coming back to us, the door will be open to you."

Mr. Halpern walked around the desk to shake Rylee's hand, then turned to Thom.

"May I have one of your cards, Mr. Richardson? It's always a wise idea to know good attorneys and state legislators."

Thom produced a business card from his coat pocket, while motioning Rylee to the door.

"Ms. Blackman, you will have to tell me if we have anyone else the caliber of Ms. Vance in our ranks," Mr. Halpern added.

Ms. Blackman stood blinking in the doorway. "After you, Ms. Vance. Excuse us, Ms. Blackman," Thom said.

"What are you doing?" Rylee hissed. Thom beamed down at her.

"Hiring you."

## Chapter 41

Thom held the door for Rylee as they left the Halpern facility. Rylee had not said a word to him that wasn't directly related to packing out her desk. Thom wasn't certain whether she was angry with him or not. She had talked easily enough with her surprised co-workers who were coming to see what was going on. They loaded her things into her car before she turned on Thom.

"Okay. I know that I said I would take the job last night, but it would have been nice if I had some input into what just happened."

Thom's face and tone were serious, but his twinkling eyes showed Rylee that he wasn't.

"What? You don't want to work for me?"

Rylee crossed her arms and glared.

"Guess you're mad, huh?"

"No. Yes. It's just so sudden. You could have told me."

"We'll discuss this later."

Rylee glanced up at the building and waived to several of her old co-workers who were watching from the windows.

Thom glanced up at the windows and waived as well.

"Great. I'll see you at the office."

Rylee glared.

"Rylee, it's going to be okay. You'll see. Trust me."

Her eyes narrowed as she watched him get into his minivan and pull away.

"Who does he think he is? Okay. I really want this job,

but the point is I need to be a part of decisions that impact me. This is not the kind of surprise I like to get. How in the world did I let myself get carried along by Mr. Blue Eyes?"

She wrinkled up her face at the memory of crying on his shoulder like a baby.

"Oh, yeah. Boy, talk about responding at an emotional weak point. What exactly did I say to him? I know he's just doing something I asked for, but what am I doing driving away from a steady job? Mr. Halpern even hinted at a promotion."

Rylee remembered how Ms. Blackman looked at her as they left Mr. Halpern's office. Ms. Blackman had been the obstacle preventing her from advancing at Halpern's and making her feel bad about doing what Rylee knew was right.

"What do I know about being a legal secretary?"

Her stomach churned as she pondered her new position.

"What if I hate the new job? What if I'm not any good at being a legal secretary? Why did I accept this job? I'm not thinking things through. This isn't like me at all."

## Chapter 42

An aide stepped briskly into George Dawson's office, a sober look on his face. George looked up from the folder he was reading and arched an eyebrow in curiosity.

"What is it now?" George asked.

"Mr. Dawson, Robin, one of the girls we sent to Richardson's office to apply for the secretary job, was told it had already been filled."

"That was fast," George replied, a glint of interest sparking in his eyes. "Do we know who they hired?"

"Not yet. I'm work on it."

George leaned back in his chair with a calculating smile.

"Maybe we can convince them to do a little work for us on the side."

The aide nodded and left the office.

The gears of George's mind were spinning rapidly.

"This position was filled fast. Faster than expected. Maybe they had already known who they wanted."

He wondered who had managed to catch their attention. A shrewd grin crossed his face as he considered his options. George's skill at playing this game had served him well in his career.

He called another aide into the office.

"Tell the boys to put out some feelers. I want to know who Richardson brought on board. I have an idea or two about how to make this interesting."

"Yes, Mr. Dawson."

George pulled a cigar from the box on his desk and sat

down again. Even if the secretary's position was snapped up, there were other ways to get what he wanted.

The thought of his influence spreading unseen into this kid's law firm made him smile. The information would come to him quickly enough. Richardson's new hire would not stay a mystery for long.

He lit the cigar and went back to the folder he had been reading, crossing his feet on the desk with a supreme sense of confidence.

## Chapter 43

When Rylee walked into her new workplace, she scanned the room she had seen twice with new eyes. It was small for three people and needed some color. Thom followed her through the door with the largest of the boxes.

"Mr. Fallon, you here?" Thom called.

"I'm here in the back. Hold your horses," Chip said.

Thom smiled at Rylee and called out to Chip again. "We have a new member of our little firm, so make certain you're presentable."

Rylee had been trying to stay angry, but she found herself returning Thom's engaging smile.

Chip walked out of the only other room and shook her hand.

"Well, Ms. Vance, welcome aboard," Chip said warmly.

Rylee took a deep breath. She had been swept along so far, but some rules needed to be set down.

"Thank you, Mr. Fallon."

Her gaze turned to Thom and then back to Chip. "You both certainly have a unique way of interviewing. I had no idea that I would start working for you until I came into work this morning, and you were pulling a little proactive stunt with my current employer. Is proactive the right word?"

She paused to glare at Thom, who could barely suppress his grin, before she continued.

"I don't know that I can even do this job. And this is the last time," she pointed at Thom, "that either of you will make a decision that impacts me in any way, without including me in the decision-making process."

"Ouch. Sounds like you made the right choice there buddy," Chip said.

"I'm serious here," Rylee said.

She planted her fists on her hips and glared at them both.

There was an uncomfortable silence as Chip looked at Thom. Thom held his eyes steady with Rylee's. She glared back, fighting the urge to stamp her foot.

"Well?" she demanded, "Well?"

Chip started laughing, and Thom broke into a grin.

"Please tell me this means you're taking the job?" Chip asked.

Thom fought to contain his amusement at Rylee's anger and defiance.

"Rylee, we're not making fun of you," Thom said.

Rylee's head snapped around to face him. She was furious. "What is wrong with you two? Am I not speaking English here?"

Chip stepped forward, still laughing, and said, "Ms. Vance, the best legal secretaries need to be able to give as good as they take. It looks like you can."

Chip paused and looked over at Thom.

"Ms. Vance–Rylee, let me tell you a story. There was this first-year law student who was, of course, poor and needed a job. This student wanted to find a job that would also give a ground-level view of the legal profession. So, when the student read the ad for a legal secretary, it was immediately appealing. However, most lawyers want the secretary to commit to at least eight-hour days. With no previous experience, and the burden of needing to work around a class schedule, the student applied with this sole proprietor lawyer," Chip said.

Thom looked down at the ground.

"Thom hired me over several very experienced legal secretaries and paralegals. I'm just finishing up with law school. I can't even practice law until I pass the bar, and this guy," Chip pointed at Thom, "makes me his partner. To answer your question about what's wrong with us, we're not your normal law firm. To make matters even more complicated, Thom is also in politics."

Rylee turned to look at Thom, who looked embarrassed, and then she turned back to Chip. Thom walked toward Rylee and Chip, taking Rylee's hand.

"I'm sorry that I acted for you, without having you be part of the decision. We talked about it last night You're right; I should have told you what I intended before I did anything this morning. It was wrong to spring it on you like that. But we really need you to start right away, and I got the feeling that you also wanted to start immediately. Was I mistaken?"

Chip nodded his head and gave Rylee a meaningful look. She sat down in a chair.

"Okay," she finally said. "I can type." Thom shot a quick look at Chip.

"Here's the deal. Chip and I don't just need a secretary. I need a political aide. It isn't appropriate for Chip to fill that role for me anymore. You have proven to me that you can. You will be an important part of our little team, unlike your last job, where you were barely noticed. Besides, we pay a lot more."

"But I've never done this before," Rylee protested.

"But you do it so well." Thom grinned at Chip.

"Today, you and I – rep and aide - will put on our political hats. We will drive up the road a few miles to talk with some folks about free clinics, just like you wanted to do last night. While we're on our way, we can discuss your terms of employment. I also want to take Lexie along."

Chip sucked air between his teeth, leaned in, and said to Rylee in a stage whisper.

"Rylee, if you value your life, make sure Lexie is always in the car when Thom drives."

Thom's eyes narrowed, but he did not respond.

"Don't worry. We'll both be here to coach you; I promise. You are taking the job, right?" Chip pressed.

Rylee stood up and smiled, shaking Chip's hand. "Mr. Fallon, Mr. Richardson, I accept. This job will be interesting, if nothing else. But before you do something that will impact me again, you will talk to me first. Okay?"

## Chapter 44

They decided to drive Thom's car, because Lexie's car seat was already in it. After running by daycare and picking up Lexie, they headed east.

"So, where are we going?" Rylee asked

"The Grant Hospital and then to visit with the free clinic there."

He checked his rearview mirror and eased the car into traffic. Rylee was silent as she watched the passing buildings thin to more rural scenery. Thom glanced over at her from time to time.

"Penny for your thoughts?" Rylee didn't turn around.

"No thoughts. I'm still stunned. I don't have the job that I had when I left for work this morning."

Thom bit on his bottom lip. "You still mad?"

He could see her shoulder move as she sighed. "No. Well, yeah, a little bit. Maybe. This has all happened too fast to absorb."

She started to say something, but looked back at Lexie, who was asleep in her car seat. She took a deep breath to control her tone so as not to alarm the little girl.

"Look, how would you feel if someone made a life altering choice for you, and you didn't have anything to say about it? It didn't matter if you wanted it or not; it's what you're going to be doing. Period. End of discussion."

Thom felt the words like a physical blow. He suddenly remembered the helplessness and anger that he had felt six months ago. He could find no words to respond to her. She was right; he had acted presumptuously and taken away an important life choice.

Rylee stared at Thom, waiting for him to say something. He just sat there, not even looking at her or acknowledging her comment. She jerked her head back to the window.

Thom had been watching her out of the corner of his eye. He wanted to say he was sorry, but he knew a simple sorry wasn't enough. Thom pulled over to the side of the road and glanced at the still sleeping Lexie.

"Look, Rylee, I screwed up. I understood what you said last night to be the truth. That you didn't want to work for the evil Ms. Blackman anymore and wanted a job that would let you give back to people. You said that it was upsetting you to not be able to go out like everyone else and visit hospitals. I wanted to help you."

He bit his lip to keep from raising his voice.

"I apologize, but you accepted the position. You need to get over it and move on. You're right. If and until we end this arrangement, Chip and I will be your bosses, and we are going to make professional decisions for our firm and for you. We need a secretary as well as a political aide. If you can't put your anger behind you and do your job, I'll take you back to the office and you can help Chip today instead."

He didn't wait for her to respond. He threw the car into gear. He was looking in the side view mirror when he heard the sob catch in her throat. He turned on her, angry this time.

"Oh please, Rylee, not again! That isn't going to work again!"

Lexie stirred in her seat. Rylee returned Thom's glare, with

158

tears on her now very pink cheeks, and her eyes were hot with anger.

"Mr. Richardson, I accepted the position, and I am good at what I do. This is my project anyway. You're not going to take me back, because we are going to get the job done. However, I don't find it unreasonable to feel some anger at being railroaded the way I was."

Thom opened his mouth, but she held up her hand. "I understand it was what I was asking for, and I do want to participate in talking to people around the state."

She dropped her voice and her eyes. "And I really do appreciate your kindness. I really do appreciate that you are trying to help me save the clinic. I really do appreciate that you are giving me a job that will allow me to be a real part of something important. You're right. I am being ungrateful. Thank you."

She looked up at him with her eyes dilated from tears and emotion.

"Thanks, Thom. Really."

Thom sat open-mouthed, and when she raised her eyes to him, all he could think about was kissing her. He turned off the car and unbuckled his seat belt.

Rylee continued to look at him, watching him slide toward her. And feeling his arms around her, pulling her toward him, she watched the lips that she was longing to feel on hers. Finally, at first with gentle brushes, and then as she responded, with more urgency his mouth did touch hers.

Rylee wanted to pull him closer. The very air sizzled. She wanted more. But this was quickly moving in a direction she was not ready to go. A car went whizzing past, honking at them, and a young woman shouted out the window.

"Get a room!"

Rylee was thrilled as Thom chuckled, his breath brushing against her cheek.

"Sounds like a good idea. Maybe we should," he whispered in her ear.

He ran his finger around her sleeve cuff until he found the button. His finger deftly unfastened the button. Rylee felt, rather than heard, the moan escape from her when Thom bent his mouth to hers again, with the warmth of his breath on her lips.

"Rylee," he whispered.

Lexie began to gurgle in the back seat.

Thom groaned and rested his head against Rylee's forehead. He sat up and brushed Rylee's lips with his, his eyes clouded.

"I'll be right back. Don't go anywhere." He turned to attend to Lexie.

Rylee's head was spinning. The thought of more was tempting, and her mind was alive with sensation.

Thom turned back around and reached toward Rylee.

She longed to fold back into his arms, but this was too much, too fast. She let her emotions run away from her, so she pushed gently against his chest. She could feel the hard muscles under the soft cotton of his shirt.

"Thom, we have some hospitals to visit today."

Just inches from her, Thom opened his mouth to say something in protest, but Rylee stopped him.

"We need to sort this out later. Cooler heads need to prevail here. Let's get the job done first. A lot has happened to me today that I need to process. Now isn't the time for any of this."

Her tone was firm, but her eyes were singing a softer tune.

She did want more. Her skin was alive with desire for his touch.

"Thom, I don't know what to think. You're my boss now."

Thom sat up, suddenly pushing away from her without touching her.

"Oh. I'm sorry. Yeah. Listen, I don't expect, you know, whether we, uh, this isn't going to impact your employment in any way. Okay. Rylee, um, Ms. Vance, you have my assurance that I am not asking for any, um—"

She placed her fingers over his mouth. Her cheeks, already warm, deepened in color.

It was everything he could do to keep from kissing her hand.

"It's okay. I just don't think we need to go the direction we're heading right now, okay? I don't believe that you're sexually harassing me. I'm just as guilty. I'm glad you kissed me. I just don't know how to handle this right now. We're fast approaching an area that I'm not comfortable going to. And now you're my boss, so things need to be," she paused to find the right word, "different."

It was hard to stay in control when she looked at him like that. He was ecstatic that she didn't regret the kiss. How could a church lady taste so good?

"Right. Okay. Job," he said.

## Chapter 45

They wound around the curves in the parking lot as they drove around the hospital looking for an open spot. They had to park some distance from the entrance.

"Okay, we're supposed to be meeting a Ms. Jordan at the reception desk."

Thom said from the backseat, as he changed Lexie's diaper. "She will be giving us a tour of the emergency room and hopefully be answering questions."

Thom stood holding Lexie, and Rylee reached to take her from him. He turned back to the car to retrieve the diaper bag.

"Why didn't you pick a place closer to home?" Rylee said.

Thom's deep chuckle warmed her.

"That's a good question. This is far from all my fellow representatives and may escape their notice for a time. It's important to have the element of surprise on our side as long as we can. A few rabble rosing armatures isn't going to worry our opponents. Having a representative fighting against the bill would alert them. The vote is close."

He grinned at Rylee. "And having Lexie with us makes us more incognito."

Rylee was beginning to appreciate that Thom was much more than he seemed. They entered the hospital and approached the reception desk. An elderly volunteer greeted them and called the public affairs office. Within a few minutes, they were approached by a pleasant-looking woman in a blue suit.

"Senator Richardson?"

Thom took the hand that she was offering to him. "You must be Ms. Jordan," he said.

He turned slightly, indicating Rylee.

"This is my aide, Ms. Vance, and," he nodded at Lexie, "Miss Alexia Simms."

Ms. Jordan's only reaction was a slightly raised eyebrow. She smiled at Rylee.

"Nice to meet you, Ms. Vance."

"I don't want to take up a lot of your time. I'm here to find out the impact that closing the local free clinic would have on this hospital." Thom said.

Ms. Jordan nodded her head.

"To tell you the truth, Mr. Richardson, the impact is purely economic."

"Economic?"

Ms. Jordan nodded her head and smiled.

"Yes, that's the horrible secret. Let's walk down to the emergency department, and I'll explain. People often think an emergency department is for people who don't have insurance or can't pay for health care. They think people in those circumstances will get treated and someone else will pick up the bill."

She paused at the hospital entrance to the emergency department.

"Believe it or not, an emergency department is for emergency situations, sometimes life or death. Emergency departments are not a substitute for a family doctor."

Holding the door open for Thom and Rylee, she gestured toward the waiting room.

"The sad thing is, most of these folks don't have

163

insurance for one reason or another. We will, of course, treat them."

Ms. Jordan's gaze swept the room. "I would guess that none of the people in the waiting room have conditions will be considered urgent."

Rylee looked around and saw a room full of people of various ages. As she watched, a quick and efficient ambulance crew wheeled someone on a stretcher past the woman at the reception desk and through the double doors.

"That appears to be something urgent."

Ms. Jordan nodded to the still closing doors to the emergency room.

"Our emergency room can only treat a certain number of people at a time. People with life-threatening emergencies go to the front of the line. When someone comes in here with a non-life-threatening illness or injury, things get backed up, as they are now. This is normal."

Thom looked around at the people waiting. "You said, 'economic reasons,' Ms. Jordan?"

She nodded. "Yes. For those people who can't pay for services, that cost gets passed on to others who can, either directly through our costs or in the form of Medicaid or Medicare. To pick up the load from the free clinic, we would need to increase the size of the emergency room, which would incur a cost that someone would have to bear. We would also need to increase the size of our emergency room staff, which would again be a cost that someone would have to pay. Hospitals are in business—even non-profits— those higher costs will be passed to the public."

Ms. Jordan glanced around the waiting room. "The free clinic treats non-life-threatening illnesses and injuries that we aren't structured to handle efficiently." Her arm made a broad sweeping gesture around the room.

"As you can see, it is early afternoon and we're full. Things will probably get worse after five."

Thom nodded.

"You must remember that not only will the number of physicians increase, but also nurses, lab techs, x-ray techs, and other support personnel," she added.

"I see," Thom replied.

Rylee had not considered that the free clinic's loss would have a widespread and costly impact on the hospital. But it made perfect logic. Someone would be paying for the increase in services; the taxpayer would ultimately be footing the bill for higher medical costs overall.

"Let's walk back and see if we can catch one of the ER doctors," Ms. Jordan suggested.

She walked across the room and stopped to hold open the double doors that the men with the stretcher had passed through earlier.

Rylee turned to Thom and looked down at Lexie. "Mr. Richardson, if you don't mind, I'll just talk with some of the people out here," Rylee said.

"I'll see you in a few moments then, Ms. Vance," he replied.

Ms. Jordan looked at the registration clerk at the counter. "Sue, this is Ms. Vance, she is Mr. Richardson's aide. Please provide her any assistance she might require."

Ms. Jordan and Thom entered the interior of the emergency room. There was a man in a white coat sitting at a computer.

"Dr. Goldman, this is Representative Richardson," she said.

The man frowned before giving his attention to Thom and Ms. Jordan.

"Nice to meet you. A little early to be campaigning, isn't it?"

Thom smiled and glanced around the room.

"Not today. I can see you're busy, so I have just one question. If the free clinics were to lose funding, what impact would that have on the work you do here?" Thom asked.

"You mean, close?"

Thom nodded.

Dr. Goldman whistled. "Today I've had to deal with one multiple injury automobile accident, one home repair gone horribly wrong, two heart attacks, a necrotic gallbladder, and one DOA. That might seem like a pretty full day, but it's only 12:30.

I've also seen several sprained ankles, numerous kids with head colds, heartburn mistaken as a heart attack, removed a splinter, dealt with earwax buildup – I could go on. And that's just today. There is a room full of people out there who have similar ailments, no family doctor, and some with no way to pay. All of them are going to have to wait. If the free clinic were to close, you could triple that number, easily."

"Doctor."

Dr. Goldman turned to the nurse who called him and smiled over his shoulder at Thom as he walked away with her.

"Nice to meet you, Mr. Richardson. Don't let them close the clinics, okay? Keep 'em open!"

"Wow," Thom said.

# Mayzie Sterling

"Do you understand the impact that closing the free clinics would have here?" Ms. Jordan asked.

"Yes, I believe I do. I don't think I need to see anymore here. Let's go find Ms. Vance."

Chapter 46

Rylee moved to the reception counter as Thom and Ms. Jordan entered the bustling emergency area.

"Sue, are the people coming into the emergency room told about the free clinic in town?" Rylee asked.

Sue wrinkled her face.

"Not told. We do have brochures out here. The problem is that we can't turn anyone away. Sometimes, when people have waited without being seen for a while, they will pick up the free clinic brochure and leave. Sometimes they just leave. I hope they're going somewhere to get medical care, but I don't know. They're usually mad if they must wait a long time. I'm the one who gets to hear about it. I usually don't try to engage people in a lot of conversation, because I don't want them to yell at me."

Rylee scanned the waiting area. Some people looked angry.

"Do you think you see many patients here who could actually use the free clinics?"

Sue leaned closer to Rylee. "There is a room full of them waiting now."

Rylee looked back at the people in the little waiting area. There didn't seem to be anyone in distress, just cuts, a few people in wheelchairs, someone in a homemade sling, and what looked like good old-fashioned colds.

"I understand why folks get mad when they must wait; it's just that people who are dying or seriously ill get in first. We are an emergency room, not a substitute for a family doctor. And we only have a certain number of rooms and doctors."

"Well, that certainly seems to be the case."

Rylee shifted Lexie on her hip and patted Sue's hand. "Thank you for doing such a good job, Sue."

Rylee looked at the brochure rack again before sitting beside a mother and two children in the waiting area. The oldest child seemed to have a clotting cut on his forehead, and blood on his face. Rylee settled Lexie on her lap.

"Excuse me, could you tell me how long you've been waiting?"

The woman glanced at the clock. "Over two hours. They're taking people in ahead of us and look at Jimmy!"

Jimmy grimaced melodramatically to emphasize the pain that the cut caused, and his little sister started poking at Lexie.

Rylee smiled and moved Lexie to the other side of her lap. While she wasn't a medical professional, she had seen similar injuries before and knew that they weren't as bad as they looked.

"Oh, two hours."

The woman looked down at Lexie.

"What's wrong with your baby?" the woman asked.

"Oh, Lexie is—"

Rylee paused. She could be Lexie's mother. They had the same dark hair. Rylee's eyes were a dark hazel, not brown, but it wouldn't be a far reach to think that Lexie's brown eyes came from her.

The woman put a hand gently over Lexie's forehead. "She is a little warm," the woman said.

Rylee stared at the woman, who thought Lexie was her baby.

"You know you'll have to wait for her to be seen if she just has a fever. Probably just cutting teeth. The doctor will tell you that they don't run a fever with teeth," the woman said. "But I'm here to tell you they sure do."

Rylee recalled the reason they were there and spoke up.

"I saw a brochure for a free clinic."

Rylee held out the brochure she had taken from the rack to the woman.

"Have you been there?"

Shaking her head, the woman took the brochure. "No, I haven't. I don't believe I've ever heard about it."

The woman read the brochure and then walked to the front desk. She asked Sue if she could borrow the phone. Sue directed her to a pay phone. The woman returned to where Rylee was sitting.

"I called them. They said to bring Jimmy down, and it won't cost us anything. You should go too," the woman said.

"Maybe I will," Rylee said with a smile.

"Beats waiting here forever," the woman said.

Lexie started to fuss, and Rylee pulled a bottle out of the diaper bag, adjusting Lexie in her arms. As Lexie settled into taking her bottle, Rylee thought about how much they looked alike and how much Lexie didn't look like Thom.

Thom hadn't talked about Lexie's mother once. When he introduced Lexie to Ms. Jordan, he didn't call her his daughter.

Lexie smiled up at Rylee around the bottle's nipple. "You, little pumpkin, are at the center of a mystery."

## Chapter 47

Thom was listening to Ms. Jordan, but his gaze kept drifting over to Rylee.

"You see, Mr. Richardson, losing the free clinic will cost taxpayers more money in the long run. They will ultimately be funding the additional cost to the hospital one way or another. The free clinics are a cheaper solution for everyone."

Thom reluctantly pulled his eyes away from Rylee. "I would appreciate it if you could fax me those figures," he said.

"Not a problem, Mr. Richardson. I would be glad to."

"Thank you so much for taking the time to talk to me, Ms. Jordan."

"Just keep the clinics open, Mr. Richardson."

Thom crossed the waiting room and sat down beside Rylee.

"So, my new political assistant, what did you discover?"

"Well, people get mad having to wait for services in an emergency room."

Glancing around, Thom chuckled softly. "You think?"

Rylee glanced around, making certain no one was overhearing. Her eyes glinted softly as he leaned toward her. "Yeah, Sue said that people yell at her because they can't get in right away, or see other people being taken in ahead of them. And the staff isn't allowed to refer people to the free clinics because they aren't allowed to turn people away. There are brochures from the free clinic on display, but the hospital must see whoever comes in."

"Ms. Jordan said the same thing to me."

Rylee continued her report.

"The people here waiting today probably don't even know about the clinics. I sat next to a family who didn't need the emergency room. They didn't know about the clinic. When I gave a brochure to the mom, she called the clinic and left to go there instead of waiting here."

"I think I saw her talking to you. Tall woman with two kids?"

"Yeah."

Thom walked over to the brochure rack. After a brief pause, he seemed to meander around the room before returning to Rylee. "Looks like the brochure rack can be seen from every vantage point in the room." he said.

Lexie pushed away the bottle with sleepy hands. "Ms. Vance, how about lunch before we head to our next stop? It's one o'clock, after all. It looks like Lexie has already finished her lunch."

He rubbed Lexie's head and gently whispered in the baby's ear.

"You probably need to be changed again. I should buy stock in a diaper company."

An older woman, carrying some medical records, stopped in front of the threesome. "What a beautiful family," she said.

The woman smiled at Thom.

"Your little girl looks just like her momma. You're lucky to have such lovely women in your life."

Thom's hand stilled, but it remained on Lexie's head after the woman walked away.

"We must really look alike, pumpkin. That's the second time that's happened."

With stiff abruptness, Thom took Lexie from Rylee, jerked up the diaper bag, and walked out the door without another word.

Stunned, Rylee sat, mouth open and arms still holding the baby who was no longer there. In amazed silence, she watched him walk away. Coming to herself, she quickly followed them to the car.

"Thom?" she called. He didn't respond. "Are you okay?"

Rylee knew that something was wrong, as she watched the hard line of his jaw. One minute, he was thrilling her with his kisses, his gentle touch, and murmured passion. The next he was cold, angry, and withdrawn, and she didn't know why. She had the fleeting thought that he was behaving like someone with a split personality.

## Chapter 48

"Thom?" Rylee called again as she rushed behind him. He ignored her.

"He is deliberately walking even faster. Does he want to leave me behind here?"

She took a breath before trying one more time. "Are you okay?"

Nothing. Not even a glance back.

He'd drawn her into his deep, urgent world with his gentle touch and whispered words. The next minute, he'd got cold and angry, pulling away from her with no explanation.

"How could he change like that," she thought, "from warmth to complete withdrawal?"

As they climbed into the car, an overwhelming silence took hold. Thom started the engine and drove away from the hospital; his eyes fixed on the road. Rylee studied the carpeting on the floor without seeing it, her mind filled with confused thoughts.

"This is getting scary," she told herself.

"How about this place? Does it look good to you?" Thom's voice broke through the silence.

Rylee jerked, startled by the suddenness of his words. She blinked a few times, trying to gather her composure.

"Sorry, I didn't mean to startle you." he said, a hint of warmth returning to his voice. Rylee looked over at him. His features were still set in a hard line, but his eyes held concern that softened his expression. It was almost as if he were two different people.

"Oh, I was just drifting off like Lexie."

Thom turned his head to look at Lexie, who was dozing softly.

"Let's stop here. They have picnic tables outside, so Lexie can move around a bit."

Rylee barely had time to nod before Thom pulled the car into a lot crowded with families, all happily eating. Children galloped around, and a giant cow statue stood out in front. The prospect of an ice cream cone caused Rylee's mood to lift, but sharing the moment with someone so mercurial didn't sound like a fun time.

Once he parked, she climbed out and placed their order at the window while Thom changed Lexie's diaper. Awkwardness hung in the air between them. Rylee shifted from foot to foot as she waited for the order. When it finally arrived, they moved to one of the tables by the grassy area with their sandwiches. The silence between them was so loud it hurt her ears.

Lexie contentedly crawled in the grass at the side of the table, and Rylee felt she had to ask again. "Thom, are you all right?"

She wasn't sure how much patience she could keep summoning.

Thom's shoulder sagged, and his eyes dropped down instead of meeting hers.

"Did I do something wrong?"

She hoped that he would tell her what this was all about.

His head shot up, and those blue eyes, filled with tenderness and passion just that morning, were now hard and cold. It was plain to see that this man was angry. But what had she done?

Rylee sat silently, stunned, watching the emotions play over Thom's face. She swallowed, trying to be patient with this man. His expression was distant and unreadable, as if he were a million miles away.

"What is going on with him?" she wondered.

After several painful moments of silence, Thom buried his head in his hands. It was almost as if he were trying to hide from something.

## Chapter 49

Thom's head dropped into his hands, and his thoughts roiled around in his mind. He desperately tried to clear his head and make sense of what he was feeling.

"How can Rylee look so much like Lexie? How can she be precisely the type of person I don't want to get involved with? This whole thing was getting way too complicated."

Yet he couldn't seem to stop himself from being drawn to her. Thom glanced up, seeing Rylee playing and laughing with Lexie on the picnic table.

"She really does look like Lexie." His thoughts were bitter. "It isn't her mother Lexie looks like."

The hated promise he had made resurfaced in his mind. Even the smells of the hospital room came back to him.

"She's not Lexie's mother." The idea was nagging at him.

"Just what am I doing? I've known her, what? A couple of days? No way am I letting some church lady get close. The last thing I need is to let my guard down."

Rylee couldn't understand why Thom was shutting her out. She had been patient—more than patient. Didn't he realize she was trying to help?

Lexie was back next to her, trying to climb onto the bench. She lifted the baby up and gave her a piece of a sandwich. With a sigh, she looked over at Thom. He still had his head buried in his hands.

"Thom?" she said, gently, reaching across the table to him.

He straightened up before Rylee could touch him. He was

determined to stay closed off from her, afraid to let her in.

"I'm okay. I don't want to talk about it. It doesn't have anything to do with you."

His voice hard and distant as his eyes. "You done yet?"

Rylee sat back, stung and frustrated. She didn't know how much longer she could put up with this.

"What on earth had made him so angry?"

She replayed the events at the hospital repeatedly.

"What is wrong with him? Did he really mean it when he said it didn't have anything to do with me?"

She wasn't sure what to think anymore. Lexie returned to the ground and was happily pulling at the grass.

Thom tried to keep his thoughts straight as he picked up Lexie and grabbed the diaper bag, a look of determination on his face.

"There isn't any possible way I will allow myself to get close to someone like Rylee. She is my secretary. I am her boss. Getting involved with her would be crazy."

He recalled that it was God who took his family from him. It was God who left him unprepared to care for an infant. It was God that he no longer believed in. Who in the world would be more wrong for him than a church lady like Rylee? He shook his head, still unable to make Rylee fit into his life.

Lexie succeeded in rubbing grass into Thom's hair and down his back.

"Oh, um, let me brush you off. You have grass everywhere."

Despite his determination not to become involved with Rylee, Thom felt a thrill run through him at her touch. Her hands moved up and down his back, and he knew he couldn't keep blocking her out, no matter how hard he tried.

"I can't do this. She's my secretary, and she believes in God. Why in the world did I hire her?"

He wasn't supposed to feel like this. Not this soon. Not ever.

He walked back to the car, struggling with his tangled thoughts, and changed Lexie out of her grass-stained clothes into a clean romper. He settled her into her car seat, taking more time than necessary in a final attempt to clear his head.

"Let's go visit this free clinic. It's getting late," Thom finally muttered.

## Chapter 50

The clinic was tucked between crumbling brick buildings on a narrow side street, not easily located. It was street only parking and a bus stop took up most of what was close. Thom was forced to leave Rylee and Lexie on the cracked pavement right in front of the clinic.

When Thom finally slipped back into the clinic's modest entrance, his ears caught the familiar tone of Rylee chatting animatedly with the same middle-aged woman he had seen Rylee talking to back at the hospital. The little girl tugged persistently at Lexie's leg, her tiny fingers gripping the fabric of the romper.

Thom's footsteps crunched on the uneven flooring as he stepped toward the group. The woman spoke with a mixture of worry and relief.

"I'm so thankful this clinic exists."

Her eyes glistening under the fluorescent lights. "My husband lost his job, and without insurance, every day is a struggle just to put food on the table. The idea of paying for medical care? It's beyond reach."

Rylee nodded in quiet agreement.

With gentle care, the woman lifted a well-loved, pastel-colored doll from a worn fabric tote and pressed it into her daughter's small hands.

"Their father is out searching for work right now, and I work nights. I'm so pleased to find a different—a friendlier, more caring approach."

After giving brief instructions for the children to head to the car parked under a leaning streetlamp pole, she turned back to Rylee and offered a warm smile.

"Nice to meet you and your sweet little daughter." Thom's jaw clenched imperceptibly as he scooped Lexie from Rylee's outstretched arms.

"That was the woman I mentioned from the emergency room—the one whose son had that nasty, slashing cut on his head."

Rylee's tone carrying a teasing edge at what sounded like a clipped retort.

"Yeah, I saw." he grumbled.

Rylee arched an eyebrow. "Great. Mr. Hyde is still here."

Before long, a woman clad in a crisp white lab coat approached them briskly.

"Can I help you?"

"Yes, my name is Thomas Richardson; I called earlier.

I'm here to discuss matters regarding this clinic." Thom's voice was steady as he adjusted his shirt under a squirming Lexie.

The doctor's eyes flickered over his spikey hair—and a few stray blades of grass tangled within.

"I didn't think you were here as a patient." A wry smile tugging at the doctor's lips.

Rylee stifled a small laugh as Thom hastily brushed his hair to remove the uninvited greenery.

"Please, follow me."

They soon entered a cramped office space, about the size of an oversized closet, cluttered with a battered wooden desk and faded plastic chairs.

Thom, balancing Lexie on his hip with practiced ease,

motioned for Rylee to occupy the lone spare seat.

As Rylee reached out to retrieve Lexie into her arms, Thom intercepted gently with a measured, if curt, response accompanied by a smile that never quite reached his eyes.

"We're okay here."

He turned to the doctor.

"Let me introduce my aide, Ms. Vance."

"I'm Dr. Yan. And who might this other young lady be?"

A slight warmth replaced the stiffness in Thom's posture as he quickly corrected himself. "Oh, pardon me, this is Lexie."

"Hello, Lexie. It's lovely to meet you, Ms. Vance." Her sharp eyes refocused on Thom. "What questions do you have?"

Thom's voice was firm and business-like. "Thank you for meeting with me, Dr. Yan. There's a bill under consideration before the legislature that—if passed—would slash funding to free clinics. Officially, it's about eliminating redundant services to cut taxes, but in practice, it's a direct blow to health and human services."

Dr. Yan nodded slowly as if weighing her words. "Yes, I've heard about it. Frankly, I doubt the bill's authors understand the intricacies of what they're proposing. They clearly haven't consulted with any of us in the field."

Thom's eyes narrowed, his tone sharpening with urgency.

"That's exactly why I'm here. Tell me, why do you think these legislators are so misinformed? And why should free clinics exist when hospitals seem to offer the same services?"

Dr. Yan allowed herself a brief, reflective pause.

"Take a look around—this is not an emergency room. This is a modest clinic designed for cases that do not require the services of a hospital. Imagine if every person coming here for colds, stomach aches, prenatal care, or skin rashes were redirected to an emergency room—it would overwhelm the system. Here, we care for those without the means to afford traditional healthcare or the necessary insurance to visit a regular family doctor."

Her gaze softened as she glanced fondly at Lexie. "I imagine Lexie has a pediatrician who handles her well-baby checkups and immunizations, a luxury not available to everyone. For many families, this clinic is the nearest they come to that level of routine, attentive care. Hospitals, with their daunting bills and endless forms, simply aren't accessible."

Dr. Yan's voice grew resolute.

"People often avoid hospitals out of fear—fear of incurring debts that they simply cannot pay, and of being caught in an aggressive system of reimbursement. Here, we provide care freely to those who are just trying to get by."

Thom's expression shifted, a mixture of determination and concern in his eyes.

"Dr. Yan, could you arrange to have the clinic's financial records sent over to my office? I'm preparing my opposition to this bill and require concrete data to back my arguments."

Dr. Yan's smile reappeared as she nodded in acknowledgment. "Of course. It's all public information anyway."

## Chapter 51

"I would like to see the clinic you volunteer at instead of going to the Merico facility. Can you call ahead and make the arrangements? I'm going to want the financials there as well."

Rylee was surprised.

"The clinic here is pretty much the same as at home. I don't think that you'll hear anything different."

He grinned.

"That's good. But I would like to get the financials on a couple of other clinics, too. See if you can also get some information from other hospitals in the state. Get me a cross-section of different-sized communities. I want to compare them."

"Sure, Mr. Richardson."

Rylee pulled a small notepad from her purse and started making notes. She would have to carry something larger to write on in the future. Her pen wasn't working; she shook it. She would need better pens as well. Thom frowned, plucked a pen from the cup holder in the car, and thrust it at her.

"Here," he said.

Rylee took the pen and started writing.

"Can you see if you can get your friends together tonight or tomorrow morning? Tonight would be best," he said.

Thom was barking orders at Rylee in rapid fire. She was having trouble keeping up. At first, she thought he was being mean, but the more he talked, the more she realized that he was just thinking at a furious pace.

His tone was not cruel; it was intense, and Lexie

responded by fussing. Rylee turned around to give her a bottle.

"It's been a long day for you, hasn't it, little one?"

His eyes glanced up at the rearview mirror, a pensive look in his eyes.

"Tell your friends we'll meet at my apartment. That way, Lexie can go down at a decent hour," he said.

Rylee noticed that his tone had suddenly changed and was softer. He was concerned about Lexie getting some rest in the middle of his brainstorming. Thom handed Rylee his cell phone.

"The office number is in there; call your friends and tell them we'll get together at my place at six o'clock tonight. If they can meet tonight, call Chip and have him pick up some sandwiches. I'd like Chip to be there as well. I don't think he has classes tonight. When you talk to him, check to see if he is available. Ask him to bring a couple of dozen copies of the phone list and addresses for all the state representatives and newspapers around the state. And remind me to get you a phone."

"Um, Mr. Richardson, what's your home address?"

## Chapter 52

On the way to the clinic, Rylee's mind was a storm of conflicting thoughts as she made calls on Thom's cell phone. With each ring, she arranged for their visit to her clinic and the evening meeting, but an unsettling tension gnawed at her. Her final call was to catch up with Lisa.

"Miss Ants-in-Your-Pants, listen up—a good number of folks are coming. Many were off checking with other state hospitals, but they practically flocked when I mentioned free food. It'll be intriguing to hear their findings. Dave's college buddies and Jim Hooper are on board too."

Lisa's tone equal parts excitement and mischief.

"That's great, Lisa! Thanks."

"You can thank me when you finally explain what's really going on. Word is you quit your job and jumped ship to Mr. Blue Eyes."

Rylee's eyes darted nervously toward Thom, a silent plea for reassurance.

"Lisa, we'll talk about that later." she whispered.

"You're with him right now, aren't you? All day long, I mean—lucky girl! Just yes or no, please."

"No. Stop."

"Have you kissed him yet?"

Rylee's cheeks burned red with unspoken confessions.

"I knew it—he's been giving you those looks. Spill it: did he initiate, or did you?"

Abruptly, Rylee ended the call, her heart pounding with uncertainty. She couldn't decide whether she was entangled with a madman who could be passionate yet volatile or a man who might slip into anger at the slightest provocation. His unpredictability was a serious red flag for Rylee.

Rylee's anxiety was palpable. She felt imprisoned by her own hesitations and desperately wished to avoid any misstep that might lead Thom astray into the darker corners of his temperament. Lisa's teasing, ill-timed as always, only added to her discomfort.

"Lisa has gathered quite a crowd—friends of Dave are coming as well, along with Chip, who'll bring phone lists and sandwiches."

"We should reach the clinic around four-thirty. Can you ask them to compile their financial info so we can grab it swiftly? That'll give me enough time to feed Lexie and bathe her before the chaos begins."

He glanced at Lexie, then softened, "How's my little trooper?"

A pang of guilt struck him; perhaps he should have left her at daycare. His eyes flickered to Rylee, who sat rigid and silent in the passenger seat. The day had weighed heavily on everyone. He realized he was a jerk.

Despite noticing Rylee's inner turmoil, Thom was impressed by her ability to orchestrate tonight's arrangements with clinical precision. She was far more rattled than she let on— and he suspected he was partly to blame.

Thom stayed behind while Rylee went to retrieve the financials. When she returned, he tried for lightheartedness.

"I didn't realize how close the clinic was to the new office. Want to drive by and see it?"

The question caught Rylee off guard.

"New office?" she thought bitterly. "Great. Not only am I stuck with a volatile boss, but now I'm also tasked with moving his office."

"Since Chip's my partner now, he needs his own space. This place is the perfect size us. It's not the necessarily the spot I would have picked, but I suppose it will do for now."

Thom's attempt at being upbeat fell flat.

As the building came into view, Thom's forced smile "The painters have started already! What do you think?"

Rylee's eyes skimmed the sign over the door—simple black with gold letters that now read, 'Law Offices of Richardson & Fallon.' Inside, the building looked markedly better than its worn exterior.

Thom gestured toward a mid-sized room at the back. "There's the conference room there—solves the accessibility issue for client meetings. And here's the bathroom."

He continued, "Maybe, hmm, it could use some plants. I'm basically a plant murderer."

Rylee's expression remained unreadable, her smile vanished. Thom then set Lexie's carrier down on the floor, making another attempt to bridge their emotional gap. "We're getting all new furniture. Maybe you can help pick it out—I'm hopeless when it comes to décor. Do you want to see the inner sanctum?"

Carefully lifting the carrier to avoid waking Lexie, he led Rylee up the stairs.

In that quiet moment, Rylee's thoughts churned.

"He seems so normal—a decent father to Lexie. Then why does he shut down so suddenly? Why does he become so angry?"

"We've got a sort of kitchen up there, and Chip and I have

our designated office spaces. You'll be sitting in the open area here with the file cabinets."

His words sent another wave of uncertainty through Rylee. They strolled back down as Thom rambled about paint colors and office furniture. Lexie wriggled urgently in her carrier, demanding attention. Thom eventually scooped her up and set her gently on the floor to rummage for another bottle, only for Lexie to dart away.

Giggles followed as Thom crouched to fetch her, and in a sudden burst of energy, she tried to climb the stairs.

Despite her protests, Thom quickly gathered her back into his arms. "We might need a couple of child gates around here."

Rylee, scanning the room, silently wondered how a man could discuss child gates for an office as if it were mundane. Afraid of another misstep causing his anger to flair, she adopted a purely professional tone.

"Mr. Richardson, whatever you decide will be just fine."

Her cold, flat words cut him.

"Look, Rylee, you can choose your own desk if you want. I know the location isn't ideal, not the greatest neighborhood, but we have plenty of parking."

He turned to face her with an earnest openness that only underscored his vulnerability.

"It's close to your free clinic." His words hung in the air.

Thom hesitated before softly saying, "Well, we'd best get going."

"Certainly, Mr. Richardson."

The icy formality in her voice was painful. Even as Lexie began wriggling wildly in his grasp, the tension between them lingered heavy and unresolved. Lexie had all but wriggled out of his arms.

"Shall I take your daughter?"

She might as well have just slapped him, the way her tone tore at his heart.

## Chapter 53

Thom merged into the traffic flow, keeping silent as they left the new office. The silence between them was palpable. "Do you want to go and get your car before or after the meeting?"

"Oh, it doesn't matter to me. Whatever works for you, Mr. Richardson."

Rylee's tone indifferent but her mind racing with conflicting thoughts.

"The meeting could run late, so you might want to head home directly from my place tonight. We should probably pick up your car now."

His suggestion was practical, yet she felt a pang of reluctance at the thought of more time spent with him.

Rylee nodded, although she preferred to limit her time in the car with Thom. She turned her eyes to Lexie, wondering how such a sweet child could have a father she found so difficult to understand.

Pulling up behind her car, Thom placed the car in park to let her out.

"Excuse me, Mr. Richardson, what are you planning to do with all the old office furniture after replacing it?"

Thom frowned, realizing he hadn't considered it yet. "Uh, well, sell it or something, I guess."

Rylee tried to interpret his frown, unsure if it was a sign of frustration or just him thinking.

"I don't mean to presume, but the free clinics could really use it, and you could benefit from a tax write-off."

"Right."

Thom recalled the worn-out equipment he'd seen at the Grant clinic. A flicker of realization crossed his face.

"Yeah. Do you think they could use the old computers too?"

"Yes. That's terrific! It would be amazing to have some better equipment."

Rylee's face lit up with a smile, momentarily forgetting her reservations.

"Thom, this is wonderful."

He noticed her slip into using his first name and sat quietly, processing the shift in their dynamic.

"Everyone at the clinic will be thrilled. June will be at the meeting tonight. I can't wait to tell her."

Thom, suddenly reminded of the meeting, glanced guiltily at Lexie.

"We should get to my place."

His abrupt tone cut through Rylee's moment of happiness.

She looked at Lexie, "Right, it's nearly that time. I'll handle the arrangements for getting the old stuff to the clinics."

## Chapter 54

Rylee followed Thom to his apartment, her mind spinning, trying to process the events of the day. Somewhat guilty, she suspected he would be exciting as a lover. There were sparks. "Too bad he's so weird."

Thom kept watching the blue GTO in his rearview mirror all the way to his apartment. It was ironic that she would have a car like that. Car and driver certainly matched each other well, both powerful classics.

Thom walked into his apartment and groaned. "Sorry about the mess, it's kind of hard to stay on top of it."

Lexie woke up at the sound of his voice and started crying.

Rylee smiled, despite herself, at Thom's panicked expression.

"Why don't you go and take care of her, and I'll pick up."

With a look of relief, Thom headed down the hall with Lexie in tow.

"Dinner and then bath-time, little girl."

Looking back over his shoulder, he smiled with obvious relief. "Thanks!"

Rylee finished picking up the toys, dusted, and straightened pillows and various objects. The apartment was spacious enough, certainly larger than her apartment.

The room was decorated as she would expect of a single man with a baby. Along with numerous soft toys, there was a bicycle hanging from hooks at the end of the hall, and a couple of snow boards and a stroller piled in the back corner of a closet.

193

Rylee could hear Thom in the kitchen, coaxing Lexie to eat, and then a little later in the bathroom with a giggling Lexie.

Having finished straightening, Rylee moved around the living room, looking at trophies and photographs.

Several featured Thom dressed for winter, in the snow, holding one of the snowboards she noticed in the coat closet. There was a vast collection of photos of Thom with friends. Rylee smiled at the adorable picture of a very tiny, crying Lexie, sitting on Santa's lap. There was one of a younger Thom with an older couple, who were probably his parents, and a blue- eyed, very blonde girl. Next, she saw what appeared to be a wedding photo of the same blonde girl, now a woman, and a dark-haired man. And again, another family shot—parents, Thom, the blonde woman, and the dark-haired man. Only this time, the woman was pregnant. Another of an infant Lexie, with the dark-haired man and his blonde bride.

Stunned, Rylee picked up the photograph. "It's his sister's baby! Something horrible must have happened, and not that long ago."

"Lexie is my niece."

Rylee jumped, nearly dropping the photograph.

His mouth was tight and there were small creases in his forehead. Without making eye contact, he took the photograph from her and placed it back on the shelf.

Rylee's mind raced, as she watched Thom's retreating back. She turned back to the photographs. Lexie resembled her father.

"Thom?"

Thom paused without turning to face her. "Later, okay?" he whispered.

His shoulders sagged, and he rubbed his forehead again

before proceeding down the hall.

Tears filled her eyes as they encompassed the room, taking in all the photographs. Without thinking, she moved slowly down the hall and paused just outside of Lexie's room.

Thom was tunelessly singing to the baby, tucking her into her bed, and turning down the lights. Once Lexie settled, he sat in a rocker and put his head in his hands.

Rylee's tears ran freely down her face. It was the same posture that she had seen earlier today. Her heart broke, as she realized that it wasn't anger, she had witnessed today; it was grief.

She had been so wrong about him.

She heard the rocker creek as he stood up. Rylee thought about going back to the living room but decided to wait by the bedroom door for him. His eyes lingered on her tear-streaked face for just a moment, before he walked past her and continued up the hall. Rylee's arm shot out and grabbed his.

"Thom, I'm so sorry."

He stood with his back to her. His shoulders seemed to be carrying the burden of Atlas.

"Look, I can't do this now. There are people coming over. Rylee, I can't do this."

She moved to face him, and wrapped her arms around him while he stood, motionless.

"Thom, you can't keep this inside. It will eat you up. I don't know what happened, but I know that you're hurting. I just want you to know that I'm here when you're ready."

He looked down at her head resting against his chest.

Without thinking, his hands went to her hair and started stroking it.

"I barely know this woman; what am I doing?" Thom tried

to push her gently aside. "Later, Rylee. Okay?"

She didn't let go. She raised her head to find him looking down at her. Her lips found his and the world stopped, as his instincts took over for a few precious seconds.

"Rylee, we can't do this. I can't do this now."

Rylee drew air into her lungs. She hadn't been breathing. His eyes searched her face. "Rylee, I'm sorry. I just can't."

She put her hand on his chest. "Thom, I'm so sorry."

His lips tightened. Very gently, he wiped away her tears. "I'm not ready yet to talk with you about this."

"It's okay. When you are ready, I'll be here to listen."

## Chapter 55

Outside the apartment, the sun cast long shadows stretching endlessly over the still neighborhood. Each moment carried an air of uncertainty, thickening as the day surrendered to evening. In the quiet, a sharp click broke through—then another, a quick succession of clicks and whirs disrupted the approaching night's whisper.

A young man with a thin frame moved like a specter, hidden among the shadows, unnoticed by the two people in the apartment directly across from him. He adjusted his camera with brisk, eager motions, ensuring every dramatic, heart-wrenching scene was captured.

His vantage point allowed him to see every raw, unguarded moment through the wide window. Rylee and Thom, faces suffused with emotion, were unaware of the camera chronicling their fractured intimacy.

He crouched for better angles, shifting positions with the stealth of someone who had done this many times before. Every movement spoke of his dedication to capturing their story, even as he remained disconnected from its humanity.

With each frame, the young man's mind raced with the potential these images held for his employer— what they meant now, what they might mean if ever they were exposed. His enthusiasm was mixed with a darker, more opportunistic thrill as he framed each shot with an appraising eye.

He lingered on Thom's anguished face, buried in his hands, and another of Rylee's outstretched arms caught in a blurred motion of comfort and desperation. Beside him, the camera bag lay open, crammed with extra equipment as he watched through the lens, a flickering light illuminated scenes inside the apartment—Rylee's silhouette standing alone, her hands on her face in the aftermath of Thom's retreat.

Caught up in his voyeuristic narrative, the young man played the role of chronicler, his fingers never pausing. He was a purveyor of truths and details out of context. Stories only half-understood, without regard to the impact of their telling. He chuckled with satisfaction. Being able to capture something so intensely personal on the first night out was pure gold.

"This is going to be easy money."

The young man's intrusive venture finally reached its end as he noticed the arrival of a visitor and then another— he smiled again and retreated only to return a few moments later with only his cell phone. Boldly, he followed a larger group into the apartment.

Later that evening, as everyone was leaving Thom's apartment, he pulled a phone from his pocket.

"Yeah, tell your boss that I got what he needs."

## Chapter 56

Chip strode into the room carrying a well-worn box filled with neatly wrapped sandwiches, several bottles of soda still glistening with condensation, and a stack of papers tucked under his arm. Without a pause or a knock at the door, he confidently made his way directly to the refrigerator, his strides speaking of a familiarity with Thom's space that left no doubt he was a regular visitor.

Within mere minutes, the knocks at the door began as people arrived. The living room soon transformed into a lively hub of chatter and activity—a mix of animated conversations, and the rustling of sandwich wrappers.

Among the faces, some unfamiliar to Rylee, there was an unmistakable air of camaraderie. Almost as if on cue, Jim Hooper entered as one of the final arrivals. His measured pace and quiet demeanor a counterpoint to the lively group.

With a practiced ease, Thom rose from his seat and gathered the crowd's attention.

"For those who might not know me, I'm Thomas Richardson—Thom for short—and I proudly serve as the state representative for this district. I was elected in the last cycle, so I'm still finding my footing as a freshman."

His voice carried the authority of someone who cared deeply about his new role.

With a sweeping gesture toward Rylee, Thom continued in a firm, measured tone. "Ms. Vance has brought to our attention that one of the bills coming up for a vote would, in effect, force the closure of free clinics throughout our state. Many of you have taken it upon yourselves to visit healthcare facilities and find out what they have to say about the potential loss of these free clinics. I'd like to hear what experiences you've had."

One by one, voices filled the room with detailed accounts: a speaker described how the shutdown of these clinics would overwhelm hospital staff and drain vital resources, while June painted a picture of collateral damage to other health and human services if they were to lose funding. Throughout these personal narratives, Rylee listened intently, piecing together a mosaic of concern and urgency.

Jim Hooper sat quietly, his eyes reflecting a deep attentiveness as he absorbed every word. When the murmurs subsided, he gently cleared his throat. "Excuse me, Mr. Richardson, may I say a few words?"

Thom nodded, welcoming the input with an open gesture, and handed over the floor.

"Years ago, even before some of you were born, a small group of community doctors saw people falling through the system because of their inability to pay for routine care. Recognizing the dire need for accessible health care, we volunteered our skills to create a system that treated people with dignity, providing a no-cost or low-cost alternative outside the conventional healthcare setup."

"Today, as you've witnessed, these free clinics allow hospitals to concentrate on more severe cases and critical emergencies. I am proud to say that our efforts have borne fruit in that those who would not normally seek out health care are using these free clinics. Despite receiving funds from multiple sources, every single dollar is vital. Losing Medicaid and Medicare

200

reimbursements could devastate the good work we started."

His words resonated in the hushed, intent silence that followed.

Thom's eyes sparkled as he addressed the attentive crowd.

"I see a wave of enthusiasm here, and I believe that with all this energy, we can stave off this impending disaster. Now, allow me to outline our plan. I've heard firsthand the issues plaguing our emergency rooms and the struggles of free clinics to simply keep their doors open. I've spoken with frustrated doctors who warned us of the fallout if these clinics were shuttered."

Thom gestured toward Chip.

"Mr. Fallon has prepared detailed lists with every state representative's contact number, and he's also distributing email addresses of major media outlets across the state. I want each one of you to call and email as many as possible. Make copies of these lists, rally your friends to join you, and let every representative know that support of this bill risks their reelection. We must act quickly, as time is running short."

Thom raised his voice over the ensuing hubbub to ensure everyone was with him.

"Dave and June have already kicked off a letter-to- the-editor campaign. Don't confine your efforts to one newspaper—spread this message to every outlet statewide. Let's harness the power of free advertising to amplify our voice."

As Thom moved through the crowded apartment, pausing to speak individually with each person for a few minutes, Rylee couldn't help but notice his transformation. The confident, almost charismatic leader before her was a far cry from the broken man she had glimpsed only hours earlier.

She marveled at how seamlessly Thom had tucked away

his pain, burying it beneath a calm exterior. The playful hiss of a voice beside her abruptly disrupted her contemplation.

"Rylee, introduce me to Chip Fallon. Where on earth do you find these guys?"

Lisa's eyes were wide with excitement as she handed Rylee one of the contact lists.

Startled, Rylee protested, "Lisa! They're both my bosses now. I'm not exactly in the matchmaker business."

Lisa's face lit up in feigned surprise, eyebrows shooting upward as she retorted.

"Both of them? No, way you're that lucky!" She leaned in conspiratorially.

"So, do you think they need another pair of hands around the office?"

Rylee shook her head, her tone slightly amused, "I don't think so; it's just the three of us."

Lisa's expression fell into a dramatic frown. "Next time, I'm going to talk to the representative." Grinning once again, she said, "So, tell me—how are you planning to get me close with Mr. Fallon?"

Rylee's smile widened in quiet amusement, but she took a moment before replying. "I can't believe I'm even being roped into this matchmaking scheme." Rylee sighed and rolled her eyes theatrically. "Look, we're moving into a new office space soon. Why not come help with the move?"

Lisa's eyes lit up instantly.

"Is Chip going to be there?"

"Absolutely," Rylee replied with a laugh.

Lisa grinned broadly.

"I was also hoping to get closer to Mr. Blue Eyes, though

I doubt he'll spare much time for me. Seems he's already smitten with someone else."

Rylee's cheeks flushed a soft pink as Lisa teased.

"You look pretty smitten yourself. Count me in on the move!"

"Lisa, you're shameless."

"Maybe you should try being a little more shameless. You might find you like it."

As Lisa was flitting away, Thom approached once again. Sitting down with a patient smile, Thom patted the empty seat beside him, inviting her to join him.

"Come sit down, Rylee. You must be exhausted. I haven't properly thanked you for your persistence today. I can't predict the outcome, but your determination drives all this forward."

Rylee accepted the seat and smiled softly. Thom continued, his voice soft and sincere.

"Rylee, had you not raised your voice with me earlier, I might never have taken these steps. Even if victory isn't ours in the end, fighting for this cause is the right thing to do for people that need it."

"You've been incredibly understanding today, and I know it hasn't been easy for you. I apologize if I've been a jerk, and I'm grateful for your willingness to listen—even if I'm not quite ready to share all of myself."

Rylee, overwhelmed yet touched, found herself utterly speechless. Thom rose slowly, and as he moved across the room, Rylee could only watch his every measured step, her breath catching in her throat.

Nearby, Lisa nudged June.

"There's definitely something there."

Chip, on the other side of the room talking to Dave, caught the interaction as well. He nodded with a grin as he noted the lingering, genuine look in Thom's eyes.

"It's about time, buddy."

Jim Hooper stepped forward, shaking Thom's hand firmly. "You're a real godsend, young man."

Thom chuckled.

"Well, a Rylee-send anyway."

Jim smiled and walked away. He spent a few moments looking at the photographs around the room. "That baby is his niece."

As Jim's gaze fell on the scattered photographs, he remembered a multi-vehicle accident in the mountains a few months ago. Among the fatalities and injuries, one was more tragic than the others.

One family was all but wiped out, with only an infant girl surviving the accident unscathed and a son who had gone ahead to the ski resort.

## Chapter 57

"Isn't that interesting. Are you telling me he just followed the crowd right inside?" A note of incredulity mixed with intrigue in George's voice.

His aide nodded, eager to provide details.

"Just strolled in like he owned the place. And he got some good shots beforehand as well."

"So, Mr. Fallon thought he could outmaneuver me, huh? Crafty."

George's wry grin stretched across his face.

"Their plan might have worked if it hadn't been for my vigilance. Let's look at those photographs. Sounds like we can use Mr. Richardson's reputation and that little secretary after all."

The aide quickly spread the prints across George's desk, each picture a moment frozen.

There were several shots that looked like they were taken by a cell phone. Faces from the assemblage in the apartment stared back, animated and alive, capturing the urgency and energy of the gathering.

Thom held his own in the center of several photos, a look of earnest determination in his eyes. Chip was clearly visible, directing people with a steady focus, and Rylee appeared engaged, eyes bright and lit with passion for the cause. A couple of shots even caught Lisa in the background handing out contact lists, her expression was one of amused excitement.

"Looks like he's got quite the following."

The aide tapped a finger on one of the images where attentive supporters surrounded Thom. "We could pull up information on the people who attended as well."

George leaned back in his chair, all confidence and calculation. He nodded in agreement with his aide, his mind already plotting the next steps.

"Get the staff working the phones. Let's call some representatives as well. It's time to see where the chips fall."

As the aide scurried out to relay his boss's orders, George studied the photographs with keen interest. He saw opportunity in every frame, a chance to turn the tables on Thom Richardson—a naïve newcomer.

"Far too fresh to survive in this game of political brinkmanship, Junior. You should have accepted my offer. You won't survive this."

He leaned back further, clasping his hands behind his head, and considered exactly how long it would take to undermine Richardson and his upstart campaign.

He knew how to make a story like this sizzle and aimed to stir up as much trouble as possible. When the aide returned, George was already on the phone, his voice smooth and persuasive.

"Hello, this is Senator Dawson," he said, as images of Thom, Chip, and Rylee stared up from the desk.

## Chapter 58

Rylee was wide awake at six the next morning, the urgency of their cause ringing in her mind like a persistent alarm clock. The sun was barely up, and despite the restless night, she felt like she needed to dive right in, but she remembered Thom's advice from the night before: let the caffeine kick in before you start making calls.

The clock barely crept toward nine as she paced the small living room, Squeaker trotting after her with curious but sleepy eyes. She finally plopped down on the couch; the list of numbers Chip had given her in one hand and a steaming mug of coffee in the other.

"Okay, Squeaker. Let's wake up some politicians!"

The feline settled lazily next to her, as if already knowing how this would turn out.

Eagerly, she dialed the first number and waited while the line rang. And rang. A robotic voice answered, and she rolled her eyes.

"Hello, my name is Rylee Vance. I encourage you to vote against legislative bill number 68. This bill, if passed, will cut funding to free clinics. I would very much appreciate having the opportunity to talk with you about why this would hurt voters in your district."

She looked down at the scribbled note stuck on her phone that read 'leave your number,' and quickly closed the message with her contact information.

Rylee hung up the phone and groaned, gently hitting

herself on the forehead with her palm.

"Squeaker, of course, I got the answering machine. Do you know any politician who works on Saturday?"

The cat regarded her with a lazy yellow eye before returning to sleep, clearly less concerned about legislative matters.

Undeterred, Rylee steadily navigated the list, leaving the same message on every machine. She willed herself to believe that somebody would listen and that all these efforts weren't in vain.

With each call, she felt a mixture of determination and weariness, wondering if anyone would call back. When she reached Thom's number in the stack, she smirked.

After yesterday, he'd probably be doing the same thing as she was. She ran a mental image of their new office space and couldn't help but smile—the current workspace was cluttered with the chaos of boxes, and potentially a meddling Lisa.

She moved on to the next name: Representative Woodford. At least Thom was on their side, she thought. By 11 o'clock, the Saturday silence echoed, and she was so tired of talking to answering machines that she didn't want to talk to anyone else right then. She needed a break from this one-sided conversation.

On top of the morning's monotony, the emotional ups and downs of the last days swirled around her. From Thom's unexpected gratitude—had she imagined that look in his eyes—to Lisa's unabashed schemes, she felt like she needed time to breathe and prepare herself. For what exactly, she wasn't sure. Maybe to weather the storm that was Mr. Thomas Richardson. She set the list down with a sigh.

The apartment was quiet, save for Squeaker's rhythmic

breaths. Rylee stretched out next to the cat, closing her eyes momentarily. Her mind drifted back to Thom, and her cheeks flushed with the memory of his soft words. Before she knew it, the phone was forgotten, and the early start had led to a late-morning nap.

## Chapter 59

Thom was startled awake Saturday morning by a small giggle. He stumbled into her room, and there she was. With her bright eyes and even brighter smile, Lexie bounced enthusiastically in her crib.

"Good morning, sweetie. How are you today?"

Having to get up early on Saturdays was made slightly less painful by the joy radiating from his young niece. Lexie squealed and reached for him, filling the room with cheerful energy.

Relenting, Thom picked her up, snagging a diaper from the stack on the dresser.

"I can see you're ready to start the day."

A grin stretched across his face as he carried her toward the kitchen.

"Let's see what we have for breakfast."

His Saturday mornings fell into a routine that was both exhausting and endearing. He shuffled around the small apartment, balancing Lexie on his hip and talking cheerfully to her about their plans.

Breakfast was oatmeal, most of which ended up on Lexie's face and Thom's shirt. After they cleaned up, he bathed her and marveled at how quickly she splashed water all over the bathroom. He soon found himself building towers of blocks and chasing her around piles of laundry.

He could hardly keep up with her tireless spirit and playful demands.

"Up, up!"

She insisted with outstretched arms, only to want to go down a minute later. Amidst all this playfulness, he caught up on the news and battled dust bunnies, knowing that his life was this delightfully because of Lexie.

Once Lexie finally drifted off to sleep for her morning nap, Thom gathered his thoughts and his breath for a few moments. He walked outside and watched the quiet street from the front porch, soaking in the day's promise. The sky was almost cloudless, a vivid blue stretching endlessly, and a hint of a warm breeze whispered through the trees.

Days like this constantly stirred something in him, a nostalgia tugging at old memories of running outside with his sister. He felt an urge to give Lexie a taste of that carefree joy. A trip to the park might be the thing, letting her play free on the grass and enjoy the simple pleasures of sunshine and laughter.

Whistling with newfound enthusiasm, he walked back inside, determination in his steps and a plan forming in his mind. He decided she needed open space and the colors of the playground. He was sure she'd love the sandbox and the swings, even if most of the adventure would be coaxing her tiny fingers to let go when it was time to leave.

He set about packing the diaper bag with all the essentials: snacks, several changes of clothes, diapers, a changing mat, toys, and both milk and juice bottles. Thom was prepared, especially for Lexie, and he added baby safe sunscreen to the mix. Though she was young, he wanted to make sure she had every chance to experience the world around her and all its wonders.

Chapter 60

In the warm glow of the afternoon sun, Thom sat Lexie down on the grass beside the bench he was sitting on. He had held her until she was ready to explore this new environment. As her curious eyes and fingers examined the texture of the grass, Thom gently picked her up and carried her to the brightly colored baby swing. The creaky chains of the swing complemented the melodic squeals that burst forth from Lexie as Thom carefully pushed her in smooth, rhythmic arcs beneath the vast, blue sky.

Thom's attention turned to the sandbox that sported a cluster of toddlers energetically playing, their laughter mingling with the soft chatter of nearby mothers and nannies. Wanting Lexie to join the spirited mix, Thom sat at the edge of an old, worn sandbox, while Lexie happily scooped up clumps of tiny, sprinkled particles.

She chose not to engage the other toddlers, happy to settle in a quiet corner. Her bright eyes absorbing the animated play of her peers for several seconds before she shyly reached for Thom to lift her up, her thumb instinctively finding its familiar place in her mouth.

Thom looked up as her heard someone clearing their throat. A woman in a light, floral dress approached, her presence as graceful as the summer breeze. With a knowing smile playing on her lips, she approached Thom and Lexie.

"You have a shy one, don't you? Is she the only one so far?"

Her tone carried both genuine curiosity and a hint of flirtatious amusement.

Thom's mind raced for a response. He opted for honesty. "She's my niece, and yes, she's the only one."

In that moment, he couldn't help but notice the subtle but deliberate way her eyes drifted to his ring finger—a silent inquiry about his life beyond the playground.

Encouraged, the woman leaned in slightly. "So, do you live around here?"

Thom's amused laugh filled the space between them. "Not within walking distance."

She continued her probing.

"Do you have your niece often?"

"Pretty often."

With an inviting glimmer in her eye, she tilted her head.

"Well, it might help her overcome her shyness to join our play group when you're over here."

Her suggestion, laced with a hint of friendly advice, made Thom grin.

"Oh, you think so?"

Her eyes locked with his briefly, then wandered delicately down to Lexie's gentle features.

"I know so."

Thom found himself pleasantly engaged by the playful banter—a familiar feeling in an unfamiliar setting.

"Do you have a pen or something to write on?"

The woman gestured toward the diaper bag slung over his shoulder.

Thom glanced into the bag and admitted with a sheepish smile, "No. Sorry."

"That's all right. I didn't catch your name."

Thom's smile deepened as he listened, and the woman

introduced herself,

"My name is Candice Reynolds—Candy, for short."

Standing upright with an inviting posture, she waited expectantly for him to share his name.

"Nice to meet you, Ms. Reynolds."

Thom replied, his voice was steady yet cordial.

"Oh, please call me Candy. What should I call you?"

Once again, Thom found himself struggling for a response. He opted for subterfuge.

"Chuck."

Almost immediately, Candy took his hand, and with a deliberate, confident motion, wrote her first name and phone number right onto his skin. Her fingers lingered as she locked eyes with him.

"Give me a call anytime."

Her voice dropped to a sultry whisper. "And I mean anytime, day or night, Chuck."

In one final, teasing gesture, Candy bent over slightly, ensuring her top shifted just enough to reveal a playful view of cleavage, as she scooped up a toddling child. With her hips swaying in a rhythm all her own, she walked away slowly, turning her head to flash him a smile that was equal parts invitation and mystery.

"That was interesting,"

Thom looked down at the small script on his hand, now bearing the name Candy and a phone number. The ease of their meeting struck the realization that even on a humble playground, serendipity could materialize in the most unexpected moments.

Scooping up Lexie once more, he whispered into her ear.

"Stay away from desperate women. They'll corrupt you, and men like me will take advantage."

His tone was playful yet laced with a knowing irony. As he gazed at his hand again, the number slowly blurring in his thoughts, Thom mused about the possibility of stepping away from Rylee. She was now his employee after all. Perhaps Candy would be the distraction he needed—a spark to lead him into new territory.

Looking around the park with renewed interest, Thom recognized that he might have to return more often. Even as Candy and her friends watched him depart with lingering, intrigued glares, his mind danced between the familiar responsibilities of caring for Lexie and the tantalizing mystery of a new connection.

Taking a seat on a weathered bench near his car, Thom offered Lexie a small juice bottle. The cool liquid was a comforting routine amid the swirl of unexpected events.

As his eyes lingered once more on the phone number etched on his hand, warmth spread through him and curiosity spurred by the memory of Candy's inviting gaze.

"I really need to come here more often." Thom's thoughts sharpened with self-mockery. "Lexie, what's wrong with me? Yesterday, I was all over Rylee in the car, and today I'm here, thinking about someone else I barely know." His hand absently rubbed the number, as if trying to erase the new temptation. "We'd better go. We should stop for diapers and more rice cereal, and you, little Miss, are about to nod off before I'm ready."

And so, with the golden light of the afternoon sun casting long shadows on the playground, Thom gathered Lexie in his arms and began to walk away—his thoughts filled with the strange magic of unexpected encounters and the brief, delightful flirtation of a summer day.

And the man standing behind a stand of trees with a camera clicked away.

## Chapter 61

Rylee barreled into the store with a mission to grab cat litter. Her eyes locked onto the pet section until she froze—there was Lexie. With a swift pivot, she advanced down the aisle where Thom and Lexie were, just as Thom had crouched to snatch diapers from the lowest shelf. Rylee's pulse jumped; she hadn't realized how powerfully sculpted he was beneath his suit coat and crisp dress shirts. Now, casually clad in a T-shirt and jeans, he exuded an effortless magnetism that made her heart race. He rose with his back to her, nonchalantly tossing the diapers into the cart.

"All right, baby girl, that's enough. Let's go home."

Lexie's warm and teasing smile flickered over Thom's shoulder towards Rylee, who remained transfixed by the strong line of his back. Catching Lexie's lingering gaze, Thom turned, his eyes locking onto Rylee. As he slid the grocery list into his jeans pocket, Rylee's eyes widened at the sight of a name and number boldly scrawled on his hand. Thom glanced down in alarm before hastily tucking his hand out of sight.

Rylee's expression hardened as she spoke.

"Hello, Lexie. Hello, Mr. Richardson. Fancy running into you here."

Now bending over to rummage through the diaper bag for baby wipes, Thom tried to keep his voice casual as he replied. "Oh, yeah. We swung by after the park to grab a few things before heading home."

His words tumbled out, laced with a defensiveness that belied his calm exterior. Inside, his mind raced.

217

"Why am I feeling guilty? I haven't done anything wrong," he thought.

Forcing a smile on his face he said, "What brings you to this thrilling hot spot?"

"Cat litter," she replied, each word dripping with irony.

"Cat? You have a cat? What kind?"

She pointedly looked at Thom's hand, still partially hidden behind his back.

"Just a big yellow and white tomcat. He was quite the Don Juan before I got him neutered. Do you expect me to ignore that name and number on your hand?"

Thom's eyes darted around, scrambling for an excuse. "Yeah," he muttered weakly.

"Why do you have a phone number written on your hand?"

Now his annoyance flared, and he bristled with anger. This wasn't any of her business. Flipping his hand upward, he examined it openly.

"Some woman at the park jotted it down for me. Neither of us had any paper on us. She wants me to call her about Lexie joining her play group."

His declaration was defiant, his hand resting on the cart in plain view as if daring her to challenge him.

Rylee's eyes burned as they fixed on his exposed digits. "Play group? For Lexie?"

"It'd do her some good. Surrounding her with kids her age might even help her overcome her shyness."

Rylee's hand swept past Thom to stroke Lexie's hair dismissively. "I don't see anything wrong with being shy." Her accusation hanging in the charged air. Her gaze snapped back to his hand.

"So, whose play group exactly?"

Thom's jaw tightened.

"I don't think my personal life is any of your concern, Ms. Vance."

"With all due respect, I came in for cat litter; I didn't sign up to be an audience for your fairy tales."

With that final barb, she turned sharply and stalked back up the aisle.

Lexie began to fuss, tears welling, as Thom, in a fit of frustration, spat on his hand and tried futilely to erase the incriminating number. As Lexie's crying escalated, with a weary sigh, he maneuvered the cart and a heartbroken Lexie toward the front of the store.

At the checkout, Thom couldn't ignore that Rylee was also in line, just a few registers away. Despite the clamor of Lexie's tears, Rylee kept her focus, deliberately avoiding eye contact with him. When she finished her transaction, she strode out of the store with a resolute flair.

After dumping everything into the back of his van and securely fastening Lexie into her car seat, Thom fastened his seatbelt with a heavy, conflicted sigh.

"Why should I care what she thinks? I don't give a damn."

Despite his declaration, he scanned for her blue GTO before he backed out of the parking space.

"I can tell Monday is going to be a wonderful day for everyone!"

Once outside, Rylee stormed away from the store, seething.

"One day, he's passionately kissing me; the next, he's

flaunting some Candy person's number like it's no big deal. Unbelievable! As if a flimsy play group excuse could ever be the truth from a supposed lawyer. He may look like the cute guy next door but underneath lurks the heart of a reckless playboy. It's a relief to discover that little personality flaw now rather than after I've given him my heart."

Tears of hot, betrayed anger streamed down her cheeks as she drove away, leaving behind nothing but the echoes of shattered trust.

## Chapter 62

"Lisa, let's go to a movie or something. I need to get out."

"Sounds good. How about a little shopping? I need a pedicure. We can go to Franny's."

"Sounds great. See you about five o'clock at the Nail Emporium?"

Rylee leaned back in the pedicure chair beside Lisa enjoying the soak in the warm soapy water.

"You've been quieter than usual, girl. I'm assuming that something's up, or you wouldn't have sounded so desperate on the phone."

"I really don't know what to do. I've got to keep working for a jerk because we need him to help us with the bill, and I need a job. But as soon as we've finished with that, I'm gone. I'm going to start looking for another job right away."

Lisa's eyes widened.

"No kidding. You've only worked one day. You looked okay yesterday."

"Yeah. Maybe. I was interested when I saw him at church just last Sunday. But when I got into work and saw him there, talking with Mr. Halpern about me starting a new job right away, I should have known then."

"Go on. I've been dying to hear this story."

"It all happened so fast that I felt like it wasn't happening. Like I was just watching a movie or something."

"If you're serious about quitting, would you put in a good word for your best friend? Both those guys are dreamy."

"Lisa, I'm not kidding. I should have listened to that little voice that said, 'Don't do it.' But for some strange reason, I didn't pay attention to the warnings I was sending myself. I left with this stranger, who had kidnapped me from my job, to drive up to Grant, alone in his car. Well, okay, his niece was in the car."

Franny, who had been giving Rylee her pedicure, and the other nail technician working on Lisa were listening now.

"Wait. The baby is his niece!"

Looking for sympathy, Rylee continued, "Can you believe this guy? I mean, really. Deciding for me without talking to me about it first and going to my boss before I got to work! Would a normal person do that?"

Franny put Rylee's foot back in the bath and pursed her lips.

"Hmm," was all Franny offered.

"And how could I let myself be trapped with a psycho? We had this big fight on the way to Grant. I told him I was angry at him for going to my old boss. He told me that I had asked him to do that. He pulled off the road. I started crying. He started shouting. It was awful."

"This is getting good." Franny said, "Tell me again how you end up in this situation, anyway?"

Rylee leaned back in the chair and looked at the ceiling.

"There was this bill in the legislature that was going to cut funding to the free clinics in the state. A group of us from church got together to try to fight it and this jerk joined us. After the meeting about, I realized I couldn't visit other hospitals because Ms. Blackman wasn't about to let me off work. Thom walked me to my car, and I started crying. I didn't think he would do anything about what I was saying, and I don't even remember everything I said. He was looking for a secretary and said I could have the job."

Franny gasped.

"Let me get this straight here, Rylee. You're telling me that you told this guy you wanted another job. He fixed it for you the next day, and now you're mad at him?" Franny asked.

"Yeah. But he's crazy."

"And really cute," Lisa said.

Franny waved her hands. "Okay, don't interrupt. What happened next in the car, honey?"

The nail salon had gone silent as everyone was intently listening to Rylee's story.

"Well, then he kissed me."

Lisa nearly jumped out of her chair. It was good that the nail technician had stopped working on her nail polish to listen.

"I knew it! Did you kiss him back?"

Rylee nodded.

Lisa clapped her hands.

"I knew it! I knew that you guys had kissed. I could tell by how he looked at you and how you looked at him. So, what's the problem?"

"I was a little confused, things were moving too fast, and I asked him to cool it."

Franny stood and put her hands on her hips. "You what?"

"Look, not everyone thinks it's okay to jump in the sack with someone you're not married to. And besides, he's my boss now. Things are different."

"Oh, okay. Whatever." Franny rolled her eyes.

"So the plucky friend asks again, what is the problem?" Lisa demanded.

"He got all weird later in the day. I mean, strange. All cold and distant."

"Well, honey, what happened?" Franny asked.

"I don't know. Everything was good, and he just changed when we were getting ready to leave. This lady talked about how Lexie looked like me, and the walls just appeared."

"Who is Lexie?" another customer asked.

"His niece, the baby."

The nail technician working on Lisa asked, "So, this baby looks like you?"

"Sort of," Lisa answered. "They have the same coloring. Thom is very blond, blue-eyed, and tight in all the right spots. The baby has dark brown eyes and soft brown curls."

Rylee frowned at Lisa.

"Anyway, he got all bossy and mean. Wouldn't let me hold the baby anymore. Then, when we got to his place—"

"Wait. His place?" another nail technician interrupted. Franny shushed her.

"—for a meeting. With other people. Who would be there real soon." Rylee snapped.

"At his place, I saw pictures on his shelves of his family, of Lexie's parents. Thom's sister was Lexie's mother."

"Name's Thom? How old is the baby? What happened to the baby's parents?" Franny asked.

"Lexie is about a year old," Lisa responded. Then, Franny stopped working on Rylee's feet.

"Rylee, it's obvious that they're probably dead if he has the baby full-time, and he doesn't hate them because he has the baby's parents' pictures displayed everywhere. It probably didn't happen long ago, if Lexie is just a baby. Also, it was probably horrible for him, and he's still a little sensitive about it. When the lady said you looked like the baby, it may have hurt him. When my mother died, I was sensitive about all kinds of weird stuff for a long time."

Rylee nodded her head.

"Yeah, I know. I had decided that he was probably a great guy in a lot of pain. He's doing such a good job taking care of his niece."

"But?" Lisa pressed.

"But today, I ran into him at the grocery store, and he had a phone number written on his hand from some woman named Candy, whom he claimed invited Lexie to a play group."

Franny picked up the bottle of polish Rylee had selected and studied it. Glancing sharply at Rylee, she stood and headed over to the nail polish rack on the wall. She turned and studied Rylee again.

"I don't think I'm going to use the pink polish you picked out. You need this green color here. The one called 'Jealously.' Honey, you've got it bad."

Rylee's mouth dropped open. "What?"

"Honey, you aren't a pink today."

Rylee turned to look at wide-eyed Lisa and pulled her feet back.

Franny sat back down and patted Rylee on the foot. "Give it up, girl. You know you need this color."

Franny pulled Rylee's foot forward and started to paint her toenails green.

"What if he was telling you the truth, and the baby had

225

been invited to a play group?" Franny suggested.

Rylee sat, open-mouthed.

"But he tried to hide it from me!"

"Sounds like he knew that you would get the wrong idea. Sounds like you are important enough to him that he cares about what you think," Franny said.

"Rylee," Lisa interjected, "this is strange for you. You're always giving everyone the benefit of the doubt. What's different this time?"

Rylee's eyes filled with tears.

"But I've known him for less than a week!"

Lisa smiled at her friend. "I know."

Rylee bit her lip. All eyes were on her.

"Honey, you may have just met him, but there is some connection here. You must pay attention to what your heart tells you about this guy. You're jealous of a guy you claim is weird, distant, and mean. You need to relax and just let it happen. I'm not going to charge you for the polish. When you come back in, I'll paint these toes pink for free," Franny said.

Rylee turned repentant eyes to Franny. "What do I do now?"

Franny's advice was simple. "There isn't any mystery there, girl. Listen to your heart."

"I know it's off the subject, but I'm curious. You said there's a bill that got all this started? What's that about?" another nail technician asked.

Lisa looked at Rylee's grief-stricken face and grinned. "Well, it all started when Rylee found out about this fake tax cut."

Before they left, Lisa collected names and phone numbers, and a handmade petition was taped to the counter.

"I'll put the word out for you. We'll get this thing stopped," Franny said.

Franny grabbed Rylee's hand before she left. "Baby, you need to hang on to this boy, hear?"

## Chapter 63

George nodded his head as he leafed through the photographs. They were spread on the table in front of him, and the dull light in the room made them look even more incriminating than they were.

"Well, they're tame. Won't bother Mr. Richardson much."

The disappointment in George's voice was obvious to his aide, who was fumbling with notes and papers.

The aide tried to sound hopeful. "We can use them. This girl seems to be straight-laced. She's the one driving this whole campaign against the bill. When these pictures get out, people won't know what to think of her."

George nodded again, stopping as one of the photographs caught his eye. He picked it up and held it towards the aide.

"Why do I have a picture of a car here?"

The aide shuffled and looked sheepish.

"It's her car. I think the guy we hired to take the photos just likes it."

George shook his head, annoyed. "I'm not paying for pictures of cars."

He tossed a few more of the photographs back onto the counter and sighed. "Let's use these shots." He gestured for the aide to collect them. "Be discrete. No direct contact."

The aide nodded, eager to please. "We've got people on it already."

"And see if we can get some more of our guys planted on Mr. Richardson's team. If we can make it look like even his people are turning against him, it'll have a big impact."

The aide scribbled down notes. He had an idea of what George would say next, so he was ready.

"Do we have a number yet for the vote count?" George asked, looking seriously at the aide.

"Nearly, sir," the aide replied. He was trying to sound reassuring.

"Mr. Richardson's support would be helpful, but if we swing a few more votes our way, we still have a chance."

George tapped his fingers on the counter. He looked over the photos again, his mind racing with possibilities.

"This campaign is going to be trouble if we don't get in front of it," he said. "I want those pictures out before this girl can build any more momentum. Let's see how she likes the heat."

The aide nodded, gathering the photographs quickly. "We'll get on it right away. She won't know what hit her."

George smirked. "It better work. Otherwise, you won't know what hit you."

The aide swallowed nervously and turned to leave.

The sound of George's fingers still drumming on the counter followed him out of the room. The aide couldn't tell if the work was exciting or terrifying. He decided that it was both.

## Chapter 64

Rylee picked up the phone a dozen times, if she picked it up once. Each time, she set it back down, feeling more hopeless than before.

"Squeaker, I just can't believe that I messed this up so badly."

The apartment seemed filled with an uncomfortable silence. She felt her thoughts spinning out of control as she paced from the living room to the kitchen and back again. She needed some air. She pushed aside the curtain and looked out at the quiet parking lot.

"I need to get control of myself here. I'll talk to him tomorrow."

Her finger hovered over Thom's number on her phone until the truth was undeniable: she was just too chicken to call him tonight. She walked back to the window and leaned her forehead against the cool glass.

She tried to make sense of a situation that felt crazier than anything she'd ever been through. She was convinced she'd find a way to make it up to him.

Dragging her feet as she returned to the couch, Rylee felt lost and on the verge of giving up. But she refused to. There was no way she was going to sleep with things so mixed up. She turned around and approached the window again.

"May be I'll go for a drive."

A motion in the parking lot caught her eye. She stood very still, trying to see what was moving.

"Good grief. I need to sleep; now I'm seeing things!" She

rubbed her eyes and squinted into the darkness.

The man in the shadows froze, eyes locked on the second-floor window. He waited until the curtain started closing again before he moved.

"That's right. Go to bed, little girl."

He took one more photograph of the car.

He hadn't planned on doing more than the job. But then he didn't know about the GTO. It would be too easy. This parking lot was too visible. He knew he shouldn't push his luck. He glanced at the window and muttered under his breath.

"That girl is too jittery to risk staying much longer. Get what you came for and then get out."

He crept towards the street, keeping an eye on the apartment as he went. His heart raced with the thrill of how easy this was going to be. He allowed himself a smirk, knowing that if anyone figured out what he was doing, he'd be in a tight spot, but for now, it felt like he had it all covered.

He ducked low near a pickup truck and took another quick shot. He knew that George wasn't going to pay for these shots, but he was going to be compensated in another way.

He took a hard look at the complex behind him and watched the steps leading upstairs. No sign of movement. That meant he was safe. He moved stealthily down the street, careful not to leave any trail.

The man was nearly two blocks away when he allowed himself a chuckle. "You'll never know what hit you, little girl."

## Chapter 65

Rylee painstakingly chose her outfit for worship, her nerves a tangled mix of excitement and dread. Her heart pounded as she sifted through her closet, trying on and discarding three different ensembles before finally landing on one that felt somewhat right.

Still, uncertainty gnawed at her, leading her to switch shoes multiple times and end up with her original choice.

A glance at the clock sent a jolt through her—she was dangerously close to being late. She missed the ominous brown envelope tucked under the wiper blade in her hurried flight down the stairs to her car.

At first, anyway.

Her mind was a chaotic whirlwind, slowing her typically swift movements. Her steps faltered, freezing her when her eyes caught sight of it. The urgency of worship services receded into the background, overshadowed by the chilling discovery.

Rylee's gaze darted nervously across the parking lot, scrutinizing the vehicles surrounding hers. Her heart pounded with fear. Last night's concern about the parking lot was not merely a product of her imagination.

With shaky hands, she tugged the envelope from beneath the wiper and slipped into her GTO, her entire body trembling with a blend of anxiety and defiance. The word on the front struck her like a physical blow.

"Whore."

She tore open the package, her breath catching as she absorbed its contents. Denial wavered against the undeniable evidence. Someone was watching her, documenting her every action. Rylee was shattered. The realization pulling her in conflicting directions, the weight of it all crashing down like a relentless wave.

## Chapter 66

Thom felt torn about church this morning, especially with Rylee there. His determination was already crumbling as the day barely began, making him question everything. It wasn't just that she'd expect him to skip worship because of yesterday's awkwardness, but the thought of sitting in a service while knowing she was present made him want to disappear.

Even after scrubbing Candy's number from his hand with soap and alcohol until the skin stung raw, it still felt like a lingering charge against him. He kept repeating to himself that he hadn't lied to Rylee—but Candy's eyes, revealing far more than her chatter about a play group, unsettled him deeply. With a conflicted glance at the ghostly imprint on his hand, he picked up Lexie's diaper bag.

"I didn't do anything wrong."

Doubt gnawed at him. Nothing he'd done could really justify Rylee's cold dismissal. She was judging him more harshly than he deserved. But knowing that on an intellectual level and feeling what he was feeling were two different things. He couldn't comprehend why this internal struggle was eating him up.

As he shifted his attention to Lexie, who intently observed every move with the earnest focus only a toddler possesses, his inner turmoil bubbled up into a proclamation.

"Your teacher has no right to make judgments about my life. She ought to appreciate that I did what she asked me to do. What she agreed to."

Even though Lexie's giggles—knowing full well how theatrically he was reacting—should have lightened his mood, the conflict within him intensified.

"I will not cower away from my secretary—I am in charge; I will not be swayed by others' unrealistic expectations. Why am I letting a church lady scrutinize my personal life anyway."

Yet even as the words left his lips, he felt an undercurrent of doubt. It felt like he'd betrayed some sacred promise.

Taking a deep, conflicted breath, he cast Lexie a determined yet wavering look.

"I know, sweetie. She doesn't really look or smell like a church lady—but she's my secretary, and I must stay professional, or everything will just fall apart, and we'll all end up miserable. Kind of like I am now."

Lexie fixed him with a comically serious stare, as if weighing every word with all the gravity of her little world, before bouncing on the floor, laughing hard enough to momentarily blur the edges of his self-doubt.

"Alright, little miss bossy. I got it. Let's get moving before I change my mind."

With Lexie in his arms and the diaper bag slung over his shoulder, Thom headed for the car, feeling as though his decision to attend church was more a reluctant test against his own resolve. Yet amidst all his internal wrangling, it still felt like a small victory.

The drive was a quiet battleground of thoughts—with Lexie absent-mindedly sucking her thumb while Thom fought hard not to spiral back into thoughts of Rylee. He chastised himself for overthinking, insisting she might not even be as upset as he was.

Arriving in the church parking lot almost in a rush, he

felt a tentative relief. And then, almost disappointed, he noticed the GTO was not in the parking lot.

## Chapter 67

"Where is Ms. Vance?" he asked one of the parents.

"Now that is a good question. It's unlike her not to let someone know when she's going to be late," the woman said.

Puzzled, Thom carried Lexie back up the stairs, intending to leave. "May be Ms. Vance is the one to chicken out of coming to church."

Out front, where he had first seen Rylee, he saw her standing again.

"Thom, can I talk to you?"

He was dumb struck at her statement. Now was not the time to rehash their argument.

"Thom, I need to talk with you," she said more firmly.

"Ms. Vance, nice to see you. I was surprised that you were not teaching Lexie's class."

Then he noticed she'd been crying. He could see that her eyes were red, and her makeup was mussed. He reached out toward her.

"Rylee, what's wrong?"

The tears spilled from her reddened eyes, and her chin quivered.

Alarmed, Thom moved closer. "Rylee, tell me what's wrong?"

Her hand, which held the envelope, twitched.

He glanced at it and then back at Rylee's stricken face. He took hold of the envelope.

"What is this?"

Rylee released the envelope into Thom's hands before dashing into the building and disappearing.

Thom stood with his mouth open and watched helplessly as she ran out of sight. The word 'whore' was crudely written across the front of the package.

With his eyes turning to ice, he bit his lower lip before opening the envelope and pulling its contents out. A minute later, he patted for his phone. "It's in the car."

Thom glanced into the auditorium and looked at the stairs.

From the front of the auditorium, Jim had a front-row seat for Thom and Rylee's exchange. He watched as Rylee fled and how Thom looked at the package.

Catching the preacher's eye, he excused himself.

Jim moved at a steady pace toward the back of the building.

"Thom, slow down; I'm an old man."

Thom had paused to examine the envelope's contents again at the end of the sidewalk. He stuffed them back in before turning to Jim.

"Thom, I just wanted to thank you again for helping us. It's so hard to get people willing to make this much effort for no pay. That says a great deal about you. We are certainly blessed to have you."

Thom looked at the church building.

"I'm a public servant. My services are always free to the citizens."

"Oh, I know that's true, but you didn't have to get involved with us. I know how these things work. You have been a gift from God."

Thom paused. He rubbed his hand through his hair. "We make our blessings. You can thank yourself."

Jim looked up at Thom with intelligent eyes. "I see."

"I need to get my phone. I have some calls to make."

"Oh, I thought you were leaving. May I walk you to your car?"

"That's not necessary. I don't think I'll be attacked in this parking lot."

Jim smiled and looked around. "Nevertheless, amuse an old man."

Thom shrugged and started walking. Jim waited until they reached the parking lot.

"Why are you here, Thom?"

Thom stopped and turned to him. "That is none of your business."

"True, true. But it does cause someone to wonder why a person who doesn't believe in God would go to a church, especially one so far from his house."

Thom glared at him and turned but only got a few steps away before he spun around. "I promised someone I would take Lexie to church. I'm keeping that promise. I don't want to be involved. Okay?"

Jim's calm expression took the fire from Thom's belly. "Look, I don't mean to be rude, but it's personal. I don't believe a kindly god is out there caring for us. I just haven't seen any evidence of that. We make our way against the tide of circumstances that befall us. If you'll excuse me, I've got to get my phone."

Jim nodded his head. "How did they die?"

Thom's mouth dropped open.

239

"From the pictures at your place, Lexie looks much like her father. I would guess it's been less than a year. That loss would make me want to blame God, too."

Stunned, Thom looked around the parking lot, seeking a frame of reference. Numbly, he turned again toward his minivan.

"You know, sometimes life seems just like what you said. I was a doctor for a long time, and I was always amazed by the suffering some very good people endured.

There were times when I questioned the existence of God. Just seeing the levels of pain, both physical and emotional, that some folks had to walk through gave me serious doubts."

Thom stopped and stared intently at the pavement under his feet. "Okay. You can stop. I've heard this one."

"I'm sure you have," Jim said. "And if you have, you know that the line goes like this: God doesn't cause these awful things. He loves us. He provides healing for us if we accept it. Sometimes the rescue comes in the form of an army of angels. Have you heard that one?"

Thom tried walking, but Jim laid a hand on his arm. If Jim had been any younger, Thom would have pushed him away. Thom wondered if he was ever going to be able to get away from this old man and his meandering explanations.

Jim ignored Thom's raised eyebrow or how he kept glancing toward his car.

"A king sent an army to capture this one old prophet. One morning, the old prophet's servant panicked when he saw the enemy army approaching. The old prophet didn't worry, because he could see the angels on the hills. So, the old prophet asked God to open the servant's eyes so he could see them too."

"Nice story, Jim. I need to get my phone."

Jim continued as if he had suddenly gone deaf. "Sometimes, it's not an army of angels. Sometimes God will lift just one person to heal our pain. "We just have to open our eyes and notice they are there."

Thom's eyes followed Jim's gaze.

He drew in his breath as his eyes widened. They were standing behind a dark blue GTO.

Jim placed a Bible he had been carrying on the back of the car.

Thom had a Bible that he had put into storage somewhere. It was a gift from his mother, and he couldn't bring himself to throw it out. Thom stood still as his thoughts reeled.

"I'm going to make some guesses here; you let me know if I'm right or wrong. Okay?"

Thom stared open mouthed.

"I remember reading a story about this terrible accident about six months ago. There was this freak twenty-something car pileup. Several people lost their lives, but the tragic thing was that one family, named Richardson, lost four members. Only one of the passengers survived: a infant girl. One of their other kids had gone to the family's winter lodge and wasn't in the car."

Jim paused and regarded Thom, who had hung his head.

"I guess that you're that kid. Everyone else, except Lexie, is gone."

Thom's hand covered most of his face, and his eyes were dark.

Jim nodded his head. He reached over and put his hand on Thom's shoulder.

"Son, you've been trying to carry this burden by yourself

far too long. Why don't you tell me about it?"

Thom drew a deep breath through his nose, blowing it out through his mouth.

"Okay. I will allow that there is a God for this discussion. But if God is such a loving and caring God, why did He let this happen to us? Why did He leave Lexie without her mother? Lexie hasn't done anything to deserve this."

Jim's sad eyes met Thom's angry ones.

"Son, you didn't do anything to deserve this either. You're not being punished."

Thom looked away.

"I don't presume to understand why things happen the way they do. Like I said, during my life I've seen a lot of what I thought was undeserved suffering. Just because it happens, it doesn't mean that God is causing it."

Thom walked a few steps away, staring at a scene from six months ago.

Jim waited.

Thom spun around.

"Okay. I didn't deserve this, and neither did Lexie. So where has this caring God been all this time?"

Jim still waited, without saying anything. Thom's pleading eyes searched Jim's face.

"Why did you come to church last Sunday? I'm not talking about your promise, but the real reason."

"I don't know!" Thom shouted.

Jim nodded at Thom's response and reached over, taking the pacifier out of Thom's shirt pocket.

"In your heart, I think that you do. In your heart, I think that you believe. In your heart, I think that you recognize God's hand in your life."

Jim handed the pacifier back to Thom.

"God gave you Lexie to care for in your grief, so that you wouldn't become consumed by the magnitude of it. It was too much for anyone to bear, so He gave you a life to focus on."

Lexie had consumed all of Thom's thoughts and efforts. Initially, he had been so tired from learning to care for her that he didn't have the energy for anything else.

"Why would a young man who loves to snowboard and race jet skis single-handedly take on an infant?"

"I'm all she has now."

"Why not hire someone else to do it?"

"She's my family."

"Exactly. A big bundle of life in a small package. And now you have another gift from God standing right before you. I bet she has had your attention since you first saw her."

Thom just looked at Jim.

"In your heart is the truth, even if your head isn't there yet."

Jim placed his hand on Thom's shoulder. "Son, you can call me anytime you want to talk. I don't think I can snowboard, but I can handle going out for coffee."

Jim turned to walk away when Thom picked up the Bible resting on the GTO.

"Jim, you forgot your Bible."

The old doctor turned around to look at the Bible, and then he turned gentle eyes on Thom.

"No, son. I didn't."

## Chapter 68

Thom sat in his car, feeling a heavy numbness settle over him, as if the weight of the world rested on his shoulders. He tried to clear his mind of the clutter that filled it.

Beside him, on the fabric of the passenger seat, lay a well-thumbed Bible, its pages creased and familiar. In the backseat, little Lexie was securely strapped into her car seat, clutching a bottle of juice as if it were her lifeline. Her innocent presence was a stark contrast to the turmoil brewing in Thom's mind.

He needed to think, to devise a plan to help Rylee. Thom picked up the stack of photographs once more, his eyes scanning over the images before hitting Chip's number.

Chip lay sprawled on his bed, the morning light filtering softly through the curtains. The persistent ringing of his phone was like an unwelcome alarm, pulling him from the comfort of sleep. Grumbling, he pulled a pillow over his head, trying to drown out the sound. But the ringing continued, relentlessly.

Resigned, Chip tossed the pillow aside and reached for the phone, rolling his eyes when he saw Thom's name flashing on the screen. "Thom, stop calling me on the weekend. I'm busy," he muttered groggily.

"You're sleeping in. Listen, we have a situation, and we need to figure out what to do about it."

"A situation on Sunday? You won't have situations if you were like me, asleep."

"I'm serious here, buddy. Rylee got some hate mail, and I

need you to look at it."

Chip sat up abruptly, the mention of hate mail jolting him awake.

"Hate mail? What kind of hate mail?"

Thom's voice was steady but with an undercurrent of worry.

"Plain brown wrapper with some shots of me holding her and kissing her at my place. Not very scandalous. But the letter that came with it is bad. Rylee is very upset."

Thom's gaze flickered to the rearview mirror, catching the sleek silhouette of a GTO backing out of a parking space and smoothly merging into the street traffic.

"Kissing her?" Chip's groggy mind locking on that detail.

"Focus, Chip. Look, can you meet me at the office?"

"Thom, it's Sunday."

"I know. I'm at church. Chip, I need you to focus."

Chip's mouth fell open in surprise.

"Okay. But you're going to have to tell me about the kiss and, and did you say you were at church? Wait a minute. Thom, are you at church?"

"Yes. I'll see you at the office." Thom left no room for argument.

On the other end, Chip sat in stunned silence, his disbelief unobserved by the phone.

Chapter 69

Lexie had drifted into a deep slumber at the office, so Thom gently nestled her back into her car seat, ensuring she was comfortable as he and his partner wrapped up their business.

"I think I'll have this one blown up poster sized." Chip held a glossy photograph at arm's length, squinting as he examined its details under the office light, a playful grin on his lips.

"Might look nice as one of those velvet paintings."

Thom reached over and selected one of the photographs from the stack, scrutinizing it with a critical eye. "As hateful as the note is, Rylee does look like she could be Lexie's mother." Thom's voice barely above a whisper, the weight of the observation hanging in the air.

Thom avoided Chip's surprised gaze, letting the photograph slip back onto the pile before picking up the venomous letter.

"I especially like that particular piece of fiction." Chip indicated the letter.

"Looks like we have a mole."

"Yeah, I thought the same thing."

The gears in Thom's mind were turning.

"Only someone who was at the meetings would know that stuff. I guess they thought she would heed their warning to keep it to herself."

"They threatened to go public if she said anything to you. Instead, she went straight to you," Chip noted.

Thom's gaze, intense and unwavering, locked onto Chip.

"This is probably going to be all over the papers tomorrow."

A shadow of worry crossing Chip's features. "And Rylee is going to get hurt. If it were just us, I wouldn't care. But it's not just us, is it?"

"Well, there will probably be a few days of Rylee getting crucified in the press." Thom's voice was heavy with resignation. "It's just so easy to disprove the allegations made in this letter, but by the time the truth comes out, the damage to Rylee will already be done."

Chip's brow furrowed in thought. "I guess they figured attacking Rylee was going to be a major distraction for you."

Thom's gaze drifted thoughtfully to Lexie, peacefully dozing in her car seat, her small chest rising and falling with each gentle breath.

Chip broke the contemplative silence. "So, what do we do, buddy?"

"We find the mole. Who has the list of people at the meetings? Wasn't that little redhead who was with Dave, taking photographs on her phone? Let's get those pictures and see if we can figure out who the rat is. Turn some rocks over."

"Okay. I'll call Lisa and Dave to see if they can come here right away. What are you going to do?" Chip inquired.

"I'm going to call some of my fellow public servants. But first, I need to find Rylee."

Chapter 70

"Rylee, I know you're in there. Open the door."

Thom continued pounding on the door. He smiled at the person standing in the door of the next apartment and waved.

"Look, the neighbors are staring. I won't stop until you let me in, or they call the cops."

He pounded the door again.

"Look, Lexie needs to get out of the sun. Open up."

Rylee opened the door. She had cried to herself to sleep after coming home and she looked like it.

"You don't have Lexie."

Thom stepped in and gently pulled her into an embrace. Rylee feebly reached to close the door.

"No. Leave it open. I don't care. Let them take all the pictures they want. I don't care."

Rylee pushed the door closed.

Thom all but carried Rylee to the couch.

"Rylee, you probably think I'm nuts. And I wouldn't blame you."

Thom took a deep breath.

"Well, here goes. Back in the day, about six months ago, I used to waste as much time as I could as a snow bum, and in the summer, I was on the water."

Rylee nodded, remembering the photographs. Her soft smile reached his heart and steeled his resolve.

"I figured you were a surfer, or something like that," she said.

"So what gave me away?"

"I think it was that sun-bleached hair that won't lie down."

"Oh."

He pawed at his hair.

A slow grin spread over Rylee's face.

Thom stopped messing with his hair, relieved that she was smiling.

"Rylee, I need you to hear this. I haven't talked with anyone about this except Chip, who was with me when it happened."

Rylee sat very still, nodding again. This was important, and she knew it. Thom forcefully blew the air out of his lungs.

"This is going to be hard for me to get through, please bear with me."

He released the air from his lungs again.

"About six months ago, my family, my parents, sister, and brother-in-law, had planned to go to our family lodge and ski for the weekend. I had even purchased a little sled for Lexie. I went up early with Chip to get extra time on the slopes before it got too crowded. They were coming up later in the day."

Thom paused.

"My parents were driving, and Jake, my brother-in-law, Andie, my sister, and Lexie, their daughter, were coming with them. It started snowing about the time Chip and I arrived."

He paused and took a drink of water.

Rylee watched him. He wasn't making eye contact anymore. She impulsively reached for his hand.

Thom bit his lip and squeezed her hand. He looked up at the wall, his eyes distant.

"All I could think about that day was how great the

snowboarding would be with all the fresh powder. Chip and I were up on the mountain when it happened. It took the police a while to get to us because of the storm. Someone lost control, and there was a big pile-up.

Mom and Dad were the third car back. Andie survived for a few hours. The only one who came out without a scratch was baby Lexie. Sweet little Lexie."

Thom let go of Rylee's hand and dropped his head into his hands, a motion that Rylee was now very familiar with.

"This must be killing him. Just six months ago. He hasn't finished grieving!" she thought.

"When Chip and I finally got to the hospital, Andie was just coming out of surgery. She was all bruised and had tubes and stuff coming out of her."

Thom raised his head, and his weary eyes told the story of his burden. Rylee's tears were washing what remained of her makeup from her face as she watched the muscles in his jaw working.

"Andie made me promise to make sure Lexie went to church. She made me promise." He barked out a harsh laugh. "You see, I was the bad boy who avoided church because it was boring. And after the accident, I was so angry that God could have done something like this, that I stopped believing altogether. I couldn't believe in any god who would be so cruel."

His eyes locked on Rylee's as he watched the silent tears stain her cheeks. He looked back down at the table.

"When Andie died that afternoon, I was sitting in the room with her. I became Lexie's guardian that day, and my life changed. Not that I regret having Lexie, but everything changed."

Rylee could feel the agony coming off Thom, like heat

waves.

"You must have loved your sister very much."

"Andie was more than my sister; she was my twin. I lost everything that day, everything. I didn't understand how any God could do that."

Thom's voice had dropped, barely above a whisper, and Rylee no longer remembered the hateful envelope.

"I ignored the promise until that Sunday, when I came to church for the first time. It had started eating at me for some reason, so I picked a church far from my house, so that church people wouldn't bother me, and off we went. I found you there. You probably think I'm crazy. I think that maybe I was. I couldn't stand it when people talked about how you were Lexie's mother."

With pleading eyes, he added, "You've got to understand that it had nothing to do with you. You do look as if you could be Lexie's mother. It's no wonder they thought that. It made me angry to think anyone else could be Lexie's mother. I didn't mean to hurt you. But this morning, Jim stopped me in the parking lot. We had a talk, and I'm beginning to think that I didn't really stop believing in God; I was just so angry. I've been angry way too long, and now I realize that I've just got to let go somehow."

His eyes were open and honest. Rylee knew that he was pouring his heart out to her.

"I apologize for my behavior. I hope you can forgive me. You look like you could be Lexie's mother, and people are trying to use that against you to stop me. Things will not be pretty for a few days. I just pray that God will let me protect you."

His anxious eyes flicked across her face.

It was her turn to take a deep breath.

## Chapter 71

Thom finished telling her his grim story. His brow furrowed with concern and anger as he turned his thoughts toward the trial that Rylee faced. He told Rylee that the false accusations were bound to make headlines. Even as he spoke, she knew that the dreaded letter and its claims would ignite a frenzy. Their enemies were counting on it to undermine them both. The strategic assault on her credibility was designed to take his focus off the goal.

The wicked implications of the planned attack had sunk in Rylee's mind like a stone in deep water.

"They're going to use this to hammer me," she said, "to get to you."

Her hands had clenched into fists.

Thom told her that they were going over the photos and his suspicions about a mole having infiltrated the group.

"Well, we'd best get over there then," she said. "But first I need to clean up a little bit."

Her memories of the conversation were vivid as she stood amid the rising steam in the bathroom. She had listened as Thom's voice was filled with determination, urging her not to lose heart. His words were a promise in themselves: she wouldn't be facing this alone.

He assured her that no matter what the reports said, no matter how they spun it, they would face the fire together and come out stronger. That part she believed—or wanted to.

The roar of the shower did little to muffle Thom as he spoke on the phone, pacing like a caged lion in the living room.

Her mind swirled with images of the chaos about to unfold, her heart pounding with the rhythm of uncertainty. She could hear his steps tapping insistently against the floor, his voice a constant reminder that he wouldn't rest until he had turned over every rock, called in every favor, and left nothing to chance.

Rylee could hear snippets of his conversation; each word laced with urgency as he implored fellow state representatives to stand firm against the proposed tax cut.

She turned off the shower, dressing quickly before turning on her laptop.

Most of the responses from the legislature members were just the automatic ones that said they received her missive. However, some of them had responded, and a few of those had said something different than the ever-so-personal 'We are always ready to talk about your concerns.'

But one legislator said that she wasn't happy with the bill herself and would like to speak to Rylee further about it, asking her to call and schedule an appointment for early next week.

"Wow, Squeaker, it looks like we're making some headway."

Rylee checked her messages. One message was from Lisa, asking where she went. The other was from Franny, asking her to call back. Some customers, including Franny, wanted to take a more active role in the cause. Rylee quickly dialed the Nail Emporium.

"Franny?"

"Yes."

"Good, it's you. This is Rylee. So, who wants to volunteer, besides you?"

"Baby, you are never going to believe this. It's only

because I have the best nail salon in the city that I get these kinds of customers. I have two very nice ladies who want to volunteer."

"Franny, that's great."

"Oh, honey, that's not the best part. Wait until you hear this."

"What?"

"Besides filling out three petition pages, and getting you two new volunteers, I have this one lady who doesn't want to volunteer, but she is very interested in finding out more. And baby, this is someone you should talk with, and right away."

"Franny, you're killing me. Who is it?"

"Only a television news reporter. You know that brunette on channel three? She is interested. Seems she has been reading some letters to the editor this week."

"Franny, you are a peach. Can you give me her number?"

"Sure sugar, but don't let this one sit too long."

Rylee's skin tingled, as she recorded the number on a scrap of paper.

"Thank you, Lord," Rylee whispered.

She ran into the living room, stopping to take a deep breath. Thom's heart quickened as she entered. Her bright eyes sparkled with excitement.

"What?"

"I've been so silly. I need to trust in God and those that God sends to me."

"Was Jim right?" he thought.

The first time Thom saw Rylee, he felt alive—something he hadn't felt in months. Jim had said that he just had to notice that God's help was there—life in a beautiful, very feminine bundle.

"We don't need to worry about how to fix this. God has taken care of it."

Her excitement was contagious. Surprised, at that moment he realized that her faith only enhanced his appreciation of her.

"I got a real response from one of the emails I sent out Saturday. Ms. Newbury responded and said she wasn't happy with the bill and wanted to talk with me about it."

Thom leaned back on the couch and whistled softly. "Really? Tanya Newbury, huh? That is interesting; I never would have guessed."

"And that isn't even the good news. The other information is much more interesting."

"Tanya Newbury," Thom disclosed, "is the most rabid tax cut person I know. I was originally a little surprised that her name wasn't on the bill. Maybe she figured it out as well. It would take a lot to top that."

"Oh, it does. Lisa and I went to a nail salon yesterday afternoon for a pedicure."

Thom smiled at the mental image of Rylee getting a pedicure. While it was amusing to think about, he didn't know what this had to do with the bill.

Rylee noted Thom's wry smile, and her cheeks warmed to a soft pink.

"Well, anyway, we talked in the salon, and the owner became interested in the whole bill thing and volunteered to put a petition out on her counter for people to sign. She's been telling everyone about it."

"Well, that's good. Is this your amazing news that you needed me to be aware of?"

She took a deep breath before continuing.

"A couple of the ladies are going to be coming by the office next week to volunteer to call, or whatever."

"And?"

She was nearly bouncing.

"Do you know the brunette reporter on Channel 3?"

"What about her?"

"Oh, she comes into Franny's place, the Nail Emporium. Anyway, she came in and saw the petition and wants to interview you as soon as possible."

Rylee stood proudly as Thom whistled through his teeth.

"So, Mr. Richardson, you see that it was important for you to know about this."

Thom laughed.

"Rylee, I honestly didn't think of a nail salon as a hot bed of political activity. This is better than I had hoped. And we can make a preemptive strike at the slander job that is certain to come out tomorrow. Talk about free advertising. Good job."

Rylee leaned close to him and smiled conspiratorially. "What should we do?"

Thom looked at her smiling face and bright eyes. She was almost dancing in her excitement.

"Never again will I let her be hurt like she was this morning," he vowed silently.

"Rylee, call the office and tell Chip to spruce up, because we're going to have a camera crew there soon. There is probably already a group of our volunteers there. Find out how many and tell them we're bringing lunch. I need to stop by and get some stuff for Lexie. I'll let you call the reporter and see if she can meet us there in about an hour."

## Chapter 72

At the office, Chip, Lisa, Dave, and June were gathered around a desk looking at photographs on various phones. Lexie squealed as Thom walked through the door and started motoring over to him.

Lisa knocked over her chair as she rushed to Rylee.

"Oh, Rylee, this is awful."

Lisa stopped several feet from Rylee. Her eyes, filled with concern, slowly narrowed as she placed her fists on her hips.

"You're grinning like a weasel."

"I've never seen a weasel. What do they grin like?" Dave asked.

Rylee started laughing and hugged Lisa.

"I couldn't possibly be more blessed than to have you all as my friends. Don't worry, because God has already fixed it."

Lisa turned to Thom.

"Okay, Mr. Blue Eyes, tell me what's happening here."

Chip's laughter startled everyone, as it rang around the room.

"Mr. Blue Eyes?" Chip choked out.

Lisa spun on him, making Chip laugh harder.

Dave started laughing as he watched Lisa's face scrunch up. Without looking at Dave, she pointed a finger at Chip.

"Are you done? Good," Lisa said.

She slowly turned back to Thom, trying to keep an eye on Chip.

"Well?"

Chip suppressed a snort, and Lisa's blazing eyes flicked to

him again. Thom was openly amused as he watched Chip struggle to keep from laughing.

"WELL?" Lisa demanded impatiently.

Thom held up his hands, fingers spread wide as he bowed his head to Lisa. "Rylee is right. Things have fallen into place nicely. This morning had a very nasty start. Rylee was targeted in an effort that Chip and I think was designed to stop me. However, due to circumstances that none of us had anything to do with, we will vindicate Rylee and push forward our cause. A reporter from Channel 3 will be here in a few minutes, and her story will probably air tonight, before the slander hits the papers tomorrow."

Thom's eyes darted to Chip. "My eyes are blue, Chip. Goes with the spiky blonde hair."

Chip raised an eyebrow, bit his lip, and suppressed his grin.

"Have you guys identified the mole yet?" Thom asked.

"There are a couple of folks who fit the bill who have shown up in several photographs," June said.

Rylee was moving toward the desk when the office door opened, and the reporter from Channel 3 entered. Thom moved forward to greet her.

"Hi, I'm Thomas Richardson. And these are some of the citizens who have asked me to help them stop the pending tax cut bill."

"Nice to meet you, Mr. Richardson. My name is Vera Upchurch. I'd like to get more information about the tax bill and why you oppose it."

Thom pulled out a chair and motioned for her to sit down. He sat across from her and grinned. When the camera crew was ready, Thom began.

"Who in the world would be opposed to a tax cut? I guess that's the big question. I am." he said.

"And why would that be? Isn't a tax cut a good thing?" Vera asked.

"If the citizens saw a decrease in their taxes, it would be. And it is good for the very small groups that will benefit from the redistribution of public funds," he said.

Vera leaned forward. "Okay. You have my attention."

The cameras were positioned so that Chip and the rest of the group could be seen working in the background during the interview.

"I see you have some volunteers here working on a Sunday. What are they doing?" Vera asked.

"That is a good question, but I don't think you would be interested in the answer.

Vera smiled. "Try me."

"Okay. The easiest thing to do is to let you see it yourself."

Thom walked over to the table and picked up a few documents. When he returned, he just handed them to Vera. After only a few seconds, Vera waved her hand past her neck in a slicing motion at her camera crew.

"Cut the cameras."

She waited until the cameras were off before asking, "Who is Rylee?"

"My secretary," Thom replied.

"Tell me about the baby."

Thom told Vera about the accident, how he became his niece's guardian, and Rylee's part in bringing the damage the tax cut would do to his attention. Thom pointed to the group working behind him.

"This is Rylee's Army, not mine. She is the one who has been pushing this—pushing me to do the right thing. Someone is getting nervous and trying to distract us from moving forward. The folks working back there are trying to find out who."

Vera nodded. "Which one is Rylee?" she asked.

Thom pointed her out.

Vera turned to the camera crew. "Okay. Get them rolling again."

## Chapter 73

Chip met Rylee at the door when she came into work on Monday.

"Hey, there's our new star. Or maybe it's General Vance."

He picked up a bag from his desk and offered it to her.

"I brought in bagels to celebrate."

"I checked the papers and saw nothing this morning about me being a whore."

"Yeah. It will be uncomfortable for you when and if that hits the papers. We all know the truth. Ms. Upchurch ran with the story about the fight against the tax bill last night. She's sitting on quite a story but wants to wait to jump on them when they go public with their lies."

Chip Rylee did get a bagel before Thom came busting in the door.

"Great! Who got the bagels? Chip, is there anything new on the Spencer thing? Did you guys see the interview last night? Pretty good stuff."

The men walked into Thom's office, with Thom still talking. He paused at the door and grinned at Rylee.

"Please join us, Ms. Vance, and bring the bagels," Thom said.

"I'll run the partnership agreement over to Mike Spencer's office. Hopefully, they'll be good with it, as it is. I'm getting tired of working on it," Chip said.

Thom nodded as he grabbed a bagel.

"It took us what, two hours to hammer out ours?" Thom said.

"Yeah, but I trust you," Chip winked at Rylee, "and I'm almost a lawyer too."

Chip also grabbed a bagel and spread cream cheese on it while he continued to relay the morning's business.

"After I finish with Mike, I've got to go to the new place. The phone guys are coming in today to run cables for the computers. I'll be on my cell phone."

He paused to look at Rylee. "Oh, I almost forgot."

Chip moved to the reception area, returned with a new cell phone, and handed it to Rylee. He laughed maniacally.

"Now you are in our complete control."

"It will do everything that I need it to do for you to do what I need you to do," Thom informed Rylee.

"Say what?" Chip asked.

Thom's eyes sparkled.

Chip said, "If you have problems with the phone's features, just ask. You can track everything from it and even listen to tunes. Of course, none of us listens to tunes at work."

Thom looked over at Chip, who was taking headphones from his pocket.

"What?"

"In an effort to get some work done today," he pointedly told Chip, "we've got another interview with Vera this afternoon at the Orchard Street Free Clinic."

"Can I do the interview this time?" Chip inquired.

"Oh. Okay. Wear a clean tie," Thom instructed.

"Maybe I can get her autograph or phone number," Chip wondered aloud.

"If the cable guys aren't done, just call me, and I'll cover at the new place," Thom said.

Thom handed Rylee a small stack of cassette tapes. "Here are dictation tapes you can get started on.

Chip, before you take off, show Rylee where things are on the computer, how to use the dictation equipment, what to do with phone messages, and where we keep the hardcopy files."

"Someone needs to show me how to use this phone," she reminded them.

"Oh, you plug the headphone in right here." Chip pointed to the headphone jack.

"No, I mean as a phone."

"What fun is that?" Chip asked.

Rylee spent the rest of the morning typing and answering the phone. Thom left shortly after Chip. It was good that the tapes contained just a few short letters, because the phone rang off the hook.

All the representative contacts made by the group over the weekend stirred the pot. Several of them mentioned the interview that ran Sunday night. At least the word spread quickly that Thom was opposed to the tax cut bill.

When Thom returned, Rylee conscripted him to help with phone duty. After about half an hour, Thom asked Rylee if she could call Dave and see if he wanted to volunteer to manage phones.

Naturally, Dave was eager to help. When he arrived, he relieved some pressure on the phones, so Thom could return calls instead of just reacting.

"Rylee, Thom's on another line right now, but I've got George Dawson on the phone," Dave said.

Rylee remembered from the list that George Dawson was the majority leader in the legislature.

"We'd better interrupt him for that," Rylee said. "Yeah, Mr. Dawson doesn't sound so happy."

"Excuse me, Mr. Richardson," Rylee said.

Thom, alerted by the tone in her voice, immediately looked up.

"Listen Stan, I've got to go, my assistant Rylee is trying to get my attention. Give Tanya a call; she's setting something up."

Rylee waited until he set the phone down. "George Dawson on three."

Thom nodded.

"Well, we knew this was coming."

Rylee exited his office and pulled the door shut.

When Chip returned, he tossed a catalog on her desk with some pages flagged.

"Rylee, take a look at these and pick one out."

He paused to look at Dave, who had a phone to his ear. He turned wide, questioning eye to Rylee.

"The phones have been crazy. Dave volunteered to come in today to help cover them, especially since you and I are going to be at the clinic this afternoon."

"Oh, yeah. You going too? You mean this isn't going to be all about me?"

Chip walked over and patted Dave on the back. "Thanks buddy."

Dave looked over at Thom's closed door.

"George Dawson called."

Chip shot a quick look at the closed door and nodded his head.

"Well, to complicate things a little bit more, Rylee, we'll be able to start moving into our new office this week, and I hope to have the doors open by next Monday. Thom has planned to take Lexie to her grandparents tomorrow for the week. Lisa said she would help with the move. Can you give her a call?"

Dave started laughing.

"What?" Chip asked.

"Dave, be nice. Lisa would love to help," Rylee said.

Dave just laughed harder.

Rylee had to answer the next call because Dave was still laughing.

Chapter 74

Rylee had called ahead to the Orchard Street Free Clinic that morning, informing them that a camera crew would arrive at two o'clock for an interview. When Rylee and Chip pulled up, the place was humming with activity. The doctors and volunteers had spread the word.

"Looks like someone was expecting us," Chip said.

Several doctors were waiting at the entrance, ready to greet them as they arrived.

"Mr. Fallon, good to meet you," said a doctor. "Ever since that interview aired, we've seen an uptick in patients. It seems a lot of people had no idea we were available. I hope this one will generate just as much interest."

"Has the camera crew from Channel 3 arrived yet?" Chip asked.

"Yes, it's just the cameraman and the reporter. They are interviewing patients now."

"It looks like you don't need me for this part," Rylee said.

They were doing fine without her. She decided to help with patient intake. June and Rob were also there, answering questions about finances and explaining how the tax cut would negatively impact services.

Rylee tried to avoid the cameras, but Chip spotted her anyway.

"Hey, Gen. Vance, want to be a star today?"

"I think I'll pass."

She continued helping check in patients. Rob and June, however, seemed to relish the spotlight and gave lengthy answers about how the tax cuts would gut the already strained clinic.

When the reporter had finished and walked out of the clinic, Rylee was exhausted from the afternoon and the whirlwind of questions and commotion. She was glad to return to the office to collect her thoughts at least.

Thom was waiting for them with the evening paper in his hands.

Chapter 75

Thom pressed the newspaper against the table, his knuckles whitening. He leaned toward Rylee, eyes sharp with concern.

"Rylee, it isn't as bad as it could've been. They only hint at some illicit relationship you're using to sway my vote on the tax cut."

The fluorescent lights above buzzed.

Rylee's shoulders snapped rigid. She inhaled slowly, then reached for the folded newspaper. The room lay hushed, save for the insistent trill of an unanswered phone.

With deliberate calm, she smoothed the page and let her gaze drift over every line, head tilted, lips parted. When she finished, she set the paper down without a word, scanned the faces around her—Chip's clenched jaw, Dave's uneasy fidget—and rose. Her heels clicked against the linoleum floor as she crossed to the ringing handset.

"Law Offices of Richardson and Fallon. How may I help you?"

Her voice was steady, professional. She scribbled on a pad, nodded as she listened, then replaced the phone in its cradle. Rylee turned, a small, wry smile tugging at her lips. She tapped the front-page photo—herself holding Lexie, both bright-eyed.

"Nice picture of me and Lexie, don't you think?"

Dave's coffee mug trembled in his hand; he set it down too fast, the liquid sloshing over the rim. His mouth dropped open.

"Rylee, they're being vicious. You can't just shrug this off."

She met his gaze, shoulders squared.

"No, I'm not okay. It's cruel. But I trust in God and my friends, and I refuse to let evil win."

Her voice rang out, unshaken, as though the words themselves banished doubt.

"This bill is wrong, and we must defeat it. No smear campaign will distract us from doing what's right."

Rylee paused, remembering the knot in her stomach when she first glimpsed the grainy photos, when the anonymous letter threatened to ruin her. She closed her eyes for a heartbeat.

"I wanted to quit—feared for my reputation. But the Bible tells of saints who endured true torture. Compared to that, this is just spiteful gossip."

She flashed Thom a quick, almost sheepish look.

"I won't let it stop me. We must expose this bill's lies and stand up for folks who can't see what's happening—or don't yet appreciate the danger. We must reach out to those in need, every single one."

She stepped back toward Thom, conviction lighting her features.

"God calls us to care for the little and big things." Gently, she took his hand, her fingers warm around his. "This isn't about me."

Thom's heart thundered. He watched her—shoulders back, chin lifted, eyes steady—radiating strength and grace. He wrapped her in his arms, relief and pride flooding him as he held her close.

## Chapter 76

Rylee wiped her damp palms on her jeans as the last rush of patients ebbed through the clinic doors. Exhaustion and excitement swirled together in the cramped reception area.

Rob hauled a battered television from a cardboard box in the corner. Electrical cords spilled across the floor like snakes.

"Looks like Channel 3 is ready to roll," he announced. Someone nudged the volume up.

"We're here at the Orchard Street Free Clinic, where patients are waiting to be seen by doctors and volunteers working around the clock, despite devastating uncertainties in their funding. When it comes to tax cuts, what is the real cost paid by those most in need?"

A flutter of nerves tickled Rylee's ribs. She pressed her back against the wall, gripping her clipboard until her knuckles blanched.

The camera shifted. The reporter shifted her position slightly, stating that there was opposition to this movement. She mentioned the newspaper article—details Rylee had barely dared to share. How Lexie's parents had died in a car accident, the anonymous letter scrawled with threats in black ink; every tragic stroke flickered on the screen.

A few gasps rippled through the assembly at the free clinic when a photograph of Lexie's smiling parents filled the frame.

Rylee's throat tightened.

At the end of the segment, the reporter stared straight

into the lens.

"Can a bill to cut taxes target the most helpless segment of our society? Rylee's Army says it is."

The words landed like stones. Rylee blinked, her breath catching.

The final shot lingered on her, kneeling beside an elderly patient, helping them fill out a benefits form. She didn't even know they'd filmed that moment. A hush stretched through the room before applause broke out, cautious at first, then boisterous.

June gave Rylee a triumphant grin. "Wow."

Rob's eyes glinted.

"Did they just call it Rylee's Army?"

Her phone buzzed. It was Thom. She lifted it to her ear. "Yes?"

"Don't you look cute. Rylee's Army sounds great"

"Thom, this is wonderful. They made the bill sound downright evil."

"Yeah. This'll work in our favor. See you tomorrow, Ms. Rylee."

He hung up.

Rylee lowered her phone and surveyed the cluster of faces all beaming at her.

Rob slapped her shoulder. "Looking good, General Vance."

## Chapter 77

By the time the sun rose on Wednesday morning, the frenetic pace that had gripped the office finally eased to something less than a full-blown panic. This reprieve was a stroke of luck, as Dave had classes and couldn't cover the phones.

Rylee, juggling her newly acquired job duties, found herself at the center of a media storm that spun relentlessly around the office. Then the rustle of the delivery of the morning paper hit her desk.

The front page featured a vibrant photograph of Thom standing confidently outside the new office, clad in faded jeans and a casual T-shirt. The bold headline proclaimed him 'The People's Advocate,' accompanied by his quote, 'I'm in favor of tax cuts, just not ones that leave people bleeding.'

Thom chuckled as he glanced at the image, amusement dancing in his eyes.

"Well, I bet that George really hates my guts now. No cushy committee for me." A smile tugging at his lips as he shook his head in resignation.

His prophetic words were spot on.

In his office, George Dawson glared at the same newspaper, his brow furrowed in irritation. With a sharp, frustrated exhale, he flung it onto his cluttered desk. The slam of a desk drawer echoed his displeasure.

"Alice, get in here," he barked.

In mere seconds, Alice appeared at the doorway, her steno pad open and pen poised, ready to capture every word.

"Fire that photographer! Tell him we don't want him to attend another meeting or take any more pictures, and he needs to keep his mouth shut. Pull everyone we have planted."

He turned to glare at Alice, who furiously scribbled down his furious commands, her pen nearly flying off the page.

"See if you can line up a photo op at one of those clinics. Write me a press release about how the tax bill is not cutting services but simply removing redundancy. Don't mention that girl or Richardson. Get everyone in here now!"

Alice inhaled deeply. Looking at George's red face, she was concerned he was having a heart attack. She understood the urgency.

"On it."

She returned to her desk, fingers already dialing the first of many calls.

## Chapter 78

Outside of George's office at the state house, aides scurried along the marbled hallway, clutching folders stamped URGENT. Inside, George stood with his back to his desk, shoulders hunched, phone pressed to his ear.

He'd spent the morning calling every ally he knew—emails, whispered phone calls in shadowed corners—trying to push today's fast-tracked tax cut vote into next week.

Too little too late, the motion would proceed today as scheduled. George slammed the receiver into its cradle so hard the desk trembled. His jaw clenched, veins throbbed against his temple, and the taste of defeat turned his mouth sour.

Lisa had cleared her calendar to help Chip with the office move. In the temporary bullpen of mismatched chairs and cardboard boxes, Rylee answered a dozen calls in rapid succession. She scribbled on Post-its: Call back Reporter Diaz. Constituent re: bill—send fact sheet, Alarm company again—sigh.

Her pen scratched so fast her hand ached.

At noon, Lisa and Rylee slipped into a corner booth at Rosa's Diner, where red vinyl seats stuck a little and the chalkboard lunch specials boasted meatloaf and mac n' cheese.

Lisa stabbed at her club sandwich.

"I swear, the security guys who installed that keypad made it super sensitive on purpose. I keep triggering it. It's embarrassing."

She flipped the sliced tomatoes off the sandwich.

"I know you dial the wrong code. I get the calls. You need

to stop fat-fingering it. At least you're spending time with Chip. Isn't that what you wanted?"

Lisa brightened.

"That's right. And you get Mr. Blue Eyes all to yourself."

Rylee tapped her spoon against the edge of her bowl.

"He's my boss. It would be inappropriate for me to --

"Phish."

"We're simply friends."

"Oh, I'm fine with friendship," Lisa said, voice playful. She traced the rim of her water glass.

"You just need to ensure it stays friends with Blue Eyes; Chip is mine."

She grinned, then added thoughtfully.

"And I need to pick out some cute snowboarding gear. He hits the slopes on weekends during winter."

Rylee laughed, imagining Lisa learning to snowboard.

At about 1:30 that day, Thom buttoned up his tailored jacket, grabbed the leather briefcase Rylee held out, and flicked through the papers—committee reports, press clippings, talking points—before snapping it shut. He beamed at her, bright as a sunrise.

Leaning forward, he brushed a quick kiss against her cheek. He pointed at the corner of her desk.

"Thanks, Rylee. Gallery passes for Chip, Dave, Lisa, Jim, June—you," he winked, "—and anyone else on your guest list. Lock up, remind Chip about the alarms—they're about as subtle as a foghorn."

He strode toward the door whistling a jaunty tune.

Rylee watched the glass door swing shut behind him, fingers lingering on her cheek where his lips had warmed her skin, realizing he'd barely registered the kiss himself.

## Chapter 79

Upon her arrival at the state house, Rylee's pulse thundered as she spotted rows of picket signs posted like sentinels, furious slogans denouncing the cold-hearted tax- cut package. The protesters' chants swelled into a low roar, and she recognized a handful of them as Dave's friends, their faces flushed with righteous anger.

Inside the chamber, the air crackled with expectation. From her gallery seat she could see the polished floor below, clusters of legislators leaning in close as huddle factions pressed Thom before the session began.

A single rap of the gavel carved through the murmur, and the Assembly was called to order. First came a handful of dutiful speeches praising the bill—polite nods, stilted applause—then wave after wave of the bill's opponents rose to speak, each voice rising higher, painting pictures of clinics shuttered, families abandoning hope, and emergency rooms overwhelmed.

At last Thom was recognized. You could have heard a pin drop. He stood, squared his shoulders, and spoke in a voice that rolled through the chamber like thunder.

"Mr. President, esteemed colleagues, before us stands a bill that promises tax relief to our citizens—who, after all, could oppose that sweet fruit? Yet I stand opposed. Because this package is a razor's edge aimed straight at the throats of our most vulnerable. Cutting healthcare services is not compassion but cruelty dressed in numbers."

He picked up a stack of papers from the podium, their

corners fluttering like trapped birds.

"Here are the financial records from free clinics across our state. Look at these figures. The reimbursements we grudgingly send them—thin slivers of support that barely keep their doors open. These clinics do not drain our coffers or sink our budget. They are lifelines."

His gaze swept the room, igniting silent sparks in every eye.

"Yes, we can cut taxes. We should. But not by eviscerating the health and human services that rescue our poorest citizens. There are fat pockets to trim, pet projects, pork-barrel spending, special-interest deals that line private pockets while real people go without. We swore an oath to serve, not to squander the hard-earned resources of every man, woman, and child who depends on us."

His voice cracked with urgency.

"It takes courage to stand against the entrenched interests who treat public funds as their personal slush fund. We must stop the backroom deals, the earmarks that benefit the few at the expense of the many. We must honor that oath we took freely, under no duress. I cannot—and will not—in good conscious vote for this bill."

He leaned forward, intensity burning in his eyes. "Let us instead craft legislation that truly cuts taxes while safeguarding those most in need. Let us strip out the pork and redirect those dollars to fully fund our free clinics, to heal our communities rather than hobble them."

Thom paused, scanning the gallery until his eyes found Rylee. A fierce, joyful smile bloomed on his face.

"And let us remember that it is our solemn duty—and

our greatest privilege—to defend those who cannot defend themselves, whether they stand with us at the ballot box or not."

Rylee's chest soared with pride. She had never seen him in his element, and he was magnificent with every word searing itself into her heart. Camera flashes cracked like gunshots. The gallery erupted in standing ovation; even some representatives stomped their feet in approval.

The uproar swelled until Thom raised his hand. "Thank you, Mr. President," he said, and returned to his seat as the chamber crackled with energy.

A few more speeches followed, hurling the usual talking points. For the most part they were George's minions. However, as the vote tally was calculated, it was clear the bill would fail. Rylee's breath caught as each name was read; the "nay" votes sailed past the "yea" with a decisive roar. Thom turned, caught her eye, winked—and gave her a triumphant thumbs-up.

## Chapter 80

After the vote, Rylee felt like she was moving through a fog. Upon descending from the gallery into the hallway below, Rylee was immediately surrounded by reporters and people who had been working with her to save the clinics.

It all seemed surreal to Rylee. Lisa was jumping up and down, elated. Dave was clapping people on the back and shaking hands. She was blinded by camera flashes.

People were talking to her from every direction. Chip stayed very close and fielded many of the questions. Time stood still for a moment, and then suddenly, the reporters were off to make their deadlines.

Dave danced with excitement. "We've got to celebrate!" he said.

Chip agreed. "Thom told me that if the bill fails, we are to go to his apartment's community room and throw a party."

"Well, what are we waiting for? Start calling everyone!" Lisa added.

The room was alive. People were coming and going until early evening. Rylee didn't remember everyone who showed up over the course of the evening, how all these people knew about it, or even how all the food got ordered. Several representatives came and talked with Thom. Jim Hooper, and several other volunteers from free clinics around the state. Of course, there were reporters present, interviewing everyone. It was after eight o'clock before Thom walked up to Rylee, who was busy chatting with June and Lisa.

"Hi Lisa, June. Big day, huh?"

June gave him a hug. "You were great! Thank you so much."

"Look guys, when we wind up here, a few of us are going back to my place." Thom said.

"Give me your keys," June offered, "and let me open your apartment. This party is far from over. There are still people here who want to talk to you. You know you have a new reputation. The lawyer in blue jeans, and the people's advocate."

Thom grinned.

"At least my wardrobe will be cheaper."

"Lisa, Chip, and I can greet the people you've invited to your apartment until you can get away," June suggested.

Thom put his arm around Rylee to prevent her from leaving with June.

"Congratulations, Rylee. You were the driving force behind this. None of it would have happened if it hadn't been for you," June said.

Rylee turned to watch the small group heading off. Thom's arm felt so comfortable around her waist. Chip and Lisa were laughing about something, as they both snatched up bowls of snacks. Rylee knew that it was a group effort that had brought them to this night. She leaned into Thom, her eyes shining.

"Thom, June was right. You were wonderful. Your voice rang across that room this afternoon."

Thom reached down and took her hand. She was warm and comforting. He realized increasingly that Jim was right. Rylee was healing his heart.

"The hard work happened before the vote. Did you see the guys talking to me before we were called into session? They were the guys who authored the bill and they were trying to bend my arm, right up until the eleventh hour. It was hard for them, because they were trying to look all friendly for the reporters, but they were not happy."

He grimaced and looked around again.

"Now, I need to put my money where my mouth was, and work on something that will cut taxes without cutting services to the poor. Tanya is already pushing me."

He let go of Rylee and spun her around to face him. He put his hands on her shoulders and looked into her eyes.

"But Rylee, it was you who made it happen. I didn't care one way or the other about the bill, and I wouldn't have lost sleep over it passing. You're the one who made me care about it. You became my conscience. People should be thanking you. But since they aren't, I will."

He leaned over and kissed her gently on the cheek.

"Thank you, Rylee." He brushed her cheek with the back of his hand. "I've put the word out to the press that this effort was spearheaded by Rylee's Army. I hope that you will not go unnoticed and unheralded. You deserved the recognition."

He kissed her again, this time gently on her lips. "Rylee, there is so much I need to say to you, but it will have to wait until later. Please make some time for me." His eyes were soft, and pleading.

"Of course, later."

She looked at the people waiting to talk with him.

"Go," she said, smiling as she pushed him away.

The gathering at his apartment was less noisy, and much smaller, but still held all the warmth and excitement of the earlier celebration. Rylee was exhausted and happy. Folks started leaving around eleven o'clock, and shortly, it was just Chip, Thom, and

Rylee sitting around his kitchen table.

"Okay. Tomorrow, we move the files," Thom said. Rylee groaned.

"Oh, come on, you little sissy. That's the easy stuff. I've been picking out drapes," Chip said.

"Tired, Rylee?" Thom asked.

He wanted to ask her to spend the night. He was trying to convince himself that she was too tired to drive home. He also knew that he wouldn't be able to stay on the couch if she was in his bed. The thought of her in his bed sent shivers through him.

"My goodness, yes. I didn't realize that this work is so draining," she answered.

"It isn't always. I'm certain there will be days when you'll be bored to tears. I usually bring in Lexie with me to help with the slow times."

Rylee thumped the table with her hands.

"I'm going home before I fall asleep. Good night, guys."

## Chapter 81

"Okay, bud, what's going on? Don't tell me you've resorted to hiring potential girlfriends because you can't get them any other way? What happened to your ban on church ladies?"

Thom picked up his cup without comment.

"Oh, it's serious then?"

Thom took a sip. "I just don't want to mess it up. I almost did. I just don't want to scare her away. For the first time since," he looked down at his coffee cup and swirled the liquid around, "well, I feel like a person again. I believe in goodness again. I think that I can be happy with Rylee. I just don't want to move too fast. I really did almost blow it several times. My motto from now on is, slow and steady," Thom said.

"Uh-huh. That'll be a first. What happened to plowing through new powder?"

Thom cocked an eyebrow at Chip.

Chip laughed.

"Hey bud, it's okay, because I happen to be a romantic who believes in love at first sight."

Thom considered this. Maybe not love at first sight, but she certainly got his attention at first sight.

"Partner, right now she is our employee. When and if we do connect, I don't want her to work for us anymore. I don't want my wife to be my employee," Thom said.

Chip spit coffee across the table. "Wife?"

Thom grinned at Chip, as Chip wiped the coffee from his face and the table.

"Chip, you bear so many similarities to Lexie."

"Thom! Old buddy! Wife? You haven't known her more than, what? Two weeks?"

"I don't think I can explain it. Sometimes when I stand at the top of a mountain and look down, it just feels right. I just know that this run is the right one. Not every trail feels that way to me. Not that they aren't all fun, but sometimes, it's perfect. That's how Rylee feels to me. Perfect."

Chip put his elbows on the table. "It's been a while since you've shown any real life. I've missed the old Thom."

Thom took a sip of his coffee.

"Yeah, me too, buddy. Me too. You know I told her about the accident."

Chip leaned back in his chair.

"Did you tell her about the rest of it?"

"No, she doesn't know. I've been okay living like this since the accident," Thom said.

"But...?"

"Lexie needs to be out in the fresh air and sunshine. Eventually Lexie may even want a pony to ride."

"Good thing you didn't sell the old homestead."

"Yeah. Thanks for stopping me from doing that. At the time, I didn't think I would ever want to live there again."

"And it would be a good place to settle with your wife."

Thom grinned and nodded his head.

Chip paused and screwed up his mouth. "Oh, no, the boy is a total loss."

Chapter 82

Rylee drove home without issue, though fatigue clung to her like a heavy fog. As she entered the front door, Squeaker greeted her with a chorus of noisy complaints, his fur bristling with impatience. She filled his bowl with food before collapsing onto her bed, exhaustion pulling her under like a warm, welcoming tide.

Her slumber was abruptly shattered by an increasingly loud pounding reverberating through the walls. Lisa's voice, sharp and insistent, pierced the morning quiet from beyond the door.

"Wake up! We have a lot to do today."

Squeaker, disturbed by the commotion, began to hiss, his tail flicking with irritation. Rylee, bleary-eyed, shrugged a bathrobe over her pajamas and stumbled toward the door, Squeaker a shadow at her heels.

"Lisa, hush! You're going to wake up the neighbors. It's Saturday morning!" Rylee protested, her voice still heavy with sleep.

"Rylee, get in the shower. We've got stuff to do. You were the one who told me to meet you at six-thirty."

With a resigned sigh, Rylee headed for the shower, the promise of hot water urging her forward, while Lisa took over feeding the disgruntled cat.

They arrived at the old office just before the agreed- upon time of eight, the morning air crisp and cool. The front door stood ajar, and Chip nearly fumbled his load of office supplies when he spotted Rylee's sleek, blue GTO maneuvering into the parking garage adjacent to the building.

"Whose car was that?" he asked, his voice tinged with awe as Rylee and Lisa crossed the threshold.

"Oh, it's mine. My father gave it to me when I moved down here," Rylee replied, her tone casual.

Wide-eyed, Chip spun on his heels and made a beeline for Thom's office.

"Marry her now," he declared to Thom, excitement in his voice. "I'll get the JP down here. You didn't tell me she was driving that. What a woman!"

Thom chuckled at his friend's enthusiasm.

"I guess the girls are here. Stop drooling, Chip, it's unbecoming."

Lisa entered with a box of doughnuts and steaming cups of coffee; her brow furrowed with curiosity at Chip's reaction.

"Why do guys always act like that when they see your old car?" Lisa asked, her voice tinged with genuine puzzlement.

*Rylee Rising*

## Chapter 83

Boxes clattered across the floor as they shoved years of clutter into cardboard boxes. Sweat beaded on Rylee's brow as she placed Thom's snowboarding and jet-ski trophies into a box. She knew he hadn't touched either sport since the accident. Lexie was his priority.

"Are you going to compete this year?" she asked, voice firm.

Thom froze. He had been crawling beneath his old desk and was holding a lost pacifier.

"Why?"

"Because you dominated it. Because you love it. And because you owe it to yourself."

Still scrunched under the desk, he turned toward her, dust motes dancing in the late afternoon sun.

"I haven't thought about it in, oh --"

"Six months," she said.

A month ago, he would have snapped back. Now, he couldn't find anger in himself. He crawled out, met her gaze— Jim was right. He was staring at his second chance.

"Yeah. Six months."

Rylee lifted a framed photograph. It showed Thom, flushed with victory, beaming beside his father in the snow. The older man's pride radiated from the image.

"Your dad was proud of you, wasn't he?"

Thom's jaw tightened.

"Yeah. I guess he was."

"Then compete next season," she said, wrapping the photo in newsprint like a holy relic.

"Will you—" he left it unfinished. Rylee waited a moment.

"Will I what?"

"Will you come watch me?"

"Of course."

She sealed the box.

"Do they make skis Lexie-sized?"

He gripped the desk's edge, pulling himself upright.

God had sent him back from the edge, and now life shone at him through hazel eyes. He wouldn't let her go.

"Slow and easy," he murmured, but his pulse thundered.

Night had fallen by the time they stacked the last box in the new office. Files for Monday's first appointments lay neatly on Chip's and Thom's desks—Rylee's trademark efficiency. They returned to the old office and grabbed take-out.

Chip volunteered to drive Lisa home.

"Chip loves your car. Says I should marry you because of it."

She laughed, the sound bright in the empty space. "I dated a guy once who only wanted my car. Cops notice it, too hard to be bad with blue lights at your rear."

After one final sweep of the old spaces, Rylee flicked off the lights one by one.

"The free clinic crew picks up the old computers and furniture Monday morning."

"And that, as they say," Thom whispered, "is that. New digs on Monday."

He offered to walk her to her car in the well-lit garage,

but she shook her head, already striding toward her future. He watched her go, determined to chase the spark she'd reignited inside him—one powerful carve through fresh powder at a time.

## Chapter 84

Rylee's fingers fumbled through her purse in search of her keys. Her eyes darted up toward her vehicle, catching a shadowy movement at the far end of the garage. Eventually she felt the hard edge of the key.

"There they are."

She pulled the keys from the fold where they always seemed to hide. The day had been grueling, the past few weeks utterly draining. As she trudged toward her car, her mind whirled with distraction.

"Did Thom actually mention marrying me?"

Her heart skipped a beat as she neared her car. She thought she recognized the man hunched over the hood, his hands busy with something sinister.

"What are you doing?" she demanded, her voice echoing hollowly in the vast, empty garage. "Can I help you?" she pressed on, trying to sound braver than she felt.

The man spun around, his eyes darting behind her with a predatory glance. Beneath the low brim of his ball cap, Rylee discerned the face of one of Thom's identified moles from the photographs.

"You're the mole. You took those pictures of me," she accused.

"Yeah. So what? It was a job, not a crime."

His voice laced with a menacing edge that sent icy chills racing up Rylee's spine.

"What you did was wrong," she insisted.

He surveyed the empty parking garage with a smirk.

"Sweet ride. And I'm not just talking about the GTO, little girl."

His words dripped with malice.

Panic surged through Rylee as she spun on her heel and sprinted back toward the office. Her heart pounded in her ears as she heard his footsteps thundering behind her, then felt his iron grip clamp down on her arm.

"Just give me the keys, and you won't get hurt. You might even like it." his grip tightening like a vise.

Desperately, Rylee struggled to wrench free. "Let go!" she screamed.

"Give me the keys, bitch."

His fist slammed into her stomach with brutal force.

She collapsed to the ground; her breath ripped from her lungs. He snatched her purse, its contents spilling out beside her head.

"Where are the keys, bitch? I don't want to damage the car."

Rylee lay crumpled, clutching the keys desperately in her hand. Gasping for air, she pressed the alarm button, the blaring sound echoing through the garage. Enraged, the man stepped on her hand until the pain caused her to release the keys.

Rylee lay there, paralyzed by pain, her breath shallow and labored. Her hand throbbed, each pulse a reminder of her helplessness as she watched him retrieve the keys and move toward her car with predatory determination.

## Chapter 85

Thom noticed Rylee's gray jacket thrown over a chair before he turned out the lights for the last time. She had just left; maybe he could catch her.

As Thom stepped into the dimly lit parking garage, the piercing blare of a car alarm shattered the eerie silence, echoing off the concrete walls like a distress signal. Turning the corner, his heart plummeted at the horrifying scene before him.

Rylee lay crumpled on the cold, hard ground, her face contorted in pain, while a sinister figure mercilessly stomped on her hand with a vicious sneer. Time seemed to stretch, each second dragging agonizingly as Thom sprang into action without hesitation.

The assailant's wild, frantic gaze shifted from Rylee to Thom, then darted to the sleek GTO parked nearby, desperation flickering in his eyes. A feral growl erupted from Thom's throat, primal and fierce, as he launched himself over Rylee with a single, fluid leap, his momentum unbroken.

The attacker lunged forward, a glint of steel in his hand, the knife flashing under the harsh fluorescent lights. He moved with a reckless abandon, but Thom's instincts took over. He deftly sidestepped, spinning away from the deadly arc of the blade with practiced precision. In one seamless motion, Thom delivered a bone-crunching uppercut, the impact resonating through his fist. Without missing a beat, he followed up with a thunderous right hook, the blow connecting with the man's jaw with a sickening crack. The attacker spun in a disjointed pirouette before collapsing like a marionette with its strings cut.

To ensure the threat was neutralized, Thom delivered a swift, punishing kick to the man's side, his foot sinking into flesh and bone with the force of his determination, making sure the man would not rise again.

Thom's entire body trembled as he sprinted back to Rylee, dropping to his knees beside her with a pounding in his chest.

"Rylee, are you all right?" he pleaded, his voice cracking with desperation.

His hands fumbled frantically for his phone, but his eyes caught sight of hers on the ground. He snatched it up and dialed 911. Though she was breathing, she lay unresponsive, and Thom's eyes filled with hot tears that threatened to spill over.

"Rylee, I'm right here," he choked out.

He sat back, straining to hear the arrival of the ambulance, rocking on his heels with anxiety gnawing at his insides.

The assailant let out a pained moan, and with a surge of adrenaline-fueled rage, Thom dragged him closer to Rylee, sitting on him until the wailing sirens of police and ambulance finally tore through the night air.

## Chapter 86

Blood pooled beneath Rylee's hand as the paramedics closed in. The sight of those ragged cuts—jagged slashes carved by her keys, crimson seeping between her delicate fingers made Thom's gut knot. Fear churned in his chest. If only he'd walked her here like he wanted to do.

"Thom, I'm okay," she rasped, voice fracturing on the words.

Hollow sounded the admission, even to her own ears.

Thom pressed her hand to his lips. "How could she be okay?" he wondered.

"Rylee," he whispered.

Her eyes fluttered open, dark pools darting to his face. "I'm okay now, Thom. You saved me. I saw you."

She offered him a brave, brittle smile but to him if felt like an admission of defeat. He wanted to argue, but all he managed was a knotted nod as the paramedics slid the gurney into place.

A uniformed officer materialized at his side, tugging him back. He pointed at the GTO. His voice was low, clipped with urgency.

"Nice GTO, sir. Only a couple thousand made, if I recall. Are you the owner?"

"No. It's Rylee's car."

"Nice." The officer nodded at Rylee. "And that is Rylee?"

"Yes."

"That what he was after?"

Thom stared at the ambulance; every siren beat

hammering in his ribs.

"He had the keys," Thom muttered.

The officer gave a sharp nod toward Rylee.

"Lucky you showed up when you did. If I were you, I'd stash that car in a vault and keep it there. Too tempting for scum like him."

Thom's nod was automatic. He felt hollow. He followed the paramedics, each step heavy with worry and something like regret.

"Excuse me."

Thom tried to inch toward the ambulance doors, desperate to climb in beside her.

Rylee lifted her head, dirt smudging her cheek, hair tangled like storm clouds overhead. She offered a wry grin that didn't reach her eyes.

"I'm fine. I want to go home. I've got to feed my cat."

Behind them, a paramedic's voice cracked, "Ms. Vance, you need to go to the hospital. You're in shock. There's a bruise forming on your temple, a possible concussion, maybe a broken hand or ribs. You'll need X-rays and someone to stay with you tonight. The hospital is the best place for all of that. Someone else will feed your cat."

Thom's voice came out ragged.

"I'm not letting you go alone. I'm coming with you."

He reached for her, his thumb brushing her uninjured hand. "Rylee, I'm scared. I won't rest until the doctor clears you."

The paramedic's tone sharpened.

"You took a solid hit in the gut. At the very least, you'll feel that for days."

Weariness overtook her and the fight drained out of her.

She nodded.

As the ambulance doors slammed shut, a paramedic blocked Thom's path.

"Sir, follow us in your car. If she's released tonight, she'll need a ride home."

Thom stood on the curb, chest heaving, every pulse pounding duty, fear, anger, and adrenaline. He watched the ambulance recede, wondering if he'd ever feel whole again. Thom swallowed hard. The night felt endless, every choice twisting inside him like a blade. He didn't know how to make it right.

In the lurid glow of the patrol car's lightbar, the arresting officer leaned into the window where the thief was handcuffed. "You just made the mistake of a lifetime," he growled. "You beat up a popular attorney's girlfriend."

## Chapter 87

"Well, what happened to you?"

The ER nurse surveyed the scrapes on Rylee's face. "Some guy tried to steal my car."

"That's what it says here."

The nurse held up the clipboard.

"You may really hurt now, but tomorrow it's going to be worse. It always hurts more the day after."

The nurse finished taking her vitals.

"The doctor will be in with you in a little bit."

Rylee lay on the gurney, drifting in and out of sleep.

"Rylee? I was hoping there was another Rylee Vance."

It was one of the doctors who volunteered at the free clinic.

"So, you were attacked?"

"Only because he was trying to steal my car."

"Oh, your car."

He grinned at her.

"I've thought about stealing your car too. However, that doesn't give anyone the right to hit you."

He flashed a light in her eyes, had her stick out her tongue, and looked up her nose. He pulled up her blouse and gently prodded her abdomen.

Rylee winced. "Ouch."

The doctor nodded his head. He continued to explore, watching her reaction closely.

He examined her hands and palms and looked at her face.

"I'm going to order some x-rays and keep you on the pain meds to start."

"Can't I just go home?"

"Uh, the answer to that would be 'No.' Maybe tomorrow. I want to keep you here tonight to watch in case you have a concussion. I'm not convinced that your hand isn't broken. Do you need me to call anyone?"

"No, a friend of mine will be here soon."

The doctor nodded.

"Okay. I'm ordering some x-rays and an ultrasound of your belly. Do you want me to have the nurse send your friend in when they arrive?"

"Yeah. His name is Thom Richardson."

"Oh, that guy. One of the nurses thinks he's the bees' knees."

He winked and leaned close to Rylee.

"She's going to be worthless if she knows he's here." Rylee blushed.

"So, he didn't get your car, did he?"

"No. Thom beat him up, and the police came and took the thief away."

"Oh, this isn't going to make things easier for me. We won't let the nurses know that he saved you, okay? But I'm glad that he pounded the guy."

He picked up Rylee's hand again and examined her palm.

"Next time, give the jerk the keys." With that, he bustled out of the room.

When Thom arrived, Rylee was almost asleep because of the pain meds. She turned her head to him as he entered. He winced at the darkening bruise and scrapes coloring her face. He pulled a chair close to her bed and stroked her hair.

"Where did you learn to hit like that?"

He smiled crookedly. "Well, hitting a bag is much cheaper than psychotherapy."

He laughed at her astonished expression.

"No, I don't do it competitively. Just an exercise program. But it's still the same punches."

She was tired and sore. She reached out to Thom. He flinched when he saw the IV and gently moved around it to hold her. Rylee snuggled into his arms as best she could, trying not to groan. Thom closed his eyes, and for the first time in years, silently prayed.

"God, thank you for sending Rylee. Please let me keep her safe."

## Chapter 88

Rylee drifted off to sleep in his arms, waking only when they came to take her to X-ray.

"Mr. Richardson, you may wait here, but there are some people in the waiting room you may want to speak with," said the nurse.

Lisa was sitting on one of the plastic chairs in the waiting room, and Chip was pacing. Chip all but pounced on Thom as he entered the room.

"Thom, what happened? How is she?"

"Rylee's getting X-rays right now and may have a concussion. They want to keep her overnight. Some guy was stealing her GTO. She had left her jacket, and I was trying to catch her before she left. I saw the whole thing. Nasty little creep. I think he's the mole. I punched him and sat on the bum. He started to talk, but I put a knee in his chest to shut him up."

"Look at your hands, Thom!" Lisa exclaimed. Chip looked down at Thom's bloody hands.

"Better get those washed off; you don't know where that guy has been," Chip said.

Thom had not noticed his hands; he was so worried about Rylee. The right one that had connected with the guy's jaw was a little bloody. Thom flexed both hands.

"Hurts when I'm not wearing gloves. Ouch, I'm not certain this is just his blood."

"Dude, you're going to get a reputation as a brawler in more than one arena. Believe me, I don't want to go up against you,"

Chip said.

Thom walked over to the bathroom and washed off his hands. He looked back over his shoulder at Chip through the open door.

"That might be a good reputation at the new digs."

"Right. Maybe we should wear tank tops that show off our tattoos," Chip said.

Lisa piped up from behind, "You have tattoos?"

Chip scooted closer to Lisa. "You want me to show them to you?"

"He doesn't have tattoos, Lisa," Thom interrupted. "But that's a really good idea there, buddy. It'll drive away our paying clients."

Thom sat down next to Lisa.

"Don't listen to him; he has impure motives."

"Thanks there, buddy. So, you just sat on the guy until the police arrived?"

Chip was clearly impressed.

"Yeah, I did. He didn't complain much, mostly because I kept shifting my weight so he couldn't."

"Driving around in a car like that is mind-boggling. You should buy her a different car and put that one in storage or on display."

"Yeah. The cop told me the same thing. I think that you guys are probably right."

"How is she?" Lisa asked.

"Okay, for now. She's on pain meds and is groggy. They'll know if there's any real damage after the X-ray. Someone will have to teach her class tomorrow and feed her cat. And someone should call her parents. I don't know who to call."

"I do," Lisa offered, pulling out her phone and moving away from the two guys to make the call.

Lisa wandered back over to Chip and Thom and finished her conversation with Rylee's mother from a few feet away. She urged the worried parents to wait until morning to make the long drive down. She explained that with the help of the pain medication, Rylee would likely sleep through the night anyway.

Lisa watched Thom's shoulders sag with weariness. "Chip, I need her in my life. I was so frightened that she was dead. I want to have her in my life permanently. I want to marry her."

Lisa, wide-eyed, stayed behind the two men, actively eavesdropping.

Thom let himself slide down in the chair.

"Yeah? That's all well and good, but does the lady know?" Chip asked.

"No. I don't want to scare her away."

"No argument here, buddy. Something in you seemed to die along with the rest of your family. The only thing that kept you connected to the human race was Lexie. Shoot. For a while, the only person you had contact with besides me was the social worker who taught you to care for the baby."

Chip slid down beside Thom and continued. "Watching you learn to care for Lexie was ugly. But after a few months, I wouldn't have known you had never cared for an infant. I've missed going snowboarding and jet skiing with you."

Chip studied his friend.

"You operated on autopilot and went into hiding until Rylee came along. I'm seeing my old friend again now. And I've got to tell you, I love Rylee, because she brought you back." He placed his hand on Thom's shoulder. "You need to tell her."

Lisa motioned for Chip to move and plopped into the chair between the two men.

"Done with your calls there, girly girl? We'd better be going, Thom. If you need anything, you know where to get me."

Chip said. He patted Thom on the shoulder and got up from his seat.

"Wait," Lisa said.

Lisa's face was set as she pointed at Chip. "You just wait."

Thom straightened in his chair and frowned at Lisa.

"Are you saying that you love Rylee and haven't told her yet?" Lisa demanded.

Chip burst out laughing.

"Cat's out of the bag now, buddy. Lisa, my dear, this poor confused soul wants to marry Rylee, but he's worried she'll run away."

"And I happen to know she adores you."

With that, she stood up and marched through the emergency room doors. A couple of nurses tried to stop her, but she just walked past them.

Chip whistled.

"She's small, but mighty."

Thom just groaned and watched helplessly as Chip roared with laughter until a nurse shushed him.

"You're in for it now. Good thing I kept all those resumes." Chip said.

Lisa navigated her way down the halls to the X-ray room and found Rylee on a gurney. Rylee smiled weakly as Lisa bustled up.

"I've called Sara, who will take over your class tomorrow.

I've also called your parents, and they're coming down in the morning because I told them to wait until then. I'll go by and feed the cat. I was planning on staying here tonight with Thom." Lisa grinned. "I wanted to have breakfast with him." Lisa gave Rylee an appraising look.

"But I think it's a wasted effort," she said.

"Lisa, behave," Rylee said weakly.

The X-ray technician walked up.

"I'll talk to you later, Rylee. Thom loves you. I heard him say so," Lisa said.

Rylee stared, open-mouthed, at Lisa's retreat. Lisa was still talking.

"I'm not kidding. He's out there talking to Chip about marrying you, but he's too chicken to ask. You should take him up on it."

Lisa looked back over her shoulder as she walked away. "And close your mouth. You look silly."

## Chapter 89

Rylee was sleeping.

The nurse closed Rylee's chart with a soft snap and glanced up at Thom under the glare of the exam-room lamp.

"She's lucky. No fractures, her spleen's intact. But she took some brutal blows, and her ribs are already bruising. That right hand is swollen solid; she won't have full use of it for a couple of weeks, but on the upside, the cuts don't need stitches, we've butterflied them, they'll heal on their own, but they're deep enough to sting every time she moves them."

Thom felt the ache of each word in his chest. The nurse leaned forward.

"She's sedated and will be groggy. She needs rest for a few days. The doctor is admitting her overnight. When she goes home, it might be good to have someone stay with her."

He ran a hand through his hair.

"Her parents arrive tomorrow morning."

"Perfect. Once they settle her in Room 256, you can come up. Right now, we need you to move out to the waiting room while we get her ready to move."

She offered him a tired smile. "Any questions?"

He cleared his throat. "Where can I grab a bite?"

The receptionist pointed to a narrow corridor. "Café's closed, but there are three vending machines at the end."

He followed the arrows and found the vending machines. He inserted coins, and watched plastic tubs spin past a window—ham sandwiches with limp lettuce, packets of chips, candy bars. He snagged a ham sandwich and a steaming cup of bitter coffee.

Thom sat heavily in one of the plastic chairs in the cafe area. He peeled back the wrapper on the sandwich, crumbs falling onto the scuffed tabletop, and bit into the stale bread.

Overhead, fluorescent bulbs hummed.

"Mr. Richardson?"

A soft voice drew his eyes up.

Dr. Miller, one of the physicians he met at the free clinic, stood there in crisp white coat, ID badge catching the light.

"Mr. Richardson? I don't know if you remember me."

Thom set down his coffee.

"Of course I do."

"Rylee's being rolled upstairs now. Room 256."

He paused, scanning Thom's face with calm gray eyes. "You can see her as soon as you like. We'll even set up a recliner so you can stay the night. You two are our rock stars. Thank you for saving the clinics."

Relief and guilt knotted in Thom's chest. "Is she all right?"

"Mentally, she's sound, thankfully. Physically, she's bruised blue from shoulder to hip. That hand of hers," he shook his head, "is sprained, cut, and swollen, but not broken. We've immobilized it, given her strong pain meds. She'll sleep."

He gave Thom a level look. "Most young women would be shaken to their cores by what happened. But they don't all have a real-life hero taking down the bad guys for them. From all of us at the clinic, thank you."

Thom's throat tightened.

"Thank you," Thom whispered back.

In Room 256, the door swung open onto a quiet suite

307

painted a soothing blue slate. A single bed held Rylee under crisp white sheets; an armchair sat beside it, its leather arms worn smooth. The only sound was the soft beeps from the monitors. Her dark hair fanned on the pillow; one pale hand peeked from the blankets, fingers slightly curled.

Thom eased into the chair, every muscle aching with the urge to hold her, to keep her safe. He wanted to crawl into the bed with her and hold her. He looked at his watch, long hours lay ahead.

All through the night, he woke up to the sound of nurses slipping in and out, hushed voices, and the beep of machines.

By dawn's gray light, the catch of a sob in Rylee's mother's throat announced the arrival of her parents.

## Chapter 90

Rylee's father walked across the room to Rylee's bed and nodded at Thom.

Rylee's mother leaned over the bed.

"Rylee? Rylee, wake up, honey. Rylee, are you awake? Do you know where you are?"

Rylee looked up groggily at her. "Mom? What time is it?"

"Rylee, honey, how are you?" her father asked.

"Oh, Daddy, I'm fine. Really. I had a knight in shining armor."

Thom was embarrassed. He turned to go, but Rylee stopped him.

"Please, don't leave, Thom. Stay here."

He grimaced at the bruises and scrapes on her face. "Mom, Dad, let me introduce you to Mr. Thomas Richardson."

"Nice to meet you. You have a real prize of a daughter here."

He turned back to Rylee.

"Why don't I go and get cleaned up, Rylee, I'll be back shortly. Your parents need some time alone with you."

Rylee's mother was crying. She nodded at Thom and then turned back to Rylee.

"Baby, look at you."

She was inspecting Rylee's face, where it was scraped and bruised. Thom shook Mr. Vance's hand, smiled at Rylee, and quietly left the room.

"Oh, it's not that bad, Mom. The doctor said I am okay."

"Rylee, how did this happen?"

"We had been moving the office all day. I went out to my car. Thom offered to walk me out, but I refused his offer."

Rylee looked at her parents.

"It was Thom who saved me. Some guy was trying to steal the car, and Thom came running across the parking lot and just pounded the guy. He moved so fast."

"An attorney pounded a guy?" asked her father.

"Yeah. The jerk who was stealing my car punched me in the stomach and then stepped on my hand to get my keys."

"Oh, Rylee," her mother gasped.

"I thought that I was dead, and then suddenly, Thom was leaping over me. The guy pulled out a knife, and Thom just kept going. He dropped the jerk with a couple of punches. The stupid guy was out cold. I must have passed out at that point, because the next thing I remember is the paramedic shining a light in my eyes. The paramedic wanted me to go to the hospital, but I didn't want to. That was kind of dumb, I guess. So, Thom made me come to the hospital and then stayed with me all night."

"Oh, my goodness, Rylee. Of course, you should have come to the hospital."

"He stayed with you all night in that chair. I would say he's a pretty good boss," her dad said.

Rylee's mother looked meaningfully at her father. Rylee started crying and told her parents the whole story from when she first met Thom at worship services until her incident in the parking garage.

"Sounds like you had a lot packed into a couple of weeks, honey. Are you sure this guy is just your boss?" her father asked.

"I don't know. I can't think about it right now."

## Chapter 91

Thom's apartment felt oppressively quiet when he stepped inside. Lexie had been at her grandparents' all week while they moved the office, and only now did he realize how the emptiness pressed in on him.

He flipped on the lights, half expecting to see boxes of files strewn across the floor, but there was only stillness. He drummed his fingers on the counter, heart thudding as if protesting the silence.

After everything that had happened, the moment stretched out before him like an exam he wasn't prepared for. He shook himself out of it and headed for the bathroom. Stripping off his clothes, he stepped under the scalding spray of the shower. The heat chased the chill from his limbs, but it couldn't wash away the knot in his chest.

His mind replayed Rylee's bruised face on a loop.

When he toweled off and caught sight of himself in the mirror, he hardly recognized the man staring back. Dark circles rimmed his eyes. His hair stuck up in every direction, no matter how he smoothed it down. He ran a hand through the unruly mess and gave a humorless chuckle. These weren't the confident eyes of someone who knew what he was doing. They were the eyes of someone about to make his biggest life decision, and he was terrified she'd say no.

In the bedroom he froze, chest tightening as he eyed the closet. He opened it and he retrieved the small, fireproof safe from the highest shelf, planted it on the bed, and fumbled with the combination lock as though his fingers had forgotten their job. When the lid finally sprang open, he lifted out a black velvet pouch with hands that trembled.

Inside lay the ring he'd taken from his safe deposit box just days ago. A symbol of a future he wanted and yet felt unworthy to claim.

He lifted the ring and rolled it between his thumb and forefinger, feeling its cold weight.

"Will she say yes? Should she? Am I even allowed to think of marriage right now, with Rylee in the hospital and her parents already on edge?"

A wave of doubt crashed over him, and he shut his eyes against the blur of possibilities, joy, rejection, guilt.

"Am I really doing this?"

His voice felt hollow in the still room.

He pressed the ring back into its pouch, lingering an extra moment to imagine Rylee's face when he asked her.

"Will relief flicker in her eyes, or rejection?"

He slipped the pouch into his pocket and exhaled a shaky breath. The safe snapped shut behind him, and he returned it to its shelf as if sealing away his fears.

The drive to the hospital felt both interminable and too short. Each red light mocked him; each green light propelled him closer to the moment of truth. He thought of how weary Rylee's parents looked. He gripped the wheel so tightly his knuckles went white, determined to be the rock they needed, even as his own doubt chafed at him.

When he parked and stepped through the sliding doors, his heart pounded in time with his footsteps. Rylee's parents appeared just outside her room; their faces lined with fatigue. Thom cleared his throat, desperately hunting for calm in his chest, and forced a tentative smile.

"Would you two like to get breakfast with me?"

## Chapter 92

"Oh, I don't know. We should stay with Rylee," her mom said.

"We can eat here, Mrs. Vance, if you'd rather. I'm told they fry a decent egg in the café here."

Mr. Vance laughed, "Sounds like a good compromise to me."

They walked down the hall in silence and entered the elevator.

"Your name is Thom?" asked Mrs. Vance.

"My name is Thomas Orlando Richardson." He grinned at her.

"I think you can understand why I prefer Thom."

"That is a mouthful. I like Thom well enough," she said.

Mr. Vance gave Thom an appraising look. "Must be a family name, right?" Mr. Vance asked.

"Yes, it is."

They went through the line and sat at the same plastic table where Thom had snacked the night before.

They ate their breakfast and made small talk.

"Do you think the flower shop is open yet? Rylee's room could use some color." Mrs. Vance said. "I think I'll run down there before I go back up."

Thom stood as Mrs. Vance got up from her chair and walked away.

"I appreciate that you're taking such good care of our Rylee, Thom, especially when she's only been your secretary for a short time," Mr. Vance said.

"Yeah, about that," Thom said.

Mr. Vance watched the retreating Mrs. Vance.

"Mr. Vance, you probably know I'm an attorney and a state representative. I know I've only known your daughter for a few weeks, but I can't imagine living without her. I don't want her to be my secretary; I want her to be my wife. I want to ask you for her hand in marriage."

"Thom, you're not being honest with me?"

Thom stammered, his eyes wide.

"What?"

"Thom, I was hoping to get you alone. Rylee doesn't know, does she?"

Thom felt his throat getting tight. It was like the room was losing all its air.

"I already know a lot about you. What's your real name? The whole name."

"Thomas Orlando Richardson, VIII." Mr. Vance snorted.

"The bad boy rich kid. You're probably one of the most eligible bachelors in the state."

Thom's clear blue eyes clouded, and he bowed his head.

"Let me continue. You lost your entire family, except for your niece, early last winter. The estate that settled on both of you is hefty."

Thom sat unmoving, staring at the floor. After all the unsuitable women who chased after him because of his wealth, he was now in danger of losing the one woman he cared about because of the money. They sat silently for a moment.

Thom was unable to meet the man's steady gaze. "Mr. Vance, when I lost my family last winter, I lost everything. It's true I had a reputation as a bad boy, deserved or not. The truth is that I enjoyed having that reputation. But my parents didn't raise me that way. They taught me about God, faith, and goodness."

Thom continued to study the tabletop.

"I lost my faith in God. I told myself that I never really had any faith and didn't like Christians in general. Through the help of an older Christian gentleman, I have recently come to understand that God didn't do this horrible thing. That God was trying to help me. I recognize that Rylee is the hand of God, rising to heal my pain."

Mr. Vance put his hand on Thom's shoulder.

"Son, I know that you've been raising your niece by yourself and have lived a simple life since the accident. I also know what you've done this past week. I couldn't miss it. It was all over the news. You didn't take a bit of credit for yourself. Regardless of your reputation, deserved or not, I would say that you've become a man I would be proud to have as a son-in-law."

Thom's head jerked up. His eyes met Mr. Vance's smiling face.

"Rylee's mother told me about a phone call from Rylee a few days ago. She called her mom to tell her about this guy who had stolen her heart. I started making inquiries. I'm impressed."

Thom was speechless.

"Do you have the ring with you? You are giving her the famous Richardson ruby, aren't you? Did your great-great-great-great-grandfather get this in Derna with O'Bannon?"

Thom was obviously surprised.

"Actually, sir, it was my great-great-great-great-great-grandfather. And yes, it was given to him as a gift after Derna fell. I was just hoping that," Thom paused, "it's just that I almost lost

316

her last night. I know I've only known Rylee for a few weeks."

Mr. Vance waived a dismissive hand in the air. "I proposed to her mother after a week. You just know when it's right. Can I see it?"

Thom pulled the ring out of his pocket. Mr. Vance took it in his hands. Thom waited, his heart beating in his chest.

"Well, isn't this pretty. Thom, you're a good man. I've always believed a man's actions were the mark of his character. I don't think your reputation was what the press wanted everyone to believe. They were only interested in selling stories. It's not words, but actions that tell the tale.

The things you have done in your life speak for themselves." He stood up and patted Thom on the shoulder.

"I said I would be proud to have you as a son-in-law; you just have to get past Rylee."

Thom nearly collapsed on the table, as Mr. Vance put the ring back in the velvet bag and handed it back to Thom.

"It's a good thing that you didn't tell Rylee you were rich. Knowing her, she probably wouldn't have had anything to do with you. I'm going to go delay her mother to give you some time with Rylee."

## Chapter 93

Thom ran up to Rylee's room, taking the stairs two at a time, because the elevator was too slow. She had been eating breakfast, and the bed was raised so she could sit up.

"The nurses think I can go home soon," she announced to Thom as he came bounding into the room.

"That's great, baby. How are you feeling? You still stoned on pain killers?"

"No, they've just been giving me Tylenol since about three. I don't think I need the stronger stuff."

Thom shut the heavy door to her private suite and crossed the room to reach for Rylee's uninjured hand. He wanted to hold her but was afraid she was too sore.

"What are you doing?"

Thom put his hand on the left side of her face and gently turned her head.

"Oh, Rylee. That must hurt."

"It looks much worse than it is. My hands hurt the most, but I'm somewhat sore everywhere to varying degrees."

The look on Thom's face amused and pained her at the same time.

"Look, the timing is off. I don't know what Lisa said to you yesterday. But the timing isn't the best."

"Lisa said you loved me and wanted to marry me."

"I do love you, Rylee. I believe with all my heart that God sent you to me to fill the void left when my family died. I can honestly tell you that I've never met anyone who makes me feel like you do. I love you. I want you to have my children. I want to grow old with you."

Tears ran down Rylee's face. Thom gently wiped the the tears running down Rylee's face.

"Baby, I'm so sorry that you're here. But I can't wait any longer. I thought that being friends would be enough for me. After last night, I realized that I can't lose you. Rylee, I love you. Please marry me and share my life. Be my conscience and remind me to rejoice. I can't bear the thought of you not being in my life."

Cradling her bruised cheek, Thom moved closer. Rylee held her breath as he kissed her. She felt like rockets were going off in her head.

"Please say yes," Thom kept whispering.

Rylee leaned into him and then quickly straightened up. "Ouch."

Thom pulled away, worried that he had hurt her.

"Yes," she said, as her eyes filled with tears. "Thom, I would love to be your wife. I don't want to be just friends with you. I consider you a friend, but I want to be your wife. I want to share your life with you. I want to watch Lexie grow up. I want to have your children. I want to grow old with you."

Rylee winced at his sudden movement as he reached to hold her.

"Sorry. Are you okay? I didn't mean to hurt you."

Thom jumped as she unexpectedly drew him closer and kissed him again, then melted when she pulled back to give him an impish grin. He pulled the velvet bag from his pocket and held her hand.

"Ms. Rylee Vance, will you do me the honor of being my wife?"

She gave him another playful grin. "Why, sir, how could

I say no?"

He slipped the ring on her swollen finger until it reached the bandages.

"It's a little big, but we'll get it resized."

Rylee stared at the ruby on her finger. "Thom, how can you afford this?"

"It's been in the family for a while."

"Well, if we're sharing heirlooms, I'll have to share my car."

"Rylee, everything I have is yours. However, that car is going into your father's garage."

She pulled him back down, searching for his lips.

"Rylee, stop. Please. I don't want to hurt you."

Rylee grinned at him again, her eyes inviting. "Then don't hurt me," she said while kissing him.

Thom thought he was going to explode. She said yes! Smiling, he gently pushed back from her, settling her carefully on her pillows.

"I don't want to hurt you any more than you already are."

She just smiled at him, tears glistening in her eyes.

"Is the ring okay?"

"Of course. It's wonderful. Everything is wonderful."

## Chapter 94

"Lisa, hurry up," Rylee urged, her voice tinged with excitement and nerves.

"Sorry, my hat isn't staying put very well," Lisa replied, fumbling with the delicate accessory that seemed determined to misbehave.

"Here, mine isn't either. Help me with this veil, and I'll see what I can do about your hat. Maybe this wasn't the best choice," Rylee admitted, glancing at the intricate lacework that stubbornly refused to sit right.

Rylee's mother approached, her presence a calming balm amidst the flurry. She secured the rebellious hat and veil with deft hands, ensuring every detail was perfect.

"Rylee, you look beautiful," Mrs. Vance said, her voice thick with emotion as she brushed away tears threatening to fall and ruin her carefully applied makeup. She beamed at the two girls.

"I've got to go. The ceremony will start soon. The mother of the bride should be seated before we begin."

She picked up the bouquet, a hand-tied marvel of white cala lilies, and gently placed it into Rylee's arms.

"Your father is waiting right outside," she added, pressing a tender kiss to Rylee's cheek before exiting the room. The door closed softly behind her.

"Oh, Lisa! This is it!"

The moment's reality settled in like a warm embrace.

"Yeah. Don't I look fabulous?" Lisa's eyes sparkled with

321

mischief.

Rylee took a deep, steadying breath, feeling Lisa's arm slip through her own as they moved toward the door.

Chip waited there, his presence a solid anchor in the sea of emotions swirling around them. He extended his arm for Lisa, and as the harpist's chords began their gentle, melodic strumming,

Lisa winked at Rylee, straightening her shoulders with newfound confidence and squeezing Chip's arm. Chip offered a reassuring smile to Rylee before beginning his walk down the aisle.

Rylee's father leaned over, his expression filled with pride and love, and kissed her softly before lowering the delicate veil over her face.

"Well, honey, this is our cue," he said, his voice a comforting rumble.

Rylee felt as if she were floating, the world around her fading into a soft blur. All she was truly aware of was Thom, standing at the end of the aisle, his eyes filled with a warmth that made her heart swell. But then, a soft, muted cry from Lexie pulled Rylee from her blissful trance.

Stopping mid-stride, Rylee scanned the seating area until her gaze landed on the little girl. Smiling at her father, she gently released his arm and approached Jake's parents.

"May I?" Rylee asked, her voice gentle and kind.

She carefully lifted Lexie into her arms, the little girl's fingers instinctively reaching for the bridal veil. Rylee carefully removed it and handed it to Jake's parents along with her bouquet.

Lexie nestled comfortably against Rylee's shoulder, her

small presence adding warmth to the moment.

Together, they returned to Rylee's father, and with a shared smile, continued down the aisle toward Thom.

# Zombie Moose

of
## West Bath, Maine
by
Marsha Hinton

Who wouldn't want to come to Maine and get their
brains eaten by a moose?
Just sayin'.

www.marshahinton.com

**BY**

**MARSHA HINTON**

You're a Hero, they said.
You saved lives that day, they said.
Kara didn't feel like a hero.
She felt like damaged goods.

www.marshahinton.com

# Coming Soon!

# Jeezley Pirates
### of
### West Bath, Maine

### by
### Marsha Hinton

www.marshahinton.com

# Mayzie Sterling

When Mayzie is not pounding away on her keyboard, she enjoys living the island life with her dachsunds, Rags and Sport.